Praise for Robert B. Parker's
Cole-Hitch Western Series

Revelation

"Robert Knott knows how to create atmospheric scenes . . . the key ingredient in a great western thriller."
—*Mystery Tribune*

"A classic plot and plenty of 8-gauge shotgun showdowns best enjoyed by those who've followed Cole and Hitch's previous adventures." —*Kirkus Reviews*

"Rapid-fire dialogue and quick-paced action."
—*Historical Novels Review*

Blackjack

"Westerns need atmosphere as much as story, and Knott has a knack for six-gun verisimilitude, sketching the land and summer heat, the horses and the shopkeepers. . . . A darn good way to pass an afternoon." —*Kirkus Reviews*

"This is the most satisfying of Knott's Cole-Hitch tales, with a shocking double-twist ending."
—*The Sacramento Bee*

The Bridge

"[A]n extraordinarily entertaining novel." —*Booklist*

"For fans of the late Parker, this book is a refreshing reunion with these cowboy characters who choose their words and situations most carefully. . . . Much to enjoy."
—*Deseret News*

Split Image
Night and Day
Stranger in Paradise
High Profile
Sea Change
Stone Cold
Death in Paradise
Trouble in Paradise
Night Passage

**THE SUNNY RANDALL
NOVELS**

Spare Change
Blue Screen
Melancholy Baby
Shrink Rap
Perish Twice
Family Honor

**THE COLE/HITCH
WESTERNS**

Robert B. Parker's Revelation
  (by Robert Knott)
Robert B. Parker's Blackjack
  (by Robert Knott)
Robert B. Parker's The Bridge
  (by Robert Knott)
Robert B. Parker's Bull River
  (by Robert Knott)
Robert B. Parker's Ironhorse
  (by Robert Knott)
Blue-Eyed Devil
Brimstone
Resolution
Appaloosa

**ALSO BY ROBERT B.
PARKER**

Double Play
Gunman's Rhapsody
All Our Yesterdays
A Year at the Races
  (with Joan H. Parker)
Perchance to Dream
Poodle Springs
  (with Raymond Chandler)
Love and Glory
Wilderness
Three Weeks in Spring
  (with Joan H. Parker)
Training with Weights
  (with John R. Marsh)

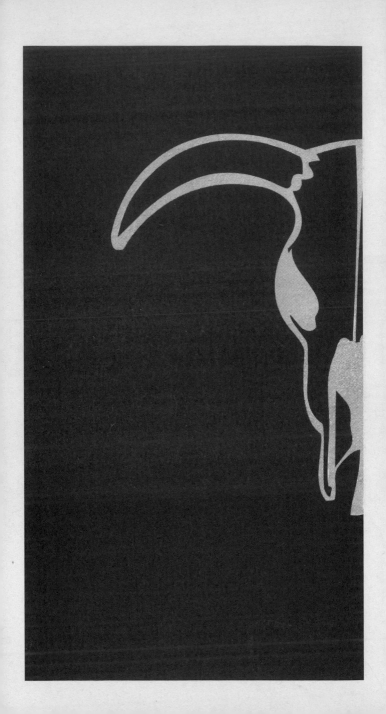

ROBERT B. PARKER'S

REVELATION

Robert Knott

G. P. PUTNAM'S SONS
New York

G. P. PUTNAM'S SONS
Publishers Since 1838
An imprint of Penguin Random House LLC
375 Hudson Street
New York, New York 10014

Copyright © 2017 by The Estate of Robert B. Parker
Excerpt from *Robert B. Parker's Buckskin* copyright © 2018
by The Estate of Robert B. Parker
Penguin supports copyright. Copyright fuels creativity, encourages diverse
voices, promotes free speech, and creates a vibrant culture. Thank you for
buying an authorized edition of this book and for complying with copyright
laws by not reproducing, scanning, or distributing any part of it in any form
without permission. You are supporting writers and allowing Penguin to
continue to publish books for every reader.

The Library of Congress has catalogued the G. P. Putnam's Sons
hardcover edition as follows:

Names: Knott, Robert, 1954– author.
Title: Robert B. Parker's Revelation / Robert Knott.
Description: New York : G. P. Putnam's Sons, 2017. | Series: A Cole and
Hitch novel ; 5
Identifiers: LCCN 2016057374 (print) | LCCN 2017004545 (ebook) | ISBN
9780399575341 (hardcover) | ISBN 9780399575365 (epub)
Subjects: LCSH: Cole, Virgil (Fictitious character)—Fiction. | Hitch,
Everett (Fictitious character)—Fiction. | United States
marshals—Fiction. | BISAC: FICTION / Westerns. | FICTION / Historical. |
FICTION / Mystery & Detective / General. | GSAFD: Western stories.
Classification: LCC PS3611.N685 R636 2017b (print) | LCC PS3611.N685
(ebook) | DDC 813/.6—dc23

LC record available at https://lccn.loc.gov/2016057374

First G. P. Putnam's Sons hardcover edition / February 2017
First G. P. Putnam's Sons premium edition / January 2018
G. P. Putnam's Sons premium edition ISBN: 9780399575358

Printed in the United States of America
1 3 5 7 9 10 8 6 4 2

FOR JULIE

Robert B. Parker's

REVELATION

1

Augustus Noble Driggs was lying inside the small *stone room on a bunk, thinking about Jesus and whatnot. He was in the Tomb. That's what the inmates called it. It was late in the evening and he was alone here, in the Tomb, in the odd April cold. He was watching gray vapors drift up from a small lantern beside his bunk that offered up rising battalions of ghostly dancers who twisted and swirled, then disappeared before they met the Tomb's low rock ceiling.*

The Tomb was solitary confinement, and the only reason Driggs was provided a lantern at all was so he could read the Bible that was left next to his bunk. It was the warden's wife's idea. She felt it a civic and moral duty—for those who could in fact read—to spread the Gospel.

The Tomb was in an isolated area separated from the main compound. This place, this penitentiary, was simply referred to by the inmates as Hell. It had another proper name when it was built, but that title was long ago forgotten and it was usually called Hell. Some referred to the massive stone structure as the Hell Hole or the Hot Box on the Hubs of Hell. The prison was meant to hold a maximum of two hundred and sixty prisoners, but it was currently overcrowded and brimming with close to three hundred. It was located in the desert—nearly one hundred miles from the closest town in every direction—and escaping Hell had proved to be near impossible. Driggs had considered escaping more then a few times but never found a way out that made any sense. Over the years a few had tried, but they all died in their attempts.

Normally this rock palace, Hell, was a sweltering-hot compound, a place where it was much easier to catch a heat-related disease than it was to catch a decent breath. But at times, when the temperature dropped, the prisoners would say, "Ol' Sam pulled the goddamn lever." Sam Satan, he was the operator, the true proprietor of Hell, and every so often he opened the gallows trapdoor that dropped in a strange, unseasonably glacial chill.

The prisoners would mostly die in the sweltering heat, of edema or syncope, of tetany, or stroke, or the galloping consumption, but the cold was also threatening. Since the place was constructed, through the consecutive hot summers and occasional cold winters, there had been more than a dozen men who couldn't tolerate the conditions and took their own lives, usually by hanging from the bars at the end of a ripped blanket snugged around the neck.

Unlike thick-walled adobe structures that kept in the cool, this place was made from stone with walls built just thin enough to allow the outside temperatures to conveniently creep inside like an unwanted guest. Then there would be stretches of time in the winter when the chill would last for weeks, sometimes months.

The earliest inmates lived in tents, shackled by ball and chain as they erected the cavernous compound that overlooked a vast desert in every direction. And after a few years of hard labor, the prisoners moved into the very cells they had built, sealing their fate.

Set high up on a rocky bluff where the harsh sun and winter gales would insult and diminish the most capable, everyone—the guards, the administration, the warden, even the governor—understood that this place was in every way damnation and most certainly the work of the Devil himself.

The week previous it had been scorching hot, but this particular night in April was for some reason freezing, and the wind brought with it some uncommon moisture. Now, miserable wetness was added to the frigid April air. It traversed through the chambers and across the rock floor tunnels of the prison compound, making a bitter cold night even colder. But Driggs was okay with it. He knew this brief bit of unseasonably cold weather was just a passing snap.

Driggs was not good being on the inside, though. Being locked up in prison just did not suit him. He was not keen on authority, and as a result his insubordination kept landing him in confinement, in the Tomb. He didn't mind it, really. In some ways Driggs preferred being in the Tomb to sharing a cell with others. Especially since the prison was overcrowded. At least this way, sequestered in the Tomb, he didn't have to listen to ignorant conversations or tolerate stupid questions by the other prisoners, who were certain Driggs would know the answer to any and all.

No one really even knew Driggs. In fact, Driggs was not Driggs, not here on the inside. He was arrested, convicted, and incarcerated under the name Donnie Lonnigan. Through the years after the war, Driggs had assumed a number of names—aliases that kept him, as he preferred to be, a man unknown. From time to time throughout his past he was not above remaining in a place and blending in as a somewhat normal person among the masses, but for the most part he was a lone wolf.

Driggs was smart and everyone knew that about him. He was by no means the standard man found behind the walls of the institution. Most were common thieves, robbers of one kind or another. Some were rapists, some were on the inside for having too many wives, and some, like Driggs, were killers.

Driggs was different, though, and everyone knew it, they saw it and sensed it. Everyone looked up to Driggs. There was something about Driggs that average men did not possess. Other men felt safe with Driggs near. It was not that Driggs took up for them in any way, but it was the simple fact that he carried himself as if he meant something, as if he had a purpose, and that purpose gave the aimless others reasons to revere him. Everyone thought him mysterious— mythical, even. Some thought Driggs was an aberration, a ghost, but most felt he was in some way—though they had no real reason to believe this—their protector, their Savior, their Jesus. Not unlike Jesus, Driggs frightened the guards.

Even though they were the ones with the guns, Driggs unnerved them. It was his simple and still manner that intimidated them, his centered, relaxed frame; shoulders lowered, his long sinewy arms comfortably by his sides. And it was the way he walked. He moved unlike the normal man. He was more like a muscled Thoroughbred stallion. Not the poised ready-to-run type with ears back and head rising and falling. No. Driggs was calm and sure as he moved, always with his body squared, his hips and torso moving together, his head up high, supported by his long, muscly neck. His face was handsome and sturdy, and his hair was a shock of varying hardwood colors—blond, brown, and dark brown—that he wore at a medium length and combed back from his strong, browed forehead. He kept his keen blue-green eyes slightly hidden behind a squint that was more relaxed and natural than involuntary or intentional. His chin was square and his cheekbones were high.

Driggs was the quiet type, too, answering annoying questions with a simple adjustment of his jawbone rather than words. He moved his tall, muscular frame effortlessly, as if he were not just a gallant steed but also a prescient, all-knowing predator. This unsettling power Driggs possessed prompted the warden to throw Driggs into the Tomb for simply being himself.

2

Driggs was educated, formally as well as self-taught. He was good with English, science, and math. He possessed skills far greater than his fellow students, but he also learned other needed abilities when he left the boring institutions and set out on his own. Eventually he ended up at West Point, but for many years previous he was a traveler, never staying in one place too long. Yet here, in this godforsaken place, he was going on close to four years. Driggs was a killer, no doubt about that, but he did his killing with precision. It started on the battlefield, that is where he got a taste for it, a bloodthirsty hankering. He was not just a good shot with a pistol or a long rifle, but he was also formidable in hand-to-hand combat. He learned his skills at the Point, where he graduated in the top in his class, but now he was here, living like a caged animal in the Devil's Hot Box on the Very Hubs of Hell.

Driggs heard someone, somewhere, call out with a mournful moan, "God help me!" And from someplace else within the dungeon another prisoner laughed, a loud, mad, and raspy bone-chilling laugh that was as cold as the chilly April air: "God? There is no God here, you pitiful fool." Driggs smiled to himself a little and thought about God. God . . . Jesus . . . God the Father, the Son, and the Holy Spirit. One and the same, so the Bible says.

He picked up the Bible lying next to the lamp and thumbed through the pages as he thought about the warden's wife. He was glad she provided the Good Book, and Driggs did not mind reading the scriptures. On the contrary, he actually got some enjoyment out of the stories. He liked the Old Testament. The stories of Noah and Moses especially, but he liked some of the new parts, too, the New Testament. He particularly appreciated one part. In fact, it was the only part he read anymore. He was drawn to the otherworldliness of it, the strangeness of it, its wildness, and he liked the way the words were put together. He understood it completely. It reminded him of the battlefield. It was as if it was written for him. He even memorized parts of it.

"'I am the Alpha and Omega,'" Driggs said out loud.

He watched the dancing vapors twisting up out of the chimney of the lamp. He put his hand over it, feeling the heat as he quietly continued reciting.

"'I heard behind me a great voice like a trumpet. And when I turned to see the voice that spoke to me I saw seven golden candlesticks. And in the midst of the seven candlesticks one was like the Son of man, clothed with a garment down to his feet, with a golden sash across his chest. His eyes were as a flame of fire and his feet were like brass as if they burned in a furnace, and his voice was the sound of raging water. In his right hand he had seven stars and coming out of his mouth was a razor sharp double-edged sword.'"

Driggs was stimulated by the words. They made him feel even more powerful than he physically was. When he read about the winds and the stars, and the horses and the dragon, he always thought of her . . . of what she smelled *like, of how she might taste. The warden's wife was not just the only woman within one hundred miles in every direction, but she was also fucking attractive, Driggs thought. It was said, though she wore dresses made from the best fabrics, that she was the one who wore the breeches in the family. Driggs could tell that just by looking at her and he liked that, that she possessed power. He had seen her numerous times and he knew it was just a matter of time until he would have her. One way or the other he would take away her power. He was certain that women like that needed him to undo the need to control. He could tell by the way she looked at him from across the yard every time he was escorted to the Tomb. But Driggs was used to that, most women wanted him to do that. He had that quality, that way about him. Driggs rested the Bible on his chest, and as he thought more about the warden's wife he heard a key slip into the lock of his door. He sat up some, thinking it odd to be pulled out of the Tomb at night; that had never happened before. Then the door very slowly opened but no one came in. Driggs reached over and turned out the lamp, then moved to the foot of his bunk, closer to the door, and sat quietly. He stayed there until his eyes adjusted completely to the dark. After a moment he could see the deep blue of the night, visible above the dark silhouette of the compound walls, but he did not move, not yet. Driggs was a cautious man, he had instincts, and his instincts for the moment told him to wait. He waited and listened but heard nothing, then he moved to the door and looked out but did not step out. He stood in the doorway for a long moment, listening, but all he could hear was the wind. Then he crept out slightly. He stopped just a step past the door and looked about. He looked to his left and then to his right. He looked behind him. There was no one in sight and there were no lamps burning. All was silent and then Driggs said quietly to himself, "Fear not, I am the first and the last. I am he that lives. I was dead but behold I am alive for evermore. And I hold the keys of hell and death. I saw heaven open and I behold a white horse and he who sat upon him was called faithful and true. And in righteousness he doth judge and make war. This is the second death. And the great dragon was cast out, that old serpent called the Devil and Satan who deceived the world was cast down to earth."*

3

"**Three thousand people living here now in Appa-**
loosa," I said.

"Two thousand nine hundred and something too
many," Virgil said.

"Well, it's a good thing for Allie," I said.

Virgil nodded.

"Hope she can make money," I said.

"Goddamn do, too, Everett."

"Cost you a cent or two to put this together."

"Two and then some," Virgil said.

"Well, it's good, even though you can't throw a rock
without hitting a human being, she don't got that much
competition that she has to contend with."

"For the time being," Virgil said.

"Gives her some independence."

"Her?"

"You, too," I said.

Virgil said nothing for a moment.

"Times are changing, it seems."

I laughed out loud.

"Goddamn right about that," I said.

"Surprises are far and few between."

"Well, she's happy," I said.

"She is," Virgil said.

"Guess it could be Mrs. Cole's?"

Virgil looked to me.

"If you and Allie were married she could have called it Mrs. Cole's?" I said.

"Could have," Virgil said.

"But you're not."

"I'm well aware of that, Everett."

"It don't bother you?"

"That we aren't married?"

"That she's using her dead-and-gone husband's name for her new business?"

"It's her name, Everett. Mrs. French."

"'Course it is."

Virgil and I were across the street from Allie's new dress shop, watching a sign man painting *Mrs. French's Fine Dresses* in fancy cursive style. We were standing on the wide covered front porch of the newly constructed Vandervoort Town Hall. It was an impressive building that was at least two hundred feet long, with tall double doors every twenty-five or so feet that opened out onto the porch. Inside, there were a few workers putting finishing touches on thirty-foot-tall draperies that were hung at one end of the room, separating the glossy wood floors from the stage.

Virgil shook his head.

"I guess you call this expansion," I said.

"That's one way of putting it," Virgil said.

We looked back to Allie's shop. The letters being painted were at least a foot tall and in colors of lavender and lilac bordered with gold. The shop was not yet open to the public, but Allie was getting ready for the grand opening.

"Fancy-looking," I said.

"Is."

The month previous, Virgil and I had experienced limited marshaling duties, so we'd been helping Allie put the shop together. It wasn't until a few days prior to today that she had even decided on just what she was going to name the shop.

"I just always think of her as Allie, and fact is, until she come up with the name for the shop, I hadn't really thought much of the name *Mrs. French* in a while."

"Just a name," Virgil said.

"Well, I think it's a good one."

"You think?"

"Do," I said. "Fact that it's European gives Allie's new sophisticated establishment sort of a sophisticated quality."

Virgil looked at me and cocked his head a little, like I was speaking a language he didn't understand.

"Does," I said.

"Hell, Everett, you might ought to be a salesman. I'm sure Allie would be thrilled to have you work with her."

"I'd make a good one."

Allie came out of the shop and stepped out into the street a bit and looked back to the sign.

"Why, that looks simply wonderful," Allie said to the painter atop the ladder.

He looked down and smiled.

"I'm pleased you like it."

"Oh, I do!"

"I should be done here in a few hours."

"Please take your time, we have all the time in the world for you to get that to your perfection."

"She has her way," I said.

"She does."

"Mrs. French," I called to Allie.

Allie turned, shielding her eyes, and looked across the street to Virgil and me standing on the boardwalk.

"Does have a ring to it," I said.

"What are you two doing over there?"

"Staying out of the line of fire," Virgil said.

Allie checked to make sure she could cross safely and walked across to where we were standing.

"Do you like it?"

"I do."

"Me, too," Virgil said.

Allie stepped up on the boardwalk next to us and looked back to the shop.

"You like the colors?"

"I do," I said.

"Virgil?"

"Sure, Allie."

"Really?"

"Well, yeah. Don't you?"

"I do," she said.

"Well, that is all that matters," he said.

"No, it's not. I value your opinion."

"Everett's better at opinions than me, and he thinks the colors are just right."

She smiled at me and said, "And the name?"

"He likes the name. Don't you, Everett?"

"And you?"

"It's your name."

"That's not what I asked."

"Everett thinks it sounds sophisticated."

"But you?"

"I told you when you decided on the name that I thought it was a good name."

"Liking it and thinking it is good are two different things, Virgil."

"Well, what do you want me to say?"

"If you don't know the answer to that, I can't help you, Virgil Cole," she said.

An Appaloosa deputy came hurrying up the street riding a little roan and pulled to a hard stop in front of us, kicking up some dirt. It was Skeeter, a small Mexican fella with a bright smile and twinkling eyes who the other deputies called Skeeter on account of his size and pesky disposition.

"Hey, Marshal Cole," Skeeter said in his heavy accent as his roan turned to the left and then, with Skeeter's nudging, turned in the other direction. "You are wanted at the office of the Western Union, *ahora*."

"What for?" Virgil said.

Skeeter shook his head as the roan shifted nervously underneath him.

"I don't know, but Sheriff Chastain told us to find you, and I find you first."

"Tell him we're on our way," Virgil said.

Skeeter turned the roan and galloped off up the street and Virgil looked to Allie.

"Allie," he said. "I *like* the name."

Allie smiled a little, the kind of smile that was more of a frown than a smile.

"Oh, Virgil," she said. "You are impossible."

"That better than possible?"

I looked across the street to see a young woman poke her head into Allie's shop.

"Looks like you have a customer," I said.

4

"Over here," Allie said.

The woman turned and looked in our direction.

"Oh, hello," she said and started walking toward us. She waited for some traffic to clear, then lifted the front of her dress and scampered swiftly to us.

"That's Margie," Allie said. "She's a new friend. Mrs. Vandervoort introduced us."

Margie was smiling as she approached. She had an enthusiastic and glowing exuberance about her. She was a petite blonde with delicate features and a smile that was as pretty as any smile I'd ever seen on a woman.

"I was just checking in on you," she said.

"Well, I'm glad you did," Allie said.

When she stepped up on the boardwalk she smiled with even greater warmth as she looked at Allie.

"Your shop, it looks to be coming along nicely," she said.

"It is," Allie said, beaming. "Look at the sign."

Margie pirouetted with a bounce to look back to the sign.

"Oh," she said with a slight squeal, "I love it."

"You do?"

"I do," she said, looking back to Allie. Then she looked to me and blushed a little.

"Oh, Margie, this is Everett Hitch and . . . Virgil Cole."

"*The* Virgil?" she said.

"Yes," Allie said with a smile. "The Virgil."

"I have heard about you, Mr. Cole."

Virgil nodded a bit.

"What'd she tell you?" he said.

"That you are a lawman," she said. "A United States Territorial Marshal."

"Pleased to meet you," Virgil said with a tip of his hat. "Miss . . . ?"

"Witherspoon," she said. "Margie Witherspoon."

"Miss Witherspoon," Virgil said with a nod.

"What about me?" I said. "Say anything about me?"

She laughed.

"I'm sorry . . . Mr. Hitch, is it?"

"Obviously she didn't," I said. "And it's Everett. Everett Hitch."

"Everett," she said with a smile. "I am afraid Allie has not mentioned you, but we are new friends, so I'm certain in due time she would have expounded on you."

I looked to Allie.

"Allie?"

"I certainly would have," Allie said. "I always talk about Everett, don't I, Virgil?"

"You do," Virgil said.

"See, Everett," Allie said. "Everett and Virgil work together, they are both lawmen."

"Deputy Marshal Everett Hitch," I said and removed my hat and bowed a little.

"Well, it is a pleasure," she said.

I looked to Allie, then back to Margie.

"New friends, you say?"

"We are," Allie said. "I told Margie that if my business got going good, maybe I could use some help running things."

"My father was a tailor," she said. "Runs in my family."

"And just look at her," Allie said. "She's a young woman with style and sophistication."

"Oh, Allie," she said, blushing.

"You are," Allie said. "Every time I've seen you, you look like one of the beauties from the catalogs."

"You are too sweet," she said.

"Where do you hail from, Miss Witherspoon?" I said.

"Margie," she said. "Please."

"Margie," I said with my best smile.

"Nebraska," she said. "Lincoln."

"Oh . . . Lincoln," I said.

"You say that like you know Lincoln."

"I do," I said. "I was stationed there for a short time during my time with the Army."

"Everett's traveled all over this country," Allie said. "He knows more than any man I've ever met."

"Not more than Virgil," I said.

"Well," Allie said affectionately as she looked to Virgil. "Virgil has his own particular smarts."

"What brings you to Appaloosa?" I said.

"My uncle passed away here and I came to sort out his affairs."

"Sorry to hear," I said.

"Thank you. He'd been ill for a while, and though it was hard on the family, it was expected."

"My condolences," I said.

She smiled.

"Anyway," she said. "I was saying to Allie that I like the place enough that I just might have to stay for a while. I have been enjoying my visit and it seems every day brings a new surprise."

"That so?" I said with another one of my best smiles.

"She has money to invest," Allie said.

"Oh," Margie said. "My family's money, not much, of course, but I thought it smart to be forward-thinking. Mrs. Vandervoort has been guiding me on what to do. Perhaps I will invest in her husband's growing empire. He obviously knows what he is doing."

"Yes," Allie said. "And Mrs. Vandervoort comes from one of the finest bloodlines in all of New York City, and who better to get advice from?"

"Bloodlines?" Virgil said. "Hell, that's sounds like horse talk, Allie."

"It certainly is not, Virgil Cole," said Allie. "And what would you know about it anyway?"

"Not much, I suppose," said Virgil.

Margie laughed. Her laughter was light and funny and she made Allie laugh, and me, too.

"Isn't she the cutest?" Allie said, looking at Margie.

"She is," I said.

5

We said good-bye to the women and left them look-ing at Allie's place: Mrs. French's Fine Dresses, a yet-to-be-fully-realized establishment, and walked up Vandervoort Avenue toward the Western Union office.

"Think that young lady might have the sweets on you, Everett."

"I'll reciprocate in kind," I said.

Virgil looked at me as we walked.

"Give back," I said.

We walked for a bit, looking at all the brick structures.

"Vandervoort is the only road called an avenue in the whole of Appaloosa, ain't it?" Virgil said.

"Is," I said. "The newest, extra-fancy addition."

"Yep," Virgil said, shaking his head. "To a town that is getting too big for its breeches."

"Allie is right in the middle of it," I said.

"Damn sure is," Virgil said.

"When we first showed up here there was but a few streets," I said. "Now there is more than you can count."

"Not hard to get lost," Virgil said.

I laughed. "Damn sure is not," I said.

When the Vandervoort Brick Factory opened in Appaloosa, it changed the face of the town almost overnight, and the change was most obvious here on Vandervoort Avenue.

Where wood and adobe had been the main construction material for growth and maintenance of Appaloosa, everything was now mostly being constructed of brick. Many of the wooden structures were transforming their tired and weathered storefronts to brick. The growing town was rapidly changing into a city, and the central figure that was bringing about that change was Vernon Vandervoort, a Dutch businessman from St. Paul.

Vernon Vandervoort was a colorfully debonair character in his mid-sixties with a slender but strong physique, and was always polite whenever we'd met. His face was healthy and handsome, his expressive blue eyes and gold-colored skin framed by a thick head of longish and unruly gray-blond hair that was always a messy contrast to his impeccable attire. Vandervoort always wore an elegant dark blue gold-buttoned coat over a leather vest. It was a look that suggested military, but Vandervoort was a civilian through and through.

He fashioned himself as a full-service building enterprise that not only offered the physical location for new businesses and institutions wishing to move to a better, more refined destination, but also provided loans for new ventures.

He was instantly an accepted and respected addition to the prominent members of Appaloosa's growing number of do-gooders, too. They liked the fact that Vandervoort brought in money and jobs, and that his plan was to create an infrastructure that grows from within. *Wealth begets wealth* was Vandervoort's motto.

Vandervoort, the brick factory, and his whole organization were a huge success.

"I reckon you could even call his endeavor here a damn near empire," I said.

"In less than three years, Vandervoort built his own goddamn avenue thoroughfare," Virgil said.

Allie's shop was on his own stretch of road with multiple business spaces—some of the spaces he owned personally and had employees operate, some spaces he rented, and others he outright sold. One of the businesses that Vandervoort owned and operated was a theater with booths and balconies where different kinds of entertainment were taking place most every night.

The fancy theater, town hall, and the impressive wide street all sported his namesake, the Vandervoort Theater, the Vandervoort Town Hall, and Vandervoort Avenue. Between the Town Hall and the theater, Vandervoort had his own stately offices and the sign above the door was simply chiseled VANDERVOORT in large block letters.

As Virgil and I strolled down Vandervoort Avenue, we noticed that almost every dwelling he'd had for sale or lease was now occupied.

"He damn sure knows how to do it," I said.

"Seems so," Virgil said.

"Good you was able to get a shop on this street for Allie," I said.

"You think?"

"I do."

"Well, she's happy," Virgil said.

"Think you being a U.S. Marshal had anything to do with it?"

"Likely didn't hurt," he said.

"No telling what might come of this," I said.

"Ain't that how it always is?"

We walked for a moment without saying anything, observing all the people supporting and managing the various businesses on Vandervoort Avenue. When we got to the end of the brick structures, Virgil stopped and looked up to the street sign.

"What's the difference between a street and an avenue, Everett?" Virgil said.

I shook my head and looked at him.

"Well, hell, you got me there, Virgil."

6

When we got to the Western Union office, Sheriff Chastain and Deputy Book were standing on the porch, waiting on us.

"Received a wire from Yaqui," Chastain said as we walked up.

"Whatcha got?" Virgil said.

Chastain shook his head.

"Been an escape . . . at Cibola."

"When?"

"Not sure exactly. Wire came in from Sheriff Stringer there in Yaqui. Said be on the lookout for escapees."

"Escapees?" I said.

Virgil glanced to me, then back to Chastain.

"How many?" he said.

Chastain shook his head.

"Don't know. Stringer said he'd be in the wire office to get into the details with you, wanted to connect with you personally."

We stepped into the office that was operated by Willoughby, a fleshy young fella with a permanent smile on his face. Virgil had Willoughby send a wire back to Yaqui to let Stringer know that he was present and waiting. A wire returned within the next minute that stated something urgent came about and Sheriff Stringer would be contacting us again momentarily. I read the original notes between Appaloosa and Yaqui that alerted us, and there was nothing else to it beyond what Chastain said.

"Be right out here," Virgil said with a nod.

Virgil, Chastain, Book, and I stepped back out onto the porch.

"Said be on the lookout. Has to mean this is not necessarily fresh news," I said.

"Why the delay, do you think?" Book said.

"Hard to say," I said.

"Cibola is a far piece," Chastain said.

"What is it," Book said. "About two hundred or so miles from here?"

"'Bout that," I said.

"So a number of days back," Book said.

Virgil looked to me and nodded a bit.

"Don't know I ever heard of anybody getting outta that place," Chastain said.

"It's a far ways, seventy-five miles from the closest town," I said.

"Used to be a lot of mining camps through there," Chastain said. "Suspect there still are."

"Dry-as-hell country, too," Book said.

I nodded.

"Wouldn't think it'd be that easy for those that get out to get gone," Chastain said.

Virgil looked at his watch.

"We'll know soon enough," Virgil said.

"Well," Chastain said as he pushed off from leaning on the wall, "Book, let's you and me get back to it."

Book nodded and lifted up off the hitch rail he was leaning on.

"We been cleaning, reorganizing the office, mending this and fixing that," Chastain said. "Tired of looking at all the shit that needed attention."

"Not sure what he's talking about the 'you and me' business. Basically it's him telling me what to do while he piddles," Book said.

"Watch me piddle-kicking your ass all the way back to the office."

Chastain halfheartedly kicked at Book, who was already steps in front of him, moving away fast.

Chastain looked back to us as he followed Book.

"You will let us know?" Chastain said.

"Will," Virgil said.

We watched as Chastain and Book walked off. Then Virgil pulled a cigar from his pocket, fished for a match, and struck it on the post. After he got the cigar going good we didn't talk as we watched the riders, buggies, workers, and women pushing their babies up and down the board-walks. I could tell, though, that there was something Virgil was thinking about other than the escapees, and after the extended silence Virgil looked at me and squinted a bit.

"What do you think she meant by if I don't know the answer, she can't help me?"

I smiled at Virgil.

"You don't know?"

"By God, if I knew I wouldn't waste time asking you." I smiled again.

"Just because French is a pretty name that borrows some sophistication from the fact it represents a world far from here doesn't mean she needs to keep it."

Virgil looked at the burnt tip of the match he was holding between his thumb and finger as if it held the answer to the meaning of the universe.

"I think she wants you to help make an honest woman of her."

Virgil flipped the match to the street, then looked at me.

"You think?" he said.

"I do."

Virgil nodded a little, considering that notion as he puffed slowly on his cigar.

"What makes you so sure?"

"Seems reasonable."

"She say something to you?"

"No."

Virgil worked on his cigar for a moment, then said, "Half the time I don't think she even likes me."

"Oh, she likes you."

"She likes the idea of me."

"Naw."

"Seems likely sometimes."

"She's just uncertain, and that makes her disposition kind of wound up at times."

"Wound up like an eight-day clock," Virgil said.

"You are everything to her."

Willoughby poked his head out the door.

"Marshal Cole," he said.

Virgil looked back to him.

"Sheriff Stringer," he said.

7

After Willoughby let Sheriff Stringer know we were present, the sounder begun clicking and Willoughby copied the incoming message. It was a fairly long message, but Willoughby was fast and efficient at his job and began reading almost before the sounder's final click.

"Start transmission: *We now have a problem here in Yaqui. Uncertain of the details at this time—A shootout occurred—Uncertain if related to the prison break—Details of the escape will be relayed directly—Currently and without question, there was gunplay at Yaqui river mill—At this time we don't know who was involved or the outcome—Have yet to ride out to mill but will do so after this telegram—The following is what we know regarding Cibola—The message we received came from Western Union office in Wingate— The message Wingate received was delivered from Cibola— Wingate is the support city of the prison—That message alerting Wingate authorities was not received by wire, but was delivered by pigeon post."*

Virgil looked to me.

"Pigeon?" Virgil said.

"Yes, sir, Marshal Cole," Willoughby said. "That's what was tapped."

"Go on," Virgil said.

Willoughby nodded.

"There is a side note here," Willoughby said. "About the post that just states: 'According to Wingate authorities, the pigeon-post messaging has been utilized since the prison was first in operation twelve years previous and has remained in operation as backup communication . . .'"

Willoughby looked up to us and said, "And the following is the post message received this a.m. from Cibola: *Post—From Kenneth Tillary, first assistant to Warden Scholes Flushing of Cibola Penal Institution—Alert—An undetermined number of inmates have escaped Cibola—Transmission lines have been disrupted—Entire prison currently under lockdown—Situation within the walls contained—Unrest, however, prevails—Evaluation is under way—Will update when more details are available—For now, be advised a number of dangerous inmates are unaccounted for and at large—Sincerely, Kenneth Tillary—End post.*"

Willoughby looked to us.

"And this is the rest from Stringer in Yaqui," Willoughby said. "Start transmission: *Wingate wire service has been dispatched for repairs—At this point in time there still is no communication with Cibola—That is all—An undetermined number of prisoners escaped four days ago—Friday, April seventeenth.* Quit transmission."

After a series of a few more questions and replies with Stringer that did not enlighten us with any more crucial details, Virgil told Stringer to go on and take care of business at the sawmill and to report back as soon as possible.

Virgil and I remained in the office and sent a telegram

to Wingate letting them know we had been notified, and after a short exchange with them we learned there was no more information to be obtained.

I tapped the square marked April 21 on the calendar hanging on the wall next to Willoughby's desk.

"If those that escaped are on foot, they could have made it to a number of towns by now if they wanted, including Yaqui."

Virgil nodded.

"Could," he said.

"They got horses? Hell, no telling how far they've ranged."

Virgil puffed on his cigar as he thought for a moment, then looked to Willoughby.

"Any other wires come in, let us know, Willoughby," Virgil said.

"Yes, sir," he said.

"I'll send a deputy here to sit with you. Word from Stringer or Wingate or any place else with information, send the deputy to us with the news of what you receive."

"Yes, sir, Marshal Cole."

With that, Virgil and I left the Western Union and walked back toward the office.

"What do you figure we do?" I said.

"Not much we can do."

"No reason to head for Wingate yet."

Virgil shook his head.

"If this situation in Yaqui is connected to an escaped inmate, then . . ."

"Wingate would be in the opposite direction," I said, finishing Virgil's sentence.

Virgil nodded.

"No reason to ride to Cibola, either," I said.

"No," Virgil said.

"What's gone is gone," I said.

"Is."

We walked for a little bit, thinking about the situation and our options.

"Wonder why the post did not come from the warden himself?" I said.

Virgil shook his head a little.

"Wondered that myself."

A wind picked up and swiveled a tornado of dirt across the street in front of us. Virgil stopped, looked at the spinning devil for a moment, then turned and looked back up the street.

"What?" I said.

"Don't know," Virgil said as he took a long pull on his cigar. "Don't know."

8

Allie, Virgil, and I were sitting in the dining room
of the Windsor Hotel, and just after we ordered dinner
Thane K. Rutledge, one of Appaloosa's newest investors,
swayed by our table with two of his worker bees, on his
way out.

Rutledge was a hefty older man residing at the Windsor who had an apparent fondness for wealth, power, and
liquor. At the moment he was prominently sporting all
three, including a diamond-studded watch fob and his
bookend associates. They were two overgrown younger
fellas with derbies and thick mustaches. They looked kind
of like twins, and the few times we'd met Rutledge they
were with him, always standing behind him like they were
there to pick up crumbs or tie their boss's shoes.

Rutledge was pleasant enough as he rambled on with
unnecessary bluster. Once he was sure his importance
was properly acknowledged and secured, he pulled back
one side of his coat and put his fist to his hip.

"I hope the three of you have it circled on your calendar, the big event. The upcoming convivial cotillion?" Rutledge said. "A ball destined to bring the who's who of Appaloosa together. Two weeks from today."

"We do indeed," Allie said.

"We do?" Virgil said, looking at Allie.

"Yes, we do," Allie said as she beamed up with bright eyes that she batted at Rutledge. "It's the talk of the ladies' social. Everyone is putting together their finest for the event. We wouldn't miss the party, let me tell you. Not for the world."

"For the world? Well, good," he said. "That's what I like to hear. I think the entire best of Appaloosa will be there. It will be the grandest party to happen here ever."

Virgil looked to me.

"It is just so exciting," Allie said. "I know all the ladies will be looking for new fineries, so I hope to have my store open and stocked soon so I can help make the festivities as grand as the parties they have in faraway countries."

"Wonderful, just wonderful," Rutledge said. "But the faraway countries will have nothing on us, Mrs. French."

"Where you gonna throw this shindig?" I said.

"The new Vandervoort Town Hall, where else."

"Wouldn't know," I said.

"It's the only place big enough. Vandervoort was kind enough to offer the place to me. It's a fabulous structure. It will be the Town Hall's maiden voyage. My idea, of course, but Vandervoort decided to bring in an orchestra all the way from Boston."

"It's so exciting," Allie said.

"Good, good," he said. "Until then, if not sooner."

Rutledge and his two shoe-tying associates made a move to go, but then Rutledge turned back. He smiled some as he leaned in toward Virgil like they were best friends.

"Almost forgot . . . What's this I hear about a prison break, Marshal Cole?"

Virgil glanced over to me. Then he rested his hands on the table and looked to Rutledge with a steady gaze.

"You tell me?"

Rutledge looked back and forth between Virgil and me like a boy knowing he's about to be scolded.

"Oh . . . sorry . . . Marshal Cole, I . . . I was in contact with one of my business partners who resides in Yaqui and that was how I received word . . . I didn't know it was something I, um . . ."

"It's all right, Mr. Rutledge," Virgil said. "But why don't you do what you can to help us by not pulling the cinch too tight on this."

"By all means, Marshal Cole, by all means. My apologies. We will see you at the gala."

Rutledge nodded, then backed away from the table and the threesome moved off and out of the dining room.

Virgil looked to me.

"Something about him don't sit," Virgil said.

"What?"

Virgil shook his head a little.

"Don't seem like the party-throwing type," Virgil said.

Allie took a drink of wine and shook her head back and forth a little.

"How many escaped, Virgil?"

"We don't know."

"My word," she said.

Virgil nodded.

"We just don't know the details yet," he said.

Allie nodded slowly and took another sip of wine.

"Well, what about me? What about my shop?"

Virgil looked at me across the table, then looked back to Allie.

"Your shop?"

"Yes."

Virgil squinted his eyes a bit, looking at her.

"What about your shop?"

"But why, Virgil?"

"Why what?"

"The prison break, you have not said a word about it."

"Well, I'm not keeping it from you."

"What are you doing if you're not?"

"Hell, Allie, we only found out about it this afternoon, after we saw you at your shop."

Allie took an unladylike gulp of wine.

"And besides, that don't got nothing to do with you and your shop, Allie."

"Of course not, Virgil, I'm sorry, I didn't mean that. I meant what about us, all of us, the people of Appaloosa, our safety, that is what I'm talking about."

"The fact that there was a break," Virgil said, "don't mean the escaped men are going to come here to Appaloosa and cause trouble and such."

Virgil looked to me and I nodded.

"Many men who escape just want a better life," I said. "Many take their newfound freedom and just hide, or do their best to stay out of trouble. Hope they don't get sent back."

"Many is not all," she said.

"I won't deny that."

"Main thing is, Allie," Virgil said. "You have us."

"I have been around you, the both of you, long enough to know exactly what this means. You and Everett will go out and pursue these convicts that are running loose, one way or another. That is just how it will be that is inevitable."

Virgil looked at me.

"Regardless of our duties, Allie," I said, "or where our

duties take us, you and the good people of Appaloosa will be looked after."

Virgil nodded.

"With Sheriff Chastain and Deputy Book," I said, "and the team of worthy deputies to look after everyone, you have nothing to be concerned about, Allie."

Allie looked at me and took another little sip of wine, then rested her hands in her lap.

"How far away from us?" Allie said.

Virgil looked to me.

" 'Bout two hundred miles."

"My God," she said.

"What?" Virgil said.

"That's close," she said.

"Hell, Allie, everything is close or far, depending how you look at it."

"Well, it's a bit too close for comfort, if you ask me."

I leaned back in my chair and saw Book enter the hotel. He caught my eye, then crossed the lobby and entered the dining room. He removed his hat as he got to our table.

"Mrs. French," Book said with a nod, then looked to Virgil.

"Sheriff Stringer got back to us and he's got more information . . ."

Book looked to Allie.

"More information," Book said. "Um . . . regarding the . . ."

"The prison break?" Allie said.

Book looked at her and smiled a little, then looked back to Virgil and me.

"Sheriff Stringer said he'd be back to the office there within the hour so you could communicate."

Allie took another sip, an even more unladylike sip, and drained her glass.

9

After dinner we walked Allie back to her shop. She said she was not in the mood to go home alone while we went about our marshaling business. She said she'd prefer to continue with getting her shop ready.

"Smells like rain," I said.

"Does," Virgil said.

"If it does, Everett will pick me up in his buggy, won't you, Everett?"

"Most assuredly, Allie," I said.

"Everett, I said this before, but I will say it again. You are forever the gentleman," Allie said.

"Sure he is, Allie," Virgil said. "You don't think I would have someone work with me who was not a gentleman, do you?"

"Well, I do what I can, when I can," I said.

"Oh, you do far more than that," Allie said as she unlocked the door to her shop.

She insisted we help her move a few trunks and hang a dressing mirror before we left. A necessary gesture on her part so as to let both Virgil and me know who was in charge. After we got the mirror hung, we left Allie standing in front of it, looking at her backside. When the door closed behind us, Virgil glanced back at Allie for a moment, then looked at me and smiled a little.

"Got a burr," Virgil said.

"Happens."

"Does."

"Don't think she has that cornered," I said.

"No."

"Goes with the territory of being a woman."

"Not hard to see it coming."

"No," I said. "It is not."

"Jug don't help."

"No, it don't."

"Nothing you can do about that."

"No, don't suppose there is."

"Shop helps," I said.

"It does," Virgil said.

"Keeps her from fueling the flame."

Virgil nodded.

"Yeah, it does," he said. "Keeps her occupied."

"Yeah, this is a good thing . . . when business is up and going, it will be even a better thing."

"Out of the goddamn house," Virgil said.

"I can see how those walls get to closing in."

"Do," Virgil said. "Things for the most go good, pleasant even, then all the sudden she will come on like a Comanche."

"I've seen it, plenty."

"I have come to the place where I just take a trip to the shed or to the barn to curry and such, just to sidestep the tomahawk."

"Least the two of you are not sitting around listening to the clock tick."

"Not doing that."

"Keeps a fella from getting too settled on his heels."

"Damn sure does," Virgil said.

"Sometimes I wonder where she gets all that piss and vinegar," I said.

"Unrest," Virgil said.

"No, hell, that we know."

"It ain't dull," he said.

"No, far from it."

"Never met a woman like her."

"No, she's been anteing up since the day she was born."

"She has," he said.

I thought about that as we walked. What all Allie had been through.

"This weather can't make up its mind," Virgil said.

The recent cold snap had passed and the night air was pleasant, but it sure enough felt like rain. There was also the feeling in the air like that when hail and tornadoes came. The evening air had a static and expectant feeling that went with it, as if something heavy was approaching.

When we crossed Main and turned up Fourth Street we saw a group of people walking from the depot, carrying luggage. Behind them the train hissed, releasing steam into the night air as it sat being replenished with water and coal.

"Here they come," Virgil said. "Every damn day another crop, Everett."

We crossed the street and waited for a handful of the newcomers that were headed for the steps of the Boston House Hotel, where some older men stood by the entrance smoking cigars, engaged in a spirited conversation as if there were no other people on earth.

As the people from the train passed, I noticed a distinguished couple bringing up the rear. The man was tall and angular and wore a polished hat and long coat, but my focus was instantly trained on the lean, elegant, and tastefully dressed woman who held on to his arm. She was wearing a high-collared dark brown gabardine dress with matching gloves and a fashionable coat and hat. She was strikingly beautiful and had a graceful air of elegance about her. She carried herself as if she was a princess, and as they reached the steps I caught the briefest look from her. Then her tall partner looked down to her and said something that made her laugh, and when he looked back up he, too, made eye contact with me just before they started up the steps.

It seemed that maybe he recognized me, and I also thought I recognized him but wasn't exactly sure.

I slowed and looked at the couple as they climbed the steps up to the Boston House.

The men standing around the entrance were still carrying on about whatever it was that made each of them do their best to talk over one another.

"Know 'em?" Virgil said, looking back to me.

I didn't reply, but as we continued walking and just before we moved on around the corner it hit me. I took a step back and looked to the couple just as they were entering the Boston House.

"Driggs?" I said.

10

The couple was already inside the Boston House, with the door now closed behind them.

Virgil looked up at the door, then at me.

I shook my head and continued walking with Virgil.

"Most likely was not him," I said.

We walked on toward the lighted office of the Western Union a half-block ahead of us.

"Don't think he heard you," Virgil said.

"Don't think it was him, either . . ."

"Pretty woman," Virgil said.

"I'll say."

I didn't say anything else as we walked, which prompted Virgil to slow some and glance back.

"Hell, go on back."

I shook my head.

"Naw," I said. "Couldn't be him."

"Sure?"

"Thought it might be this fella I knew from West

Point, fought Indians with . . . but that was another lifetime ago, when I was just nineteen, twenty."

We crossed to the boardwalk on the other side of the street.

"Well . . . you know where he is."

"Do," I said.

"Whoever he is, looks like he's done pretty well for himself."

"Fella he kind of looked like, that I was thinking of, Augustus Driggs, is maybe not even still alive. Fact is, if I had money on it I'd bet he was long gone. Besides that, even if it were Driggs, not sure I'd need to catch up with him about anything from that time. Not many good memories."

It began to sprinkle as we continued on to the Western Union office.

"Looks like you might have to be the gentleman that you are, Everett, and hitch up that buggy so's to pick up Allie like she was pleasantly saying."

When we arrived, Willoughby and Book were waiting for us.

"Sheriff Stringer is present in the office now," Book said. "This telegram there is what came in from him so far."

Book pointed to a note in front of Willoughby.

"You want me to read this?" Willoughby said.

"Do," Virgil said.

Willoughby nodded and read: "Start transmission: *Here is what we know—We have two men dead, another wounded—The wounded man, currently here in Yaqui Hospital, is one of the escapees from Cibola—The two men shot and killed in the shootout at the mill were both mill workers—There were four escapees involved—It appears they arrived here in Yaqui in buckboard pulled by*

*a single mule—Three of the four escaped here with sad-
dled horses they took from the mill—We know for a fact
that the men involved were some if not all of the escaped
convicts—Abandoned prison clothes of four men found
in buckboard—Currently we are experiencing damnable
bad weather so it's not possible to posse up just now—Plus
we wanted to communicate with you first.* Quit transmission."

"Let him know we are here," Virgil said. "Ask him
about the condition of the wounded prisoner. If he was
able to obtain any information from him."

Willoughby turned to his key and tapped out the message, and within a few minutes the sounder started to
click and Willoughby was detailing the content of Stringer's message. After a moment Willoughby sat back and
read.

"Start transmission: *We have not yet had a chance to
talk with the wounded escapee—Currently the man is in
surgery—He was in pretty bad shape and unconscious when
we found him so there is a chance we might not get any details out of him at all—Will let you know what we know
when we know.* End transmission."

We signed off with Stringer and left the wire office.
The rain was coming down steady. Virgil and I walked
back under the awnings of the boardwalk toward the
barn to get the covered buggy, which we rigged up and
drove over to collect Allie.

When we walked in she was sitting with none other
than Vernon Vandervoort and his wife, Constance, and
to my delight, Margie.

"Well, there they are," Vandervoort said as he stood
up and removed his top hat and bowed a little. "Good to
see you both."

"Hello," Virgil said.

"Hi," I said.

"Constance, you remember Marshal Cole and Deputy Marshal Hitch," said Vandervoort.

"Of course. How could I forget such handsome men," she said. "Good evening to you both."

Vandervoort's new bride, Constance, was half the age of her husband but was in every way Vandervoort's perfect counterpart. She was a curvy, full-figured woman who was always pleasant, smiling, and very attractive. She, too, had an unruly, almost violent crop of sandy blond hair that she wore piled atop her head like twisting vines, held in place with ornately jeweled hair clips. Being from New York City, she was different from most of the women in Appaloosa. She was refined and worldly in a way that suggested she'd probably traveled extensively, and she wore expensive dresses cut in the latest fashions. But she was a kind woman, and the few times we'd been in her company with Allie, it seemed she was doing her best to mentor Allie and her endeavors as a new dress shop owner.

"Nice to see you, Mrs. Vandervoort, and of course good evening to you, Margie," I said.

"Everett," she said with a giggle. "Nice to see you, too."

"We were out for a stroll," Vandervoort said. "And when the rain came we stepped in out of it to visit with our favorite tenant."

"And don't forget me," Margie said.

"Never," Vandervoort said.

Constance swiveled her head, looking all around her.

"The shop is going to be simply marvelous," she said. "And I have told Vernon I will see to it that Allison is well taken care of here."

"We most certainly will," he said. "She likes to tell me what to do."

Constance put her hand on Vandervoort's arm.

"I tell you what to do because, as has been demonstrated, you are nothing without me."

Vandervoort laughed heartily, but Constance just smiled.

"Have you told Allie the latest?"

He blinked as if he'd tasted something sour, then smiled and shook his head.

"I've not. Go right ahead, my dear."

"Vernon will be supplying all of Appaloosa with the best of the best. And that will include you and your new business, Allie."

"What do you mean?"

Constance smiled broadly.

"Vernon will be helping you by supplying you, dear, with the newest fineries from Europe," Constance said.

Constance turned to Vandervoort.

"Vernon has started an import-and-export business. He even bought his own ship."

"Well, I don't own the ship, dear, I charter the ship."

"Own, charter, what's the difference?" Constance said.

"Vernon will be importing the best Europe has to offer. From France, England, Germany, and Asia even."

I glanced at Virgil, but he remained focused on the Vandervoorts.

"Furniture, food, drink, and fineries from all over the world, and make them readily available right here in Appaloosa," Constance said.

Vernon nodded and smiled.

"He departs tomorrow for New Orleans to collect the first shipment."

"The important point is that I will be returning to Appaloosa very soon with a trainload of goods."

"My gosh," Allie said, then turned to Virgil. "Isn't that exciting?"

Virgil nodded a bit.

"What will you be exporting?" he said.

"Well, there is that," Vandervoort said with a hearty chuckle.

Vandervoort looked to Constance.

"The import-and-export moniker is a bit misleading for now," he said. "At least the export, for the time being."

"They could use some saddles," Virgil said.

Vandervoort laughed and slapped his thigh, "Quite right, Marshal Cole, quite right."

Vandervoort laughed again, then looked to his wife.

"Shall we, dear? I don't want to be inconsiderate, I'm sure they have better things to do than listen to us rattle on."

"Speak for yourself," Constance said with a smile as she got to her feet.

"Plus, I have a train to catch for New Orleans in the early morning," Vandervoort said.

"I must be going, too," Margie said.

"We will walk you, dear," Constance said.

"We have the buggy," I said. "We can drop you off if you'd like."

"We have our umbrellas," Vandervoort said.

"Me, too," Margie said.

"You sure?" I said.

"I am," Margie said. "But thank you, Everett. You are very kind and I just might have to take you up on that buggy ride one of these days."

"Most certainly," I said.

"Yes," Vandervoort said. "And we appreciate the offer, but . . ."

"Yes, we love a stroll in the rain," Constance said. "Under an umbrella, of course."

We said our good-byes and showed Mr. and Mrs. Vandervoort and Margie out the door. Allie watched them walk away, then turned to us with tears in her eyes.

"I cannot tell you just how blessed I feel," she said. "It's just overwhelming to me to know I have such supportive and helpful people in my life."

We locked the shop, got Allie loaded up, and drove to Virgil and Allie's place. When we arrived we saw a small, dark figure sitting on the porch.

"Got company," I said.

Virgil pulled his Colt but put it away when we saw who was moving out off the porch and into the rain.

11

A bolt of lightning briefly lit the interior of Hal's Café, and within a moment the thundering sound of the bolt cracked so loudly it rattled the café's front windows.

"Lord have mercy," Hal said. "Damn."

"Yeah," I said, looking out the window. "This is a good one."

Hal nodded and rubbed his hands together a bit as if he was thinking about the best way to say to us what he had to say. For some time all he had to allow was how hard the rain was coming down.

"What is it?" Virgil said.

"Yeah, I know you is wondering why I think it so important for me to come get y'all at this time of night, on a night like this," Hal said. "Why two busy and famous marshals like y'all need to be summoned by the likes of me. I know it ain't what you was planning for y'all's evening."

"Get on with it," Virgil said.

It was late in the evening and Virgil and I had just

shaken the rain off our slickers and sat down to drink some freshly brewed coffee with Hal.

"Y'all want some food?"

"No," Virgil said.

"We've had supper," I said.

Hal's Café was a place where Virgil and I would go to have some good basic grub. It was a fixture in Appaloosa mainly because Hal was always a friendly fella with a good disposition, but, most important, because Hal could cook better than most.

He was a large ex-slave who had worked in plantation kitchens for his owner for many years and in the process developed skills that were second nature, and in our opinion he was one of the best cooks in town. There were plenty of fancier places with expensive good food to be found in Appaloosa these days, but Hal's was a comfortable stopover for us. At this particular moment in time, however, Hal was not cooking and serving up food. It was well past suppertime now, and Hal was agitated and nervous about something. He'd sent his young nephew, Felix, to fetch us. Once we were seated with coffee, Hal looked to Felix.

"Go on back and wash some dishes, Felix," he said.

"Done washed all the dishes."

"Wash 'em again then."

"But I did what you asked following them fellas, then fetching Marshal Cole and . . ." Felix stopped talking for a moment when he registered the steaming look Hal was giving him. "Do I got to?"

"You don't got to, but you don't I will tan your dark hide, hear? . . . Get on, like I say."

"Here I go," he said.

Felix dropped his head a bit and sauntered off through the door to the rear of the café. Hal watched the door work back and forth on the hinges before he looked to us.

"I got a problem," he said.

"Go," Virgil said.

Hal looked out the window nervously.

"Someone is trying to take over my business."

"What do you mean?" Virgil said.

"I can see the writing on the shit house wall," he said. "I was not born yesterday."

Virgil looked to me.

"What are you saying, Hal," I said.

"Some boys a'been coming by here," he said.

"Boys?" Virgil said.

"Men is what they are, one young, one old . . . They is goddamn mean, though, both big overgrown fuckers, too. Offering me protection."

Virgil sipped his coffee, glanced to me, then looked back to Hal.

"Protection from what?" he said.

"They said someone was here to do me harm."

"Who?"

Hal looked back and forth between Virgil and me.

"From them?" I said, before Hal spoke. "They were the 'someones' that meant to do you harm?"

"Seems so," Hal said.

"They wanting money?" Virgil said.

"They is."

Virgil looked to me.

"They told me to give them money or they'd make sure they'd close me down."

Virgil looked to me, then looked to Hal.

"They say how they was planning to close you down?"

"They threatened to burn me down."

"You talk to Sheriff Chastain about this?"

Hal shook his head some.

"They told me if I said anything, if I go to Sheriff Chastain or any of his deputies they'd say that I lied.

They said to me, who Sheriff Chastain gonna believe, white man or a nigger man . . . They said they'd burn my place down."

"What'd you do?"

"I gave them some money," he said.

"How much?"

"At first it was not a lot."

"At first?" Virgil said. "How long have you been paying them?"

"Three months."

Virgil glanced to me, then looked back to Hal.

"Do you know who these men are?" he said.

"Not by name I don't."

"You seen them around?" I said.

He shook his head.

"Only when they come in here."

"Do you know or got an idea where they are?" I said.

"I do now," he said, looking back and forth between Virgil and me. "That's why I sent for you."

"Where?" Virgil said.

Hal got to his feet and paced a few times.

"Here's the deal," he said. "I come to y'all cause y'all ain't necessarily who they told me not to talk to. They said Sheriff Chastain and his deputies, don't say nothing to them, but they never said nothing about no marshals, don't know they even know you live here in Appaloosa."

"We been in here four or five times since this has been going on," I said. "Why haven't you said nothing to us before now?"

"I figured this would go away, plumb blow over. What I was hoping for, anyway."

"But it ain't," Virgil said.

"Nope. They come tonight, and they'd been drinking, I could tell. They demanded double what I gave them before."

"You pay 'em?"

He frowned.

"I did."

"Where are they?" Virgil said.

Hal twisted his big hands together.

"They down at a gambling place, over on the north end of town."

"There's more than one," I said.

"I know which one and they there now," he said. "I had Felix follow them. That's what he was talking 'bout. He said they looked to be holed up there just doing what white men do."

12

Virgil and I got our horses saddled in case some—thing went afoul and we needed to give chase. We quickly got them ready to ride in the dry of my barn. I did not have a house yet in Appaloosa, but I managed to have a place to keep our animals. It was a nice big barn I rented from the widow of a farrier who passed away a few years back, and currently she had no use for it other than to rent it to me.

I figured since Virgil had Allie to take care of and I really didn't have anybody I needed to look after, I'd take care of our horses. We had a good lot to choose from, too. Virgil still had his stud Cortez and I had big Ajax, but I had found some good horses of late, and with the exception of doctoring a few problem areas here and there, they were all in good shape to ride. We had twelve in all, and depending on the various tasks at hand, distance, weather, terrain, and surefootedness, it was normally an easy decision which horses we saddled up.

I had two fleet bay horses I'd bought from a rancher I knew who was a good horseman. We had ridden them a lot and they both had a solid step and were easy to maintain, but mainly we felt comfortable with them in rainy weather and the dark.

"How we going to go about this?" I said.

Virgil tightened his cinch and looked over the top of his saddle to me and shook his head.

"Well," he said. "Don't make sense two toughs here in Appaloosa set out to collect from a local business."

I nodded.

"Don't really," I said.

"They're just the collectors," Virgil said.

I thought about that for a moment.

"For who?" I said.

"Hard to figure."

I nodded.

"So many shits in this town these days," I said. "Could be any of 'em."

"Figure the main thing is we get to the root."

"Most likely they're not gun hands," I said. "More than likely they are just hired hands, acting big."

"Leave your eight-gauge," Virgil said. "See if we can take a friendly approach."

It was raining even harder than it was when we departed Hal's. We left the barn and rode winding through the streets of Appaloosa to Meserole's, the place Hal told us the two grifters were located. Hal gave us a good account of what each man was wearing and their physical description.

We found a place across from Meserole's to tie our horses, where they were somewhat sheltered from the rain. We covered the saddles with oilcloths and walked across the street to the gambling establishment.

There were a good number of horses hitched out front as well as a few buggies parked on the side. Most of the horses had a poncho or oilcloth covering the saddle.

Meserole's was a gambling saloon that catered to silver miners but was also known for having plenty of ladies working there. It was popular with the younger crowd and, like it appeared to be tonight, it was usually busy.

When we entered, the parlor was noisy and crowded. I did not notice the men we were looking for, not right away, anyway, mainly because it was dark. Virgil and I shook the water from our mackintoshes and hung them by the door and waited for our eyes to adjust some. Like most places that sported hustling women, Meserole's was dimly lit.

Once our eyes adjusted, we walked to the bar. It was an L-shaped bar with the long side facing the main barroom, where a crowd of men and women sat drinking, smoking, and playing cards and grab-ass. We found two empty stools on the short side of the L so we could have a good look at the gathering and ordered some whiskey. As I was watching the bartender pour the whiskey, Virgil nudged me in the ribs.

I looked to see a fella playing cards with two women in the corner under the landing that led to the second floor.

"That look like one of them Hal described?" he said.

"Might be."

Virgil nodded a little, then turned away from the man so as not to draw attention. But I could look at him as clearly as if I were looking at Virgil.

"He's big," Virgil said. "Wearing a bowler. You see a feather in his hat?"

I watched him for a moment or two, and when he turned his head I saw the feather.

I nodded.

"Do," I said. "He's the older of the two Hal described, I'd say. Looks to be mid-fifties or so."

"Don't see any other big-chested fifty-year-old fellas wearing a bowler hat with a feather, do you?"

"Don't," I said.

13

"**What about the other fella?**" **Virgil said.** "**The** young one, real tall, skinny, long hair, scraggly beard?"

"No . . . don't see him," I said. "Just the older one."

Virgil nodded a little, glancing up to the second floor.

"What's upstairs?" he said.

"I think Meserole has his office up there, but I don't know for a fact."

Virgil nodded a little and glanced around some.

"They ain't whoring here?" he said.

"No," I said. "Just saloon girls, flirting and hustling whiskey."

"We wait?" I said.

Virgil nodded a bit.

A small woman came walking in from a door near the bar and glanced around some, then looked over to me. She nodded a little to me—the friendly "buy me a drink, paying customer" nod. Then she tilted her head and casually meandered her way over and settled between Virgil and me.

"Wet enough for you?" she said.

Virgil turned toward her a little. The move put his back even more to the big-chested guy with the feather in his hat.

"Is," he said, then smiled.

"How y'all doing this evening?"

"Better 'an most," I said.

Virgil nodded a bit and looked to me.

"Real good," I said.

"That's good," she said. "That's good."

"And you?" I said.

"Peachy."

She was attractive for a woman who barely filled her dress and shoes. Every part of her was thin: her fingers, her face, her figure, everything.

"What's your name?" Virgil said.

"Betty," she said with a smile as she twirled a strand of her hair with her finger.

"Betty," Virgil said with a nod. "It's a pleasure."

"Likewise," she said as she twirled the strand one way, then twirled it in the other direction.

"You been in here most the evening?" Virgil said.

"I have," she said. "And I've yet to have a single drop, if you can believe that?"

Virgil glanced to me.

"Whiskey," I said to the bartender.

She looked to me, smiled. "Why, thank you," she said.

"Got a few questions for you, Betty," Virgil said.

She smiled and looked down at her skinny body.

"Let me see if I can find the answer you are looking for," she said, then looked back to Virgil with pouty lips that turned into a coy smile.

"I'm Virgil and this fella here is Everett. Everett and me are here on official business."

"I'm about as official as they come," Betty said with a laugh.

Virgil smiled.

"What could be more official than little ol' me?" she said.

Virgil slyly pulled back his jacket and showed her the star pinned on his vest.

"Right now we have some marshaling business to attend to."

She looked back and forth between Virgil and me.

"Am I under arrest?"

"No," Virgil said. "The official business we are here to conduct has to do with two fellas we are searching for."

Her demeanor changed and she stood a bit taller, as if she were in trouble.

"I want you to smile and enjoy your whiskey," he said. "There is no reason you need to do otherwise. Don't want you to draw attention to nothing out of the ordinary, okay?"

She glanced to me then cut her eyes back to Virgil and nodded.

"Okay."

"Just over my shoulder," Virgil said. "There is an older fella. He's a big fella sitting with a couple of gals under that stairway landing."

She leaned a bit.

"That's Debbie and Ellen."

"Just look at me," Virgil said. "Like I said, I don't want you to get anyone's attention."

She nodded.

"Smile," he said.

She smiled.

"So, real casual-like," Virgil said. "You got a good look at the man I'm talking about, sitting with Debbie and Ellen?"

"I do," she said.

"Do you know him?"

"No."

"Seen him in here before?"

She nodded.

"I've seen him before, yes, but I don't know him, honest."

"He have a friend, too?"

"He does."

"Big, tall young fella with long hair and a scraggly beard."

"That's right," she said.

"Any idea where he is?"

She nodded.

"He's walking down the stairs as we speak."

14

Just as Virgil turned, a shot was fired from someone upstairs and we heard a scream. The shot was a loud
shotgun blast and the load hit the tall, skinny man just as
he got to the landing. The blast knocked him forward
into the railing. He turned in one swift motion with his
gun and fired upstairs, then slumped and doubled over
on the rail. A moment later a body tumbled down the
stairs and slammed into the tall man and the two men
busted through the railing and fell onto a table below,
which collapsed under their weight.

The whole place erupted in a clamor as everyone
moved toward the door.

Virgil and I had our pistols out and moved through
the people toward the man with the bowler and the
other two men who'd just crashed through the railing.

After people made it by us, trying to get out, we determined that the older fella with the bowler was now
nowhere to be seen and the tall, young man with the
long hair appeared to be dead, with another man laying

facedown on top of him, who, by quick observation, also appeared to be dead.

Just behind the table where the man with the bowler had been sitting was a window in an alcove, and it was open.

"Front," Virgil said.

I moved quickly and Virgil was right behind me, trying to get through the crowd of people struggling to get out the front door, and just as we made it out, we briefly saw the man with the bowler. He was hightailing it away in the pouring rain and within a moment was around a corner and gone.

"I'll be goddamn," I said.

"I'll deal here," Virgil said. "See if you can catch the son of a bitch."

I ran across the street into the alley where our horses were tied, swung up on the bay, and followed in the direction the man rode in hopes I might get lucky. I made the corner he'd turned and rode at a steady clip. The rain was coming down in my face, making it hard to see, and so far I'd seen nothing. I rode till I got to an intersection, and in every direction I looked I saw nothing, no one moving, no one on horseback. I rode on forward for a bit to where the road dead-ended at the railroad tracks. I turned and rode up the tracks a bit, then stopped.

I looked around and saw nothing but darkness all around except in the direction of town, where the hazy light from it shimmered in the falling rain. I sat there for a while thinking I just might get a glimpse, but I saw nothing. I rode back through the streets of Appaloosa, turning down one street and then another, and after a half-hour or so I rode back to Meserole's.

When I got back to the place there was already an ambulance parked out front. Two men who worked for the hospital were loading up one of the men as Doc Burris stood on the porch under the awning, puffing on his pipe.

"Everett," Doc said.

"What do we got?"

"Two dead men," he said.

I dismounted and tied the bay to the hitch.

"One was alive for a moment, but no longer."

"Know who they are?"

Doc nodded.

"One we know is Meserole, the owner of this place," Doc said. "Shot through the heart. Don't know who the other man was."

"He say anything?"

"Not that I know of. Virgil is in there right now trying to figure out who he is and what happened."

When I entered Meserole's, Sheriff Chastain and Deputy Book were now with Virgil. They were sitting with Ellen and Debbie, the two women the fella with the derby had been sitting with, and Betty, the skinny gal that sat with Virgil and me for a bit. The bartender was sitting nearby, too. All of the employees looked as if they'd been crying. Virgil met my eye.

I shook my head.

"No such luck," I said.

Chastain leaned back in his chair.

"Virgil gave us a description," Chastain said. "I got a handful of deputies out searching."

I nodded and looked to Virgil.

"What do we know?"

Virgil shook his head.

"What we know is their boss, Michael Meserole, the owner of this place, is dead, and the other tall man nobody knows. Well, the ladies here said he called himself Charlie and the other one, the older one with the bowler, was Dave, but that is all they know."

"You figure the same situation was happening here that was happening at the café?"

Virgil nodded.

The bartender, noticing I was soaking wet from the ride I took without my slicker, went behind the bar, gathered up some towels, and handed them to me.

"Mr. Meserole was like a father to me," the bartender said.

Then he looked to the three women sitting with Virgil.

"Them, too, to all of us," he said. "He was generous and kind to us. He was tough as hell and ran a tight ship around here and put up with no shit from any of us, but he was a good man."

The women all nodded as they held back tears.

Willoughby from the Western Union office came in and removed his hat when he saw the three young women crying.

"Um . . . excuse me, Marshal Cole, but Sheriff Stringer from Yaqui asked me to find you and have you come by so to let you know what was what regarding Cibola."

15

We left Sheriff Chastain to deal with the situation at Meserole's, and Virgil and I went to the Western Union office with Willoughby and Book.

Virgil had Willoughby tap out a note on the key to Stringer, letting him know we were present. Within a few minutes the sounder started clicking and Willoughby started to write. After, he sat back and read. "Start transmission: *From Sheriff Stringer, Yaqui—No additional news from Cibola or from the support city Wingate—However, the doctor here in Yaqui operated on the wounded escapee, removing two bullets—According to the doctor, he is going to pull through just fine—He is weak, but we were able to talk with him and this is what we know as follows—According to the escapee, there were eight convicts who escaped.*"

"Holy hell," Book said.

Virgil looked to me and raised his eyebrows.

"Bunch," I said.

Virgil looked to Willoughby. Willoughby continued.

"*—Escape happened in the middle of the night—far as*

we know none of the escapees were immediately caught—
Captured escapee is a young man, twenty-one years old—
wound not critical—says his name is Bernard Dobbin—claims
he was not directly responsible for the deaths of the two mill
workers—After some necessary handiwork dealing with
Dobbin—making certain he was telling the truth, we be-
lieve him—every word he uttered."

"Handiwork?" Book said

"Persuasion," I said.

Willoughby continued. "—*Dobbin said those escaped,*
separated into two groups—He believes the other convicts, in
group opposite his, headed east out of Cibola—The other three
that were with him, here in Yaqui, are now headed to
Vadito—least that is where they had discussed going, for the
obvious reasons—we'll wait to see what you want to do,
Virgil—Vadito is, of course, closer to you there in Appaloosa—
Ready to put posse together to find others in the morning—
but will await your instructions—One other detail, the eight
men who escaped were all from compound C—According to
Dobbin, compound C is Murderers Row—houses the most no-
torious of the Cibola inmates. All inmates in compound C
are serving time for murder—including Dobbin."

Virgil looked to me.

"Vadito," he said.

"Whores," I said.

"Where's that?" Book said.

"Vadito's a river-crossing town on the Little Colorado
where cattlemen notoriously stop in to give up what
money they make on gambling, whiskey, and whores,
mainly whores."

"Mexico would be closer," Virgil said.

"It is."

"Maybe they or one of them has some connection to
the place," Virgil said.

"Could," I said.

"Damn," Book said. "Minus this Dobbin, there are seven killers on the loose."

"I suspect we'd be best to get to Vadito," I said. "Let Stringer take the posse east?"

Virgil nodded a little.

"Two days' ride," he said.

"Vadito could be busy," I said.

"Could," Virgil said. Then he thought for a moment and pointed to the key in front of Willoughby. "Need to get some descriptions of the three and their horses."

"Their names, too, wouldn't hurt," I said.

Virgil nodded.

"What about this goddamn deal here?"

Virgil shook his head.

"More to it than meets the eye," Virgil said.

I looked to Book.

"You know anything, hear anything about guys running a racket, pressuring and threatening business owners?"

"No," Book said.

"Wonder how many others this was happening to?" I said.

"Hard to say," Virgil said.

"Somebody has to know about them," I said. "Who they are, what they were doing."

Virgil nodded some.

"Like you said," I said. "There is more to it than meets the eye . . ."

"Too many goddamn people," Virgil said.

"What now?"

"First order is these sonsabitches on the run," Virgil said. "Can't have a passel of murderers on the loose."

"If they are headed to Vadito," I said, "we very well might make this notion of their new-formed freedom a little less free-feeling."

"That'd be my thought," Virgil said.

16

The rain continued through the night but stopped a few hours before daybreak. I had tossed and turned throughout and eventually gave up trying to sleep. I got myself up and dressed. Then got the horses fed and saddled for the trip Virgil and I were preparing to take over to Vadito, in search of the three convicts who had killed two men in the shootout at the sawmill in Yaqui. It was early morning and still dark, but the eastern horizon was brightening some with a faint hint of gold, and the sun would be up and showing full within the hour.

When I walked the horses toward the sheriff's office, Book was loading panniers on a tall mule tied to the office's hitch rail. Book turned quick and looked to me as I came up in the dark behind him.

"Everett."

"Morning, Book," I said.

"Gave me a start coming up like that," he said.

"Just me."

He shook his head. "Glad of it."

"How goes it?" I said as I led the horses to the hitch and tied them next to the mule.

"Okay, I guess," Book said. "Been thinking about that shooting over at Meserole's last night."

"Yeah," I said. "Hell of a deal."

"Been a long time since something like that has happened around here," Book said. "Last gunplay I remember around here was when Truitt Shirley shot that Denver policeman in front of the gambling parlor."

"Yep," I said. "Sounds right."

"I knew Old Man Meserole," Book said. "I been in his place a few times, played some cards with the guys after work and looked at the girls. One of the few good places where the gals working aren't selling their goods, too. Wonder if the place will close down?"

"Hard to say," I said.

"Damn shame," Book said.

"We'll get to the bottom of it," I said.

"Hope so," Book said.

"We ready?"

"Pretty much. Just loading everything up."

I looked to the office.

"Virgil here?"

Book shook his head.

"Not yet," he said as he continued to pack the panniers with supplies that he had laid out on the boardwalk. "Got you enough rations to make the trip over and back."

"Hard to say what direction we'll go once we get there."

"Well, I got you all kinds of stuff. A good amount—coffee, dried figs, carrots, biscuits, fatback, canned sardines, jerky, hardtack, beans . . ."

"Damn, Book, not going to China."

"Well, no reason not to be prepared."

"You got whiskey in there?"

"I do," Book said.

"Good man."

Book started back toward the office but paused before stepping inside and turned to me.

"This is bad."

"What?"

"These prisoners."

"Not good."

"What do you make of what the Dobbin fella said about how they got out?"

"Don't have a real clear picture."

"No, I know, that's what I mean. It's hard to conceive just how this happened."

"Don't think we will really get a clear understanding until we get some information directly from the prison."

"Well," Book said, "hard to figure how the whole of them overpowered the guards and just walked out."

"It does, I won't deny you that."

"What if you come across them on the way?"

"Could happen."

"Damn, Everett, maybe some of us should go with you?"

"Think we'll be all right, Book."

"And you and Virgil know one of the men on the list," he said. "Charlie . . ."

"Yep," I said. "Ravenscroft. Charlie Ravenscroft, a no-good son of a bitch. We caught him after he killed two policemen. Claimed it was self-defense."

"He's not one of the three you're after, now, though," Book said. "He's with the other bunch, the bunch Sheriff Stringer is after."

I nodded.

"What we know," I said. "That's what the Dobbin fella offered up, anyway."

"Well, if you want, I will go . . . I mean, if Sheriff Chastain thinks it's okay."

"You're needed here, Book. All of you. No telling about the other that got away from Meserole's and what kind of fallout may happen. Maybe you guys can figure out something about the tall fella that Meserole shot, too."

Book shook his head some. "That was a hell of a storm we had," he said.

"Was," I said.

"Brought in some trouble," he said.

"Did," I said.

17

Book walked back toward the office but stopped before entering and looked off down the street.

It was dark, but I could make out someone walking up the street carrying a rifle. After he got a bit closer and stepped up on the boardwalk I saw clearly it was Virgil carrying his Winchester. Book entered the office, then came back out with a handful of supplies and looked to Virgil walking up.

"Morning," Book said as Virgil came into the spilling light of the sconce hanging by the office door.

"Morning back," he said with a yawn. "Coffee?"

"You bet," Book said, then hurried back to the mule and put the supplies in the panniers. "I'll get you some . . . Everett, you, too, coffee?"

"Sure," I said.

Book walked back into the office.

"Sleep?" I said.

"No," he said. "You?"

"Like a fish outta water," I said.

Virgil nodded, set the butt of his rifle on the floor, and leaned the barrel on the wall as Book came back out with coffee.

"Fresh and hot," Book said as he handed Virgil a cup, then handed a cup to me.

"That'll work," Virgil said.

I sat on the hitch with my back to the horses and put my boots on the edge of the boardwalk. I blew on the cup's steaming surface before taking a sip.

"You pack some whiskey in those bags, Book?" Virgil said, then took a sip of coffee.

Book looked at me and smiled a little.

"I did," he said.

Virgil nodded.

"Good," he said, then sipped some more coffee and sat on the bench under the lamp.

"I got just a few more things to load and you'll be good to go," Book said, then stepped back into the office.

"I kept waking up thinking about the men from compound C," I said.

Virgil yawned and shook his head some.

"Yeah, they were running around in my sleep, too."

Book came out and held up a few small bags. "Pecans and walnuts," he said with a smile, then put them in the panniers.

Book buckled the pannier flaps and came back toward the office but stopped with a foot on the step and looked to Virgil.

"I told Everett I'd be happy to come along."

"Happy?" Virgil said.

"Well, you know," he said.

"Me and Everett will be just fine, Book, but we appreciate the notion."

"Well, okay," Book said and started back into the office but stopped shy of entering and turned, looking to Virgil, then me.

"Hard to figure how that many men got out and on the loose like this," Book said.

"Is," Virgil said.

Book walked back into the office as Virgil and I sipped our coffee thinking about that very thing—the same very thing that kept us from having decent sleep.

Book came out of the office with a small fry pan and bean pot. "Almost forgot this stuff," he said as he unbuckled the panniers and put the cooking gear inside, then secured the flap again.

"Appreciate it, Book," Virgil said.

"That should do it," he said, then pulled a packing list from his pocket and read it as he walked back into the office. After a moment Book came to the door with a cup of coffee and leaned on the doorjamb.

"How will you know what to do?" Book said. "Once you are to Vadito?"

Virgil looked to Book.

"Just have to figure that out as we go along."

"Do you think the three you're after will all stay together?"

Virgil shook his head.

"Hard to know just what they'll do."

"Seems to me they'd all go in separate directions," Book said. "So not to draw attention to themselves."

Virgil nodded a bit.

"Might well be."

"And you don't figure that they will stay away from towns?" Book said.

"No," I said.

"Don't, either," Virgil said.

"I would . . ." Book said. "I think."

Virgil shook his head some.

"Vadito gives them all the things they've not been able to have . . . pussy, whiskey, food, the basics, and Stringer said they took money, too, so they will have money to spend."

I nodded.

"Money is something they've not had in a long time," I said.

"So many people come here to Appaloosa these days . . . They could waltz in here and we wouldn't know them from the normal folk," Book said.

"That's correct," Virgil said.

"Appaloosa is closer than a lot of other towns to that prison," Book said.

"Is," Virgil said.

"You think they could come here?"

"Very well could," Virgil said.

"Hard to say about those that went east. If they got horses or not, and if so, if they do have horses and they stayed at a pace they could cover a lot of ground."

Book frowned a bit and said, "For all we know, they could be here by now."

Virgil looked to me.

"Could," he said.

"All the more reason for you, the sheriff, and all the Appaloosa deputies to be here and keep close watch," I said.

"Is," Virgil said.

Book stared off up the dark street. He turned, looking in the other direction as if he heard something, then back to me.

"Well, at least we have some descriptions and names," Book said.

Virgil pulled his watch from his vest pocket, looked at the time, then got to his feet.

We saw to a few last-minute details, then mounted up just as the sun showed a piece of its face. When we turned the corner to head south I looked back to Book. He was standing in the dark of the office overhang. He stretched out his arm and poured the remainder of his coffee into the street.

18

Driggs had no idea until he did some snooping around that he would have to wait for a while in Appaloosa until he could accomplish what he came to town to do. But that was okay with him; he was as patient as ol' Job.

Driggs raised his long, muscled arms above his head, stretching, as he stood naked looking out the window of the Boston House Hotel. It was early in the morning; the sun was just brightening the free world of Appaloosa. Behind him, in bed, lay the woman. She was naked, spent, and sound asleep. Her long, dark hair violently wound this way and that, spreading out like long tentacles across the valleys and hills of the swirling white sheets.

He stood perfectly still as he looked out, thinking about nothing in particular. Not at this moment, anyway. He was enjoying the view of the town coming to life before him, a vision he'd not witnessed in some time.

A buggy came slowly up the street that was being pulled by an old wide dun horse. The driver's face was hidden under the buggy's canopy as he incessantly urged the animal forward. The fact that Driggs could not see the driver's features made him think about how there is no real individual face of man, not really. Though far and wide there are many varied faces, they are pretty much most certainly the same. They are interchangeable, Driggs thought, all trudging endlessly toward the common goal of an end result. Survival, need, and instinct drove the masses. Driggs had determined early on that the insufferable hordes are primarily caretakers of man-made order, of the way of mankind. Driggs knew though that he himself was not part of that mundane order. He was certainly not just a driver with a face unseen.

Driggs watched the man in the buggy encourage the dun as they turned in front of the hotel, and he watched as the dun trotted on, disappearing with the faceless man down Main Street.

He stood calm and still for a few minutes, then moved from the window and picked up a tobacco pouch off the dresser and rolled a cigarette.

He looked at the naked woman, watching her breathe. She was on her stomach with only half of her rear end covered with bedding. The gentle, slow breathing forced her lips to push out when she exhaled. The move seemed childlike and made the woman appear momentarily innocent to Driggs. But she was far from innocent. After Driggs had done his necessary investigation and reconnaissance throughout the evening and into the early-morning hours, it was proved to him that nothing about the woman embodied innocence. Maybe that was true before, but now it was different. Now that she had been relieved of her preconceived self-styled notions about tolerance and suffrage, about purity and decency, what was left was only a savage beast that breathed harmonically. But he knew all that before he got into it, into the throes of it, with her. He was glad to know there was more to be extracted and that made him *feel good, that it would not simply be a matter of time before he would have to move on from her, disregard her. He rested in the comfort, however, that he knew exactly what was required and just how it would go on and what more would need to be pulled, twisted, and turned. But most important, she was his partner, his princess. His princess for the task at hand, and he was steady and patient about the process. Driggs didn't ever rush or hurry. Haste was simply not in his nature.*

He moved back to the window, and with a stick match between his middle finger and forefinger scratched the sulfur tip with a quick flick of his thumbnail and the flame ignited. He lit the cigarette, then inhaled the Virginia tobacco. He held out the cigarette and studied the smoke rising from the lit end. It had been a long time since he had fine morning tobacco after an evening of roughshod. Driggs enjoyed the smoothness as the intake stimulated spiderwebbed euphoria across his mind. When he let out the smoke he savored the refreshing morning dizziness it gave him.

He reached back and grabbed the bottle off the bedside table next to the Bible and held it up in the light of the window. It was three-quarters empty. He took a good pull from the golden liquid and savored the warmth as it slid down this throat.

Hitch, *he thought.* Fucking Everett Hitch. *It had been a long time since he had seen Hitch. A lot of men change through the years and age rapidly and drastically, he thought, but not Everett Hitch. He was still lean, strong, and youthful . . . like the Indian killer he remembered . . .* Fucking Hitch.

"What are you thinking about," the princess said with a sleepily raspy voice from the night of whiskey.

Her question did not take him by surprise. He figured it would be only a matter of time until she was ready.

"God," he said, without turning around to look at her.

"What about God?"

He did not answer immediately. He could feel his princess looking at the back of him, and most likely the three bullet holes in his shoulder that he'd received the day he was double-crossed. He turned to her and smiled.

"Just flowing with the hinges," he said.

"Hinges?"

He nodded and tapped his temple.

"This way and that, they go."

Her eyes rested on his rugged and . . . rigid nakedness. She looked up and met his eyes. She stared at him and he stared at her. She rolled over on her back, looking up at him.

He took a pull off the whiskey, put the cigarette in the ashtray, then moved a bit closer to the bed. She instinctively recoiled and moved back, but he reached out with his right hand and grabbed her ankle, then swiveled her around and grabbed her other ankle with his left hand. He stared at her eyes as he pulled the princess's body toward him.

19

We rode for a solid eleven hours, stopping only briefly for feed and to rest the animals. When it started to get dark we made camp on a finger of wooded land that diverted the river east for at least a mile before the waters turned and continued south. The peninsula, bolstered by its rocky base, served as a solid retaining wall that had withstood the years of force from the mountain spring waters.

After dinner, Virgil lit a cigar and I poured us some whiskey. I handed a cup to Virgil and we sat looking at the clear night sky and did not talk until I refilled the cups.

"We get gone by daylight, we should get to Vadito by mid-afternoon."

Virgil nodded and we did not talk again for another long moment as we just sipped our whiskey.

"Ravenscroft," I said. "Charlie Ravenscroft."

Virgil looked to me and shook his head a little.

"If there is anybody that don't need to be out and about among the innocent people," Virgil said, "it's him."

"Yep."

"Not sure how his lawyer talked the judge out of not hanging him," Virgil said.

"Cibola," I said. "Don't seem to be a much better fate."

"No," Virgil said. "It don't."

"Hard life," I said.

Virgil nodded, and he puffed on his cigar some.

"Man needs not to be locked up, though," Virgil said. "Don't do no good, really."

I looked to Virgil. He was staring into the fire.

"Man needs to be free and die for his deeds gone wrong, not fed and kept like a goddamn animal in a goddamn cage."

I thought about that, remembering back on my soldiering days, killing helpless Indians in the Indian Wars, and I thought about the man I'd shot many years ago in Tres Padres . . . a situation that just got out of hand.

Virgil looked up and met my eye.

"But," he said, "things don't go that way."

"No," I said. "They don't."

"That ain't the way of justice," Virgil said.

He looked back to the fire.

"We got the law," Virgil said. "Too many of them. Too many laws, I think."

Virgil smiled and looked back to me.

"Too many rules to live by," he said. "But . . . without law, without rules, evil takes root."

"Got hold of Ravenscroft," I said.

Virgil nodded.

"Damn sure did," he said.

Virgil held out his cup and I replenished his whiskey.

"Killed those two lawmen," Virgil said. "Trying to serve him with papers that he did not agree with."

"I remember his fancy-talking lawyer made it out it was self-defense," I said. "Even though it was Ravenscroft that rode into town and walked into the office and shot them."

"How long ago was it?" Virgil said.

"Ravenscroft went to Cibola?" I said.

Virgil nodded.

"Hell, he's been in there four, maybe five years now, I'd say."

We sipped on our whiskey for a while, just remembering.

"Of all the men we have brought in through these marshaling years," I said, "it's hard to believe that that son of a bitch Ravenscroft is the only name on that list of eight who we know."

"Is," Virgil said.

"Too bad he's in the other group and not one of the three that was with Dobbin."

I pulled the list of names and the descriptions we received from Sheriff Stringer. I leaned over to the light from the fire and read them again. "Ben Wythe, fifty-some, small, white hair, walks with a limp. Richard Skillman, thirty, average, dark hair . . . and Boyd Dekalb, forty, big, tall, Negro . . . others here, Ed Degraw, Timothy Eckford, Willard Calyer, and Charlie . . ."

"Fucking Ravenscroft," Virgil said.

"'Spect Ravenscroft is the leader?" I said.

Virgil shook his head.

"If he is, I don't think he'd be any good at it."

"No," I said, "I don't, either."

"Don't have much smarts," Virgil said.

"Mean son of a bitch, though," I said.

"Damn sure is."

"He won't want to go back."

"Don't think any of them will want that," Virgil said.

20

When we awoke in the morning the weather had
turned. The mercurial weather we'd been experiencing
had doubled back on us again and the day's ride to Vadito was wet and dark. It had rained earlier during the
ride, but now there was only dark cloud cover. They
were low clouds shaded with brown from the loose dirt
the storm picked up before the rain. Now there was no
wind, none at all, and the brown clouds hanging motionless over the small town of Vadito made the view
seem like some old oil painting.

When we got closer to Vadito, we tied our animals in
a stand of trees and walked into town. We came up on
the back of Vadito near some holding pens that were full
of cattle.

We walked through a few shacks, then edged our way
up to the road that separated one half of the businesses
from the other half.

Vadito was a little one-lane town that consisted of

buildings and tents that were mostly drinking, whoring, gambling, and bunking establishments. They lined both sides of the road for about three hundred feet.

Vadito was one of those places that existed with limited law enforcement. The township of Lancaster, a two-hour ride north, was the governing law for Vadito. The proprietors of the establishments in places like Vadito were normally capable types, and as a group, the capable banded together when trouble came about. But for the most part, cowboys in cattle heavens such as Vadito proved to be a temperate lot.

Besides having good descriptions of the men we were looking for, we also had solid descriptions of the horses they stole from the sawmill in Yaqui. We had detail regarding color, size, brands, saddles, and even bridles.

As we thought what might be the situation in Vadito, the place was busy with cowboys, and though the day was dark and dreary the businesses all looked to be lively. There were not a lot of horses, but there was a good amount lining both sides of the road from one end of Vadito to the other.

Virgil and I split up and walked down opposite sides of the road, looking for the horses stolen by the escapees. We took our time, being casual but making sure we got a good look at each and every animal, and when we got to the end I said, "Didn't see 'em . . ."

Virgil shook his head.

"No," he said. "Not this side, either."

"Could be we beat 'em here," I said.

"Maybe," Virgil said.

"Then again, maybe they went elsewhere."

"That, too," Virgil said.

"Could be they might be here and have different horses," I said.

"Crossed my mind, but I don't think they'd do that," he said. "Could, but doubtful."

"No, I don't think so, either."

Virgil looked around the building we were standing in front of, then looked back across the road.

"Let's walk the backside, too," he said.

I nodded, crossed the street, and walked the back of the buildings. Within a short amount of time I arrived at the opposite end. Virgil came to the end about the same time I did. He shook his head as I crossed the street toward him.

"Nothing," I said.

We met in the street in front of a lively place. I turned and looked up to the single sign above the door with one word: BEER.

"Might as well?"

"Why not," Virgil said.

The saloon was a narrow building with a crude bowling lane on one side and a pinewood bar on the other. When we entered, a bunch of cowhands were having a fun time gambling on a bowling game with two chubby saloon girls who were having equal fun, flaunting their goods as they reset the pins.

Virgil and I got a mug of beer and sat at a table up front, where we had a good view out the window.

"Now comes the question," I said.

Virgil nodded.

"Where do we go from here?"

"Yep."

"There's not really anything between here and Yaqui, is there?" Virgil said.

"No, not really. Some big spreads and a few crossroad stores, but that's about it. Least that is all there was last time we were through that way."

"They could have just rode to Mexico," I said. "And I

suppose they could have brought some hell to others along the way."

Virgil nodded and sipped his beer as he thought.

"I figure we stay here at least through the night," he said. "Come daybreak and they're not here we move toward the east, toward Yaqui through the spreads and stations, check on those, then get in the direction of Stringer's posse."

We sat and drank our beer and waited some, watching the street, but we did not see the men. Before sunset, we walked out to the stand of trees where we'd tied our horses and brought them back into town with us. We rented a bunking quarter on the south end of Vadito from a German fella.

The quarters were empty of other customers, so we had the place to ourselves. The bunkhouse was a simple dirt-floor room with wood sidewalls and a pitch canvas roof that was in need of repair. As we unloaded and took care of the necessities of settling in, I looked out the opening and asked Virgil to take a gander at what I was looking at. Virgil turned to see the three escapees riding slowly into town.

"Rummy," Virgil said.

21

"**That's them, all right,**" I said.

"None other."

Virgil and I stayed inside the bunk, watching as they slowly rode into town single file. Leading the way was Wythe, the older small man. He was followed by Skillman, who was described as he appeared, thirty-something, average-looking, and following him was the large black fella, Boyd Dekalb.

"Same horses, too," I said.

"Yep."

"I'll be damned," I said.

"They are."

"They're heeled," I said.

"They are at that, too."

"Don't imagine they're gonna be the type that will throw their hands up."

"No," Virgil said. "I don't, either."

"We can ask," I said.

"We can," he said. "Don't think it will do any good, but we can damn sure ask."

"How you want to go about it?"

Virgil thought for a moment, as we remained looking out from inside the bunk tent, watching them.

"I'd say let's get the saddles back on our horses in case there is a need to make haste for some unforeseen reason, before we do anything else."

We did just that. We got ourselves ready and we let the three of them get settled into the destination of their choice before we worked out the necessary details prior to letting our presence be known.

The place they chose was called Lavern's. According to the German fella that rented us the bunk, Lavern's was the main whoring establishment in Vadito. It was also the only two-story structure in town.

"They didn't waste any time," I said.

"No," Virgil said.

"They know their priorities."

"They do at that."

We watched the place from across the street for a good half-hour before we made a move.

"I'm gonna go around back and have a look-see," I said.

Virgil kept watch on the front while I went around the rear to get some idea of the paths in and the paths out. Even though the temperature was fairly cool, the evening was comfortable and the rear door of Lavern's was wide open. I could see there was a hall that led to the main room, and inside I could hear the muffled sound of women and men talking.

Behind me was a well-worn path to a piss hut that was surrounded by some supply shacks. I walked back to the hut and made sure there was no one inside. Then I walked back between the buildings and met Virgil at the front of the narrow passage between Lavern's and the building next to it.

"Can walk right in the back," I said. "It's wide open."

Virgil nodded, and then we eased from the side toward the porch to have a look in the window. The windows were covered with lace curtains, but they were thin enough and half open in places for us to see inside.

The bottom floor of Lavern's was a wide single room without divisions and had a stairway toward the rear. For a shit-hole town the place was decent, with good wood floors, nice tables, upholstered furniture, and walls with framed photographs and paintings. There was a bar with a mirror behind it, and standing at the bar there were a number of customers, including the older fella, Wythe. He was talking to a heavyset whore that was a good foot taller than he was. The other two escapees were nowhere in sight.

"Other two are obviously going about what they came here for."

Virgil nodded.

I thought about that, about what they were doing.

"Likely might be the last time for them to be with a woman," I said.

"More than likely," Virgil said.

"I can think of worst last times," I said.

"Best we wait until they're done with what they are doing up there, don't you think."

"Do," Virgil said.

We watched Wythe for a moment. He was just drinking and talking to the big woman next to him as if he had no care in the world. Then we backed up, moved off a ways, and crossed the street, where we had a full view of Lavern's.

22

From where we stood we had an angle so to see into Lavern's, where Wythe sat talking to the woman. After some time passed, the black fellow, Dekalb, came down the stairs. Then the big woman, Wythe, and Dekalb sat at a table near the entrance.

"Two present and accounted for," I said.

Virgil nodded a bit.

"One to go."

The crisp night in Vadito had a lively feel. Up and down the street there were cowhands moving out of one place and going into another. There was laughter and some hoots and hollers echoing through the street. It was the typical glee that went hand in hand with men that spent most of their time covered with dirt and sitting in the saddle. Somewhere in the distance a piano started up, followed by some off-key singing.

Virgil lit a cigar and sat on a bench in front of an eatery that was closed or out of business. We waited and waited and after about a half an hour, Skillman came down the stairs and the three men sat at the table with the big woman.

"Guess this is it," I said.

Virgil got slowly to his feet.

"Guess it is."

I stared at the men, watching them talk to one another. Their conversation was lively, not unlike the cowboys. They were free and, for the moment, full of life.

"You want me to come in the back?"

Virgil thought for a moment and nodded.

"Be good if they'd not put up a fight," Virgil said with a remorseful tone to his voice.

"I know," I said.

As Virgil and I walked across the street, we saw two cowboys exit out a few doors down from the saloon where the piano was playing but no one else close by, and the two cowboys turned and walked in the opposite direction.

When we got to the alley between the buildings, Virgil pulled out his watch and said, "Let's enter in thirty."

I pulled out my watch, looked at the time, nodded, and started walking the narrow alley toward the rear of the building. I entered through the back door of Lavern's and moved silently up the narrow hall but stopped before moving into the main room.

I put my back to the wall and stood still for a moment. When my watch got to twenty I put it in my pocket, counted ten more seconds, then took a peek around the corner. *Shit!*

Virgil was nowhere in sight and Skillman was no longer seated with Wythe and Dekalb. Then I heard a gunshot coming from outside the front door, followed by another shot. The big woman quickly got up from the table and moved to the bar as Dekalb and Wythe got to their feet.

They both had their guns in their hands as they looked toward the street, and they had no idea that there was someone behind them with an eight-gauge shotgun. They both held their pistols up and ready to shoot as they stood with their backs to me, looking out the front door. That was the direction where they thought the danger was, or where they figured the succession of trouble would be coming from, but they were wrong.

"Don't turn," I said.

But that is exactly what they did; they turned quickly. Wythe fired his short-barrel pistol, but like most anxious gunmen, the bullet was off too fast and off target. It hit the floor, splintering wood three feet in front of me just as I pulled the trigger of my double-barrel. The shot hit him square in the chest.

"Goddamn!" Dekalb yelled as he, too, fired, but I stepped back fast. His shot was close, hitting the corner of the hall wall just in front of me.

"Goddamn it, goddamn it," he continued to spew as he charged toward me, firing, cussing, and kicking chairs out of his path. I raised the barrel of my big gun, ready to fire.

"Fucking, goddamn it, son of a bitch, asshole, fucking shit . . ."

It was as if he thought he were invincible and just as soon as I saw his body I squeezed the second trigger of my double-barrel stopping him and his rant mid-word—

"*Fuc*—" The double-ought buck exploded his head before he could get another shot off.

Then I moved away quickly with my back to the hall wall. I was unsure the whereabouts of Skillman and also Virgil.

From where I stood I could see yellow shafts of lamplight streaking through the gray gun smoke that was now hanging lazily in the still air of Lavern's.

I stood with my back to the hallway wall and broke open my eight-gauge. I took out the two warm shells, refit them into the open loops of my shell belt, and reloaded with two more rounds of double-ought. There was no doubt both Wythe and Dekalb were dead, but I had no idea about Skillman. I closed the double-barrel, and just as I slid back the hammers I heard a horse on the run and a shot was fired, followed by another shot, then another. Then a louder shot followed by a second louder shot.

23

I waited, listening, then Virgil called out, "Got him."

"That'd be it," I said, calling out from the back hallway.

"So it seems," Virgil called back.

"Skillman dead?" I called.

Virgil waited some before he replied.

"No," he said. "But I got him, he's down . . . What about the other two?"

"Eight-gauge."

I moved out into the main room and, sure enough, lying dead were Dekalb and Wythe. The double-ought from my eight-gauge made a mess of both men and the room. I could see Virgil out the front door as he walked to Skillman, who was lying flat on his back in the middle of the street. Virgil kept his Colt pointed at his head as he neared. When he got close he kicked a Colt that was in the dirt beside Skillman off to the side.

Skillman moved a bit and looked up to Virgil.

"Providing you live, Mr. Skillman, we'll be taking you back to Cibola."

"Cibola," Skillman said with a moan. "Who are you?"

"Marshal Virgil Cole," Virgil said, then looked over to me. "Bring a lamp out here, Everett."

I looked to the bar, where a barkeep, the heavyset woman, and another woman, a small, skinny gal with big eyes and stringy hair, were all huddled together, looking at me.

I turned my collar and showed them my badge.

"We're U.S. Marshals, these men here were both escaped convicts, serving time for murder. The one on his back out there in the street is the same, also an escaped killer."

The barkeep nodded then reached up, grabbing a lamp that was hanging just above his head, and handed it to me.

I walked out into the street to Virgil. Skillman was on his back, looking up at him. When I got close with the light it was clear Skillman was very much alive, holding his bleeding right shoulder.

"Sit up," Virgil said.

Skillman winced in pain but did as Virgil asked.

"Shit," Skillman said.

"You hit anyplace else?" Virgil said.

Skillman looked down at his body with a disgusted look on his face, then back to Virgil and me and shook his head.

"No," he said.

"What happened out here?" I said.

"Right after you started off toward the back, Skillman here come walking out to his horse there, getting something from the saddlebag."

"How do you know my name?"

"Oh, we know your name and your prison number," Virgil said, then looked to me. "I told him to stop, and he turned and fired on me."

Virgil looked back to Skillman.

"Didn't you?"

Skillman just looked at the dirt between his legs.

"When the gunning started up inside, I took a step back around the corner and Skillman here managed to get mounted and took off."

"He thought he could get gone?" I said, looking at Skillman.

"He did."

The bay horse Skillman had been riding came walking back faithful-like, as if Skillman was his owner, and stopped. He looked at us sort of expectantly. I reached for the reins as he took a short step back.

"Easy," I said.

I got ahold of the bridle, then I looked to Virgil.

"Nobody was interested in going back to Cibola," I said.

"No," Virgil said as he opened the loading gate on his Colt and let the spent casings drop.

"Kind of what we figured," I said.

"Was," he said.

Virgil reloaded his Colt and slid it back in his holster.

"What were you getting out of this here saddlebag, Mr. Skillman?" Virgil said as he moved toward the bay.

"Nothing."

"Nothing?" Virgil said.

"A cigar is all . . . I was gonna have me a cigar."

Virgil opened the bag and looked inside.

"I got them on the way here . . . I . . . I was saving 'em," he said.

Virgil pulled out a newspaper that was folded around three cigars. He smelled one, then wrapped them up and put them back in the bag.

"Saving them for what?"

"I don't know . . . A good time, I guess."

Virgil looked to me, then moved back to Skillman.

"Think your good times are done, Mr. Skillman."

Skillman remained looking at the dirt.

"Up," Virgil said.

Skillman did not move.

Virgil nudged him with his boot and said, "Get up."

Skillman just looked at him.

"Now," Virgil said. "Let's go."

Virgil got Skillman's good arm and helped him to his feet, then pointed to Lavern's.

"Inside," Virgil said.

Skillman was a little wobbly but managed to walk back to Lavern's. A handful of onlookers drifted toward Lavern's.

"This is marshal work," I said, looking to the people gathering. "Everybody go back to what you were doing. Go on, everyone . . . go on."

When we got back inside Lavern's, Skillman stopped when he saw Wythe and Dekalb dead on the floor.

"Goddamn," he said.

"And then some," Virgil said as he pulled out a chair. "Sit."

Skillman stared at the dead men as he took a seat.

Virgil looked around the room. There were three whores sitting on the stairs, peering out between the railings like curious alley cats.

"Don't imagine there is a doc in the town?" Virgil said to the barkeep and the two women next to him.

"Not really," he said. "Me and Lavern here have done as much mending of the hurt as anybody else 'round here."

The big woman who had previously been sitting with the men was no doubt Lavern, the namesake of the establishment. She moved out and around the bar and looked down to Skillman sitting slumped in the chair, then back to us.

"Most men that come through here are good men," she said.

Virgil nodded a bit.

"They ain't most."

She stared at Virgil for a moment, then moved closer to Skillman. He raised his head, looking at her. His eyes were red and full of tears. She walked around him and looked at the back of his shoulder. Then she circled around to his front, opened his shirt a little, and examined his shoulder wound.

"You shot anyplace else?" she said.

Skillman shook his head.

Lavern looked over to the skinny woman with the big eyes. "Lucy, put some water on to boil and fetch some clean rags, salt, and liniment."

The skinny gal nodded and moved off through an open door behind the bar.

Lavern put her palms on her hips and looked to Virgil and me.

"We never know who is who here," she said. "Not really."

She pointed to Wythe.

"The old fellow there I met a long time ago, right here, when we first opened this place. He used to come in now and again, but then he stopped coming. I guess now I know why . . . I had no idea he was a convicted murderer and damn sure no idea until now that he was an escaped convicted murderer. I talked to him for a good while tonight. He seemed pleasant enough, odd but pleasant and . . . well, he never said . . ."

"No," Virgil said, "don't imagine he did."

24

It turned out the bullet that entered Skillman's shoulder did minimal damage both on its way in and on its way out. He hung his head low with the look of a man knowing he would for certain be tried for the murders of the mill workers in Yaqui and most likely hanged for his actions, but Skillman was good to ride.

The following morning we got some help from a couple of local hands and we went about the task of burying Wythe and Dekalb in shallow graves. When we finished, we stopped by Lavern's on our way out to let her know that prison officials or next of kin might come and exhume the dead in the near future.

"And if not?" Lavern said.

"If not," Virgil said, "may they do their best not to rot in hell too quickly."

We mounted up and departed Vadito with Skillman and the other two stolen horses in tow and headed toward Yaqui. We had Skillman to return to Cibola, and since Yaqui was en route between Cibola and us, we figured to collect Dobbin, the other convict wounded in the shootout at the Yaqui sawmill.

We rode for the day, and as we did, Skillman never said a word. He sat slumped in his saddle as if he had no more life left in him. When it started to get dark we stopped for the evening and made camp in a dry red-rock area not far from the railroad tracks that led to Yaqui.

We fed Skillman, then redressed his shoulder wound. He was in pain but was not losing blood, and the salve Lavern used was doing the job. We got him back into a clean shirt, put his jacket back on him, then moved him to the edge of our campsite and locked him to the base of a thick piñon with a single handcuff and chain. We left him with a bedroll and a canteen. He could move some, drink water, and lie down, but if he wanted to run off he'd have to uproot a twenty-foot-tall tree.

About an hour after sunset Virgil and I sat on a huge rock and drank some whiskey. The wide, clear night sky stretched out over us like a deep blue blanket full of pinholes.

Virgil leaned back on the rock with his cup of whiskey resting on his stomach and after a long moment of not talking said, "Hear that?"

I listened.

"What?"

"Train."

I listened some more.

"Now I do."

"I guess shooting that eight-gauge all these years has taken its toll."

I nodded.

"That and the cannons of my youth."

We sat listening to the sound of the thumping steam engine chugging rhythmically in the distance as it got closer and closer. Then we saw the beam of the engine's light sweeping across the land in front of us as the train turned and started thudding its way toward us.

"Here she comes," Virgil said.

We watched as the train came toward us, its light getting brighter and the thumping sound of the engine getting louder and louder. Then we could see the cars, and inside the cars, the seated passengers.

We could feel the tamping vibration of the engine now, and no sooner was the train upon us than it passed quickly and left us again in the dark. We listened for an extended moment as the pounding cadence of the locomotive slowly faded away.

We sat in silence for a while.

"Makes you wonder," I said. "Where they're all going."

"And why?"

I thought about that for a moment, the necessities of where and the curiosities of why.

"A lot of people coming and going these days," I said.

"Damn sure are," Virgil said.

"Not like it used to be."

"No," Virgil said. "It ain't."

"Remember when you'd never see anybody?" I said.

"I do."

"Now there is somebody everywhere, it seems," I said.

Virgil nodded.

"With something they got to do."

"Or someplace they got to go," I said.

"Needing to get there," Virgil said.

"And need to get," I said. "Get this and get that."

Virgil nodded a little.

"Saving for a good time," he said.

"You wonder," I said, "just what it will all lead to?"

"Better not to," Virgil said.

"There was a time the Mississippi felt like the edge of the world."

"Every day," Virgil said. "There is a little bit more of something."

We sat without talking as we listened to a faraway coyote.

"Times are changing right before our eyes, Everett."

"We can still get lost," I said.

"We can," he said.

Virgil looked down to Skillman sitting up with his back to the tree.

"We damn sure can," he said again. Then, without saying another word, Virgil got up. He moved down off the rock and walked over to where our saddles were. He leaned down by the saddles for a moment, then walked over to Skillman. He handed Skillman a cigar, lit a match, and cupped his hand around it as Skillman drew on the cigar.

25

Embers skittered off the waning campfire from a stiff bone-dry breeze that kicked up through the night. The wind whistled through the piñons and chaparral. Virgil was up, out of his bedroll with his Colt in hand, looking toward our animals.

I lifted my head from my saddle seat that I used as a pillow and reached for my eight-gauge.

"What?" I said. "What is it?"

"Don't know," he said.

"Horses are damn sure spooked," Virgil said.

I looked over to see Skillman move a little. He sat up in his bedroll and looked over to us. Besides the train that had come through and the occasional yapping of a coyote, the evening had been quiet and peaceful.

"Get ready," Virgil said.

I sat up and looked about in the dark, thinking maybe some critter had sniffed his way to our camp and was agitating our horses. All the grub that would attract animals was stashed in an oilcloth bag and hanging ten feet above camp by a rope draped over a tall evergreen so as to keep such pests away.

"Wind, maybe," I said. "Blowing like a son of a bitch."

"Don't think so," Virgil said.

Our horses were tied on a head-high Dutchman picket, close to camp. It was dark, but there was a quarter-moon and we could see well enough to know the horses were good and restless about something.

From the reach of the moon I figured it was near midnight. I gathered up my eight-gauge and moved toward the picket when I heard a horse blow off in the distance.

"You hear that, Virgil?"

"I heard it."

I backed up a few steps toward Virgil and cocked my eight-gauge.

"Damn sure somebody out there," I said.

"Is."

"Could be them," I said. "Or some of them?"

"By God," Virgil said.

We waited in silence for a time before we heard a man call from the dark. The voice cut through the steady breeze.

"We got you boxed in and outnumbered. Lay aside any goddamn thing you got to fight with and give yourself up or you will be killed."

Virgil looked at me.

"Sounds like Stringer," he said.

"Does."

"Do it," the man said. "Or consider being dead and gone."

"That you, Stringer?" Virgil called.

There was a bit of silence, then we heard him call back loudly, "Cole?"

"It is."

"Goddamn," Stringer shouted. "Coming in."

Stringer was once a deputy of Yaqui, but he'd out-lasted the others and was now Yaqui's top ranking offi-cial. He'd been a good lawman and a good friend of ours through the years and he was someone we trusted.

He barked out loudly as he approached, "Boys, stay put, stay where you are, I'm going in."

In a few moments, big Sheriff Stringer walked into our camp with two of his deputies lagging behind him. They were pulling their horses and carrying rifles.

Stringer was a tall man with a full mustache and was never without his bone-handle long-barreled Colt, which he wore butt forward on his left.

"Virgil," he said.

"By God," Virgil said.

Stringer shook his head some as he walked closer to us.

"Everett."

"Hello, Stringer," I said.

"Blowing like a son of a bitch," he said.

"It is," Virgil said.

"The two of you," he said, shaking his head.

"It is," Virgil said.

"I'll be goddamn if they won't let just anybody into this godforsaken territory."

"Who is 'they'?" Virgil said.

"Good goddamn question," he said.

Stringer saw Skillman under the piñon and pointed at him with his rifle.

"I'll be goddamn," he said. "That one of 'em?"

"Is," Virgil said.

Skillman sat with his back to the tree, looking at the ground.

Stringer glanced around.

"The other two?" he said.

"Dead."

"Vadito?"

"Yep," Virgil said.

Virgil tipped his head toward me.

"Eight-gauge."

Stringer looked to me and nodded.

"I'll be damned," he said. "What the hell are you gonna do with him?"

"We're gonna take him back to Cibola," Virgil said.

Skillman did not look up as his fate was being discussed. In fact, he'd kept this eyes trained down ever since we apprehended him.

"He hurt?" Stringer said.

Virgil looked over to Skillman for a moment and nodded.

"Got shot in the shoulder," Virgil said. "Bullet went clean through, but he's tough."

Stringer nodded, looked around out into the darkness, then looked back to Virgil and me.

"So what is it?" Virgil said.

Stringer leaned his Winchester in the crux of a sage scrub and shook his head.

"We are on one of them for sure," Stringer said in a serious tone, then nodded deliberately and slowly. "Got one on the fucking run."

26

"And I thought for sure," Stringer said, "you was him."

"What have you got?" I said.

"I got a posse of six with me and we been at it this afternoon. We got on their trail just about four o'clock."

"Their trail?" I said. "Thought you said one?"

Stringer nodded.

"We was following all four at first, but they split up. Three of them crossed the river twenty miles back. We went after them first but could not find any goddamn sign of them on the other side, they vanished."

"They know you are after them?" Virgil said.

"Don't know," Stringer said. "Don't think so, but they split up, that's for damn sure. The three that went into the river could have doubled back in the water for all we know. So we come back on this side and picked up the trail of the single rider."

"You sure?" I said.

"More than sure."

Virgil looked to me, then to Stringer.

"Why don't you get your men in here, give this a rest right now," Virgil said.

Stringer nodded and slid his Winchester back in the scabbard and handed the reins of his horse to one of his deputies.

"Round up everybody and bring them in," Stringer said. "Get a line up for the horses."

"Yes, sir." Then the two deputies disappeared into the darkness.

"How'd all this come about?" Virgil said. "How do you know?"

"Place called the Crosscut Depot. An outfitters' place above the Gila forty miles south of here was robbed— guns, horses, clothes, food, you name it."

"And you know for a fact it was them?" I said.

"I do."

"What about the workers at the depot," Virgil said. "Anybody hurt?"

Stringer shook his head.

"Roughed up some of them," he said. "But left no-body dead. They showed up in the early hours of the morning, got the jump on everybody. They got to the guns before anybody knew what was happening and shit went south from there real quick, leaving spent horses and taking fresh ones from the depot. We tracked them, got on their trail quick. I got an Indian with me, Kiowa, a hell of a tracker. We were gaining on them until the three broke off."

"Good chance they could have all split and gone sep-arate," I said.

Stringer shook his head a bit.

"Chance I took staying after the one tonight, but we been moving slow, taking it steady, and even found some sign in the dark. He's not been riding the railroad tracks but been keeping them close, been staying on this side of it. Using it for direction."

I looked to Virgil.

"Appaloosa."

Virgil nodded.

"I'm fucking tired and I was fixing to stop for the night, but my Kiowa caught a whiff of your fire and I thought for sure we had struck pay dirt."

Virgil glanced to me, then looked around as Stringer's men came straggling into camp.

"You fellas settle in here now," Stringer said.

The posse and their horses were moving slow and the lot of them looked tired and weary.

"We'll camp here with Marshals Hitch and Cole. Spread out over there."

The posse did as Stringer ordered and went about settling in for the night.

The Kiowa remained standing, looking off to the north, in the direction of the tracks. He was a slim, dark-skinned Indian with long braids, wearing knee-high moccasins and a buckskin shirt with a Colt holstered around it. He stood holding the reins of his pinto pony with his feet together, a picture of relaxation as he looked off, holding his Winchester by his side with the barrel pointing toward the ground.

"We give it up for tonight, Locky," Stringer said.

Locky remained looking off into the darkness for a moment, then, without saying a word or looking to Stringer, he turned and walked his horse to the edge of camp, but was careful not to be too close to the others.

"He was a runner before he became a scout for General Crook from Camp Verde. He's better than a god-damn bloodhound," Stringer said. "He could track a fucking snake across a flooded lake."

Stringer moved a bit closer. He sat his big body on a

low rock by the fire, then looked over to Skillman, who was lying down now with his back to us.

"I take it the other two weren't that interested in going back to Cibola?"

"I asked them politely-like," I said.

Stringer tipped his thumb toward Skillman.

"He say how they got out?"

"No," I said. "Won't talk, really."

"How about the one in Yaqui?" Virgil said.

Stringer shook his head a little.

"Not really. He did say he did not plan the escape or even partake in the plan. Of course, right? He said there was an opening and he took it. Said he wished he'd stayed, said he was on good behavior and had plans to work hard for an early release."

"That didn't work out too well," Virgil said.

"No," Stringer said. "He fucked that up."

"What about the prison?" Virgil said. "And the support town?"

Virgil looked to me.

"Wingate," I said.

Virgil nodded and looked to Stringer.

"Wingate? They know anything new?"

Stringer shook his head.

"No, I don't know. We just got out and after it, looking for the other four, when we last communicated over the wire. So I got no details from Wingate or Cibola. Don't know if the line is back up or not, nothing."

Virgil nodded a little.

"Got any coffee, Everett?" Stringer said as he removed his hat.

"Do," I said.

27

Driggs enjoyed his newfound freedom. It was just *a few days now since he'd been in civilization, and he was savoring it. Besides the ardent and vigorous plowing, seeding, and toiling within the confines of the upstairs chambers, Driggs enjoyed sitting in the parlor of the Boston House reading the newspaper, smoking Cuban cigars, and drinking good coffee.*

"That's fine coffee," Driggs said to the waitress.

"We're pleased you appreciate it," she said. "It comes all the way from South America."

"South America," he said. "Imagine that."

"I'm Tilda," she said. "If you need anything else at all, just let me know."

"I will, thank you, Tilda."

Driggs smiled and watched her backside as she walked away a bit before he returned to reading the paper.

He liked to read the Appaloosa Star Statesman *about the local happenings as well as current national events that involved politics, politicians, and the world. National and global news fascinated Driggs. When he was in Cibola he'd read every newspaper he could get his hands on. Most of the time it was the* Tucson Citizen *or* The Santa Fe New Mexican *or the* San Francisco Chronicle, *but he preferred* The Guardian *and* The New York Times *when he could get them. But here now in Appaloosa he was mostly interested in reading the* Appaloosa Star Statesman *and what was happening locally. At least currently, because in a short matter of time he had some particular business to attend to in Appaloosa and he felt it important to have a good lay of the land. The first article concerning the territory and the vicinity of Appaloosa was about the prison break, and this was, of course, most interesting to him. The article was a preliminary one: an unconfirmed account of the prison break, stating simply that the escape had happened but the details concerning just what happened would be forthcoming.* Good, *he thought. He read about the cattle, horses, and pigs that had been sold at the livestock auction. He read about the yearly rattlesnake roundup and how the record number of snakes caught this year would be on display through May. He read about Walter Jamison selling his ranch to a cow calf operation from Atlanta for a record price. He read about Vernon Vandervoort's trip to New Orleans and his scheduled return to Appaloosa bearing goods from abroad. He read about the newest members appointed to the Appaloosa Alderman Association and the upcoming celebration at Vernon Vandervoort's newly constructed Town Hall to be sponsored by investor Thane Rutledge. And he read about the shootout that occurred at Meserole's, and when he came across Everett's name he paused and reread the words: United States Deputy Marshal Everett Hitch, and it made him whistle.*

"Everett fucking Hitch," he said quietly to himself. "I'll be goddamned. And here he is a U.S. Marshal living in Appaloosa." Driggs lowered the paper and gazed out the

window, thinking about Everett Hitch and those days so long ago. "Everett fucking Hitch."

Later, Driggs sat in the Boston House Saloon and took a seat at the bar across from the longtime barkeep, the large but effortlessly elegant Fat Wallis.

"Whiskey, the best you got," Driggs said.

Driggs set the newspaper on the bar in front of him and had the page turned to the article about the shootout at Meserole's. He kept his head down, reading as Wallis poured the whiskey. Then he looked up.

"Heck of a deal," Driggs said friendly-like as he tapped his finger on the article about the shootout.

Wallis leaned in, seeing the article.

"Oh, yes," Wallis said. "Please know this sort of shooting is not common here in Appaloosa."

"No, I wouldn't think so," Driggs said. "Says here U.S. Marshals were at the scene."

"Yep, they live right here, well, when they are here," Wallis said. "We do have a good police department as well with Sheriff Chastain and his deputies, but having marshals here is comforting."

"Understandable," Driggs said.

"The prison break is troubling," Driggs said, flipping the page, "I read about that as well. So much discord. Your marshals I'm sure will be dealing with that."

"Oh, they already are," Wallis said. "Our good marshals are dealing with that as we speak, rest assured."

Wallis rapped his knuckles on the bar and moved on to serve another customer.

Driggs watched Wallis walk off as he took a sip of the good whiskey and lit another expensive cigar. He was fortunate to have money. It was her money, but she made it very clear that what was hers was also rightfully his. He didn't need to be told this, but he was happy to allow her the satisfaction of feeling generous.

He had yet to venture out too far from the Boston House, but he did move about through the streets surrounding the hotel, and with Hitch gone he enjoyed the unlimited free feeling of it all.

He was completely unconcerned with being found out or caught. He knew how not to draw suspicion, how to integrate. He felt more alive knowing he was a stranger among the others, but that was how it had always been with Driggs. He fondly remembered Isaiah 11:6: "The wolf also shall dwell with the lamb."

But he was a handsome wolf. He wore tailored clothes that she had procured for him. He had a thick gabardine tapered frock coat, pin-striped shirts, silk ties, and fine twill trousers that tucked into high-topped polished black riding boots, and he had a beautiful woman, a princess, on his arm everywhere he went. They even walked across the street to the church and listened to the preacher.

Driggs appreciated hearing the scriptures being read as well as the preacher's oratory regarding salvation, damnation, and the Holy Spirit. He was absorbed about the propagating notion that there is no life after death without Jesus, and if you do not ask Jesus into your heart to be your personal Savior you will go to Hell. Driggs felt like a kid in school. He wanted to raise his hand in protest but did not. He would not draw any more attention to himself than he'd already brought. But he thought about all the poor Indians he'd chased down and killed for the government who never even saw a Bible or heard the word Jesus, God, or Holy Spirit before a bullet ripped into their heads. Or the goddamn ignorant pigmies who chopped off the heads of their enemies and put them on poles around their camp to ward off evil spirits. They wouldn't know Jesus from a fucking jungle snake.

The lofty talk of God Almighty gave Driggs a strong feeling of superiority. He got the message, he understood the *alchemy of it all, it resonated with him in a way he knew others had no concept of; at least that is what existed in the reverie for him.*

The sermon was transforming, it set Driggs even further apart from all those around him. It riled him, too, in a way that nothing else could. He somehow felt that he was actually there in the beginning, that he saw it all play out before him, that he'd seen it all before.

As the sermon ended the preacher asked the flock if there were sinners who needed to come forward and ask for forgiveness. The preacher's invitation prompted Driggs to give up a low, involuntarily growl, which in turn initiated the princess to squeeze Driggs's thigh. He looked at her. She was gazing up at him with a misty, wanton look in her eyes. He peered into her soul for a brief instant, but it was long enough.

His eyes moved above the preacher and focused on the cross hanging on the wall behind the preacher's head, and he thought about Everett Hitch. He wondered if his ol' pal Hitch was going to be a problem for him. Driggs was not begrudging by nature. Hanging on to grievances for transgressions made against him was unimportant and for the weak. But the art of vendetta intrigued him. Dismantling was a precise and systematic process he appreciated. Like taking apart a deadly weapon.

28

The wind died down through the night, and when we awoke, a strange low cloud cover had crept in and the early morning was dark. We made coffee and had some hardtack.

Stringer looked to Skillman and shook his head a little.

"What will happen to him and the Dobbin fella in Yaqui, Virgil?" Stringer said.

Virgil looked to Skillman, then back to Stringer.

"Have to let the prison deal with them," Virgil said. "They are wards of congress."

"We report what we know," Stringer said. "What happened with them, what bullshit they did on the outside."

Virgil nodded.

"Yep, and the warden can deal with them whatever which way on the inside."

Stringer shook his head a little.

"Poor bastards will likely hang," he said.

We found ourselves with three directions of detail to deal with: continue dogging after the one escapee who

Stringer and his posse had been after with Locky the tracker; going back in the direction where the three crossed the river and see if we were fortunate enough to pick up their trail; and getting Skillman and Dobbin— the other escapee who was wounded and recuperating in Yaqui—returned to Cibola prison.

"What about this Dobbin fella," Virgil said. "How bad is he?"

"He'll be all right," Stringer said. "Sore more than anything. Took a bullet in the arm, buckshot in the back and on his neck. That's what shocked the hell outta him and knocked him down, but he's strong and will be good to ride. Might not be his druthers, but so be it. Should have thought about that before breaking out of prison with a passel full of no-goods."

After some discussion with Stringer, Virgil decided that Stringer and a partial of his posse should continue after the one man they were on the trail of, and Virgil and I would take a few deputies on the southward mission.

After a little more hardtack and coffee we broke camp. Stringer and four men, including Locky, headed north, and Virgil and I headed south with two deputies and Skillman in tow.

The two young deputies with us were Warren Flower, a strong, good-sized young man with a thick blond mustache and piercing blue eyes, and Bill Hart, a slight man with handsome boyish good looks.

The day did not light up much. If anything, it got darker. We stayed in heavy cloud cover as we rode. The first chance we had we crossed the river and started looking for sign.

After a few hours' ride, Bill Hart stopped and looked around a bit.

"Warren," he said. "This looks like where we lost them, don't it?"

Flower looked around and nodded.

"It is," he said, looking down and pointing to the horse tracks. "We rode back that way looking for them, these tracks here are us."

"You can see we rode this way, south," Hart said, "then cut back into the river before going back north."

"Take 'er goddamn easy," Skillman said in a low rasp.

We all turned and looked to Skillman, who was staring at us from under the brim of his dark hat. This utterance from him was the only few words he'd spoken that had any substance to them since we'd captured him. As Skillman glared at us the rain began to fall.

"The men you are after, Timothy Eckford, Willard Calyer, and Charlie Ravenscroft, are a deadly lot. The one north that the others are after is for certain Ed Degraw. Degraw is the worst of any of the men that were on Murderers Row, no question, but these three you are looking for are front-page bad news . . . so just take 'er goddamn easy."

Virgil looked to me, then back to Skillman.

"Eckford and Calyer would gut their family just for the hell of it, to watch them bleed out and die slow. That you can be goddamn very certain of."

Virgil moved his horse a bit closer to Skillman.

"And fucking Ravenscroft," Skillman said. "He would make stew out of them."

"Where they headed?" I said.

He shrugged.

"My guess is they're headed to Mexico."

"What makes you think it is this three that is headed down here and the other, Degraw, headed north?"

Skillman did not speak right away. It was like the simple mentioning of Ed Degraw bothered him.

"Let me tell you about Ed Degraw. Degraw is not fit for market. On the inside, behind bars, he was feared.

Assholes and murderers alike stayed clear of him. He is as mean as any man I have ever come across, and I come across a lot of mean men. Going an opposite direction from the others like this says for sure it is Degraw. Them others is hell-bent, but Degraw is plumb hell on earth."

29

Skillman stopped talking after that. It was as if he needed to clear out his head. Like there was a reason to be heard for a moment, get something off his chest, to offer up something that gave him some sort of comfort in his compromised situation.

We broke out our slickers as we continued on in a southward direction, looking for any sign of the men as we traveled. With the weather like it was, it was slow going. At about midday we crossed the river back toward the railroad tracks. It rained off and on for the better part of the day, and just before dark we arrived at Yaqui.

Not unlike Appaloosa, and many other towns along the tracks, Yaqui had grown to be too big for its own good. The place was overcrowded, and even though it was raining there were a good number of people out and about when we arrived.

When we stopped at the sheriff's office we were met by one of Stringer's old jailers.

"He another one?" the old jailer said as he stepped off the boardwalk, looking at Skillman.

"He is," I said.

"Got a cozy room for you," he said. "Right next to one of your good friends."

Within a matter of moments we had Skillman off his horse and into the office.

We walked Skillman through the office leading to the cells. Skillman stopped when he saw a young man with curly dark hair and a scruffy beard lying on his bunk, looking at him.

"Dobbin," Skillman said.

"I'll be goddamned," Dobbin said as he glared at Skillman. "Look what the cat dragged in."

The jailer opened the door next to Dobbin's cell.

"Dick fucking Skillman," he said.

Dobbin groaned a bit as he sat up. It was clear to see he was wrapped with bandages under a shirt draped over his shoulders, and by the expression on his face he appeared to be not just in pain but also red-faced angry.

"You left me," Dobbin said through his teeth.

Skillman said nothing as the jailers opened the cell next to Dobbin and escorted Skillman inside.

Dobbin shook his head. "The three of you, you fucking left me," he said.

Skillman didn't say anything.

"That cat that dragged your sorry ass in here also got your lying tongue, did it?" Dobbin said.

"Shut your mouth, boy."

Dobbin shook his head.

"No," he said. "Don't think so."

"Do like I tell you."

"Or what, you sack of shit?" Dobbin said. "You goddamn left me. You, the nigger, and the old man, you left me."

I pulled the key out of my pocket and turned Skillman around to remove his cuffs.

"Got nothing to say?" Dobbin said.

"What'd you expect?" Skillman said.

Skillman stared at me as I took the cuffs off him and backed out, leaving him in the cell.

Dobbin looked to me.

"He was the one that killed those two at the sawmill," Dobbin said. "It was him."

Skillman swiveled his head slowly and deliberately toward Dobbin.

"You are a goddamn liar," Skillman said, then looked back to me. "He's a goddamn liar."

"We'll see to it we get you back to Cibola first chance and get things sorted out," I said, then looked to Dobbin. "The both of you, we'll get you back to where you started and where you will end."

I closed the bars and the old jailer locked the door as Dobbin moved closer to the bars separating his cell from Skillman's cell.

"You are a murdering piece of shit," Dobbin said.

Skillman glared at him.

"I'm no squealing pig," he said.

"Fuck you."

"You was the one that fucked up, kid," Skillman said.

"Looks like I was not the only one," Dobbin said.

"Two is dead 'cause of you."

"And two more is soon to be dead 'cause of you," Dobbin said. "Me and the no-good fucking dumb-ass murdering asshole I'm this moment looking directly at."

"You two are sure two peas in a pod," the old jailer said. "Might want to give it a rest, otherwise I might have to knock you both around some so you have something to really rant and rave about."

I glanced at Virgil and we moved off and shut the hall

door to the cells, leaving the two wounded escapees to their discording banter.

"What now?" Deputy Hart said to Virgil.

"First order is to check with the wire office and find out if the telegraph line to Cibola has been fixed."

30

The rain continued to fall. It was steady and solid, and the streets of Yaqui were turning into one big puddle. From boardwalk to boardwalk Virgil and I made our way over to one of Yaqui's best and most popular eating establishments, the Altamont Steak House.

We hung our hats and slickers at the entrance, took a seat, and ordered us each a steak and fried potatoes. The waiter was pouring us each a second glass of wine when Deputies Flower and Hart entered. We looked up as they removed their soaked hats and came walking over to our table.

"Still nothing from Wingate or Cibola regarding the wire, sir," Hart said.

Virgil looked at me and shook his head.

"Damn," I said. "You think that it would be back up by now."

Virgil nodded.

"But there was something that happened to a couple

of prospectors this afternoon that you should know about," Flower said.

"Which is?" Virgil said.

"They reported to one of the deputies on duty while we were gone that they were held up by a gang," Flower said.

"A gang?" I said.

"They say what kind of gang?" Virgil said.

"Not that we know of," Flower said.

"What else did they allow?" Virgil said.

"We've not talked to them, not personally," Flower said. "Figured we'd let the two of you know."

"You know when this was?" I said.

"No, sir," Flower said.

"All we know is what we heard," Hart said. "They came to the office and reported that they were robbed."

"And where are these prospectors?" Virgil said.

"Deputy said they are staying over at the livery stables," Hart said.

"You want us to find them and bring them to talk with you," Flower said.

Virgil shook his head.

"No," he said. "We'll have a talk with them after we have our supper here."

The deputies nodded.

"What would you like for us to do now?" Hart said.

"You fellas had anything to eat yet?"

They looked to each other and shook their heads from side to side in tandem.

"No, sir," they said.

Virgil looked to the waiter and pointed to Hart and Flower.

"Bring these boys same as us," he said, then looked back to the deputies. "Hang your slickers and get a seat."

The two nodded, said thank you, then did as Virgil asked.

After supper the four of us walked over to the livery and found the prospectors camped out in one of the back stalls with their mules.

They were drinking whiskey from a jug and playing cards on top of a crate when we walked up. Both of them looked as if they'd never had a bath in their lives. They were missing teeth, chewed huge wads of tobacco, and looked nearly identical except one had whiter hair than the other.

"You the boys that got held up?" I said.

They looked up, squinting at us.

"Who wants to know?" the younger one said.

I showed them my badge.

The four of us moved into the stall and spread out in front of them as they looked up at us.

"Too little, too late," the older one said.

"For?" I said.

"Him and me," he said, "was robbed."

"We heard," I said.

"By who?" Virgil said.

"Mean sumbitches," the younger man said. "We don't know who or where they come from."

"We never seen them around here before," the older man said.

"We pretty much know everybody around these parts. When we first laid eyes on them I told Dudley—I'm Theodore, this here is my brother Dudley—I told him shit howdy, get fucking ready, and sure enough I was right."

Dudley nodded.

"How many?"

"There was two of them at first," Dudley said.

"Then one more come up behind us," his brother said. "And fucking robbed us."

Virgil looked to me.

"So there was three of them?" I said.

"That's right," Theodore said. "And I damn near shot their asses, too."

31

"Oh, bullshit, Theodore," Dudley said.

"I did," his brother said.

"You did no such thing."

"I did."

"Don't listen to him," Dudley said.

"Well, I told him," Theodore said. "I should have shot the sonsabitches as they was riding off."

"Damn good thing he didn't try," Dudley said. "You old fool. You'd gone for that carbine, we'd be fucking dead."

"Bullshit." Theodore said as he pointed to his skinny white-eared mule. "I had it right there in the scabbard tucked under the off side of Lily's pannier. They did not see it. Otherwise, they would have took it. I could have got to it."

"Where this happen?" Virgil said.

" 'Bout twenty mile this side of Montezuma," Dudley said. "We'd just come down earlier this morning when we ran into them."

"From where?" I said.

"I can't tell you that," Theodore said. "We have our places that we can't let just anybody know about."

"Our places, shit," Dudley said. "They are the goddamn law."

"So."

"You seriously think these lawmen are gonna go out there and pan us out?"

"You're the one that always tells me to keep my mouth shut," Theodore said.

"For good goddamn reason," Dudley said.

"Well, listen to you," Theodore said.

"You say near Montezuma," I said.

"Yes, sir," Dudley said. "Give or take."

"Were they headed that way?" I said. "Toward Montezuma?"

The brothers looked at each other and shook their heads from side to side like puppets.

"Could be," Dudley said.

"Do you think for any reason that was their destination?" I said.

The brothers looked at each other again.

"No idea about that," Dudley said.

"What'd they take you for?" Virgil said.

"Shit, not much," Dudley said.

"Not much, hell," Theodore said. "All the money we had. Sixteen dollars. I should have shot 'em."

"Them boys had that look," Dudley said. "Like they'd cut you down just for the hell of it but they just wanted money. They didn't go through our shit or nothing."

"And we got nothing of value in our belongings," Theodore said, shaking his head completely unconvincingly. "Nothing at all, not one thing, no gold or nothing, only thing of value is that carbine of mine and they left it alone."

"Tell us about the men," Virgil said.

The brothers looked at each other.

"They were mounted?" I said.

"Oh, yeah," Dudley said. "They were."

"And they had guns?" Virgil said.

"Damn sure did," Theodore said. "Pointed right at us."

"They all had guns?" I said.

The brothers nodded.

"They did," Dudley said.

"Some men escaped out of Cibola that we are after, and it sounds as if these men might have been them. Any reason you think it might have been them, you notice any prison clothes, anything like that?"

"No," Dudley said.

"What'd they look like?"

"Shit," Theodore said as he looked to Dudley.

"Average dumb-looking robbers," Theodore said. "They was just skinny fellas . . ."

"All but one," Dudley said.

Theodore nodded.

"Yeah," he said. "The one that come up from behind."

"He was kind of big, strong-looking," Dudley said. "No hat and bald as a goddamn baby."

Virgil looked at me.

"Ravenscroft," I said.

"I could have picked off each of the sonsabitches."

"Will you shut up? We're lucky to be alive."

32

We left Dudley and Theodore and walked by the stalls toward the front of the livery.

"Montezuma's the real fancy place near Las Vegas, ain't it?" Flower said.

"Largest hotel west of the Mississippi," Hart said. "That's what I heard."

"Never been there," Flower said.

"Me neither," Hart said.

"You think they'd go to the Montezuma?" Flower said as we neared the wide front door of the stables.

"Could," I said.

"Fancy damn place for escaped convicts," Hart said.

"I heard President Arthur went there," Flower said. "And Hays and Grant, too."

"Montezuma takes money like anyplace else," Virgil said.

"No telling who else they might have robbed besides the prospectors," I said.

"But then again, they could go anyplace," Hart said.

"They could at that," Virgil said.

"That they could," I said.

We stopped at the door, looking out at the rain. The liveryman that we'd talked to when we first entered was sitting in the office reading a newspaper. He looked up and nodded a bit.

"What now?" Flower said.

Virgil waited a second, then looked to the deputies who were both looking at him expectantly.

"For now, let's get our animals squared away, then you boys get yourselves dried out and rested," he said. "Then we'll see you at the office in the early morning and go from there."

"We gonna ride to Montezuma?" Hart said.

Virgil looked out for a moment, then looked to Hart and Flower.

"Don't know," Virgil said. "Right now Everett and me need to do some communicating at the wire office. Then we'll see you boys in the morning."

"They got wire to there, to the Montezuma?" Hart said.

"Good chance," I said.

Virgil said, "We'll see what we can find out."

"Okay," Flower said.

Hart and Flower turned up the collars on their slickers, and we watched them as they hurried off into the rain.

"Good fellas," Virgil said.

"Boys," I said.

"They are."

Virgil and I stayed out of the rain, watching it come down for a bit, then we moved on across town to the Western Union. We learned that the Montezuma indeed did have wire service, but the communication with them proved little to nothing. The hotel was crowded at the moment because of a territory political symposium, and there was no way to determine if three of the hundreds of guests might be the three men we were looking for.

We subsequently sent a wire to the Las Vegas sheriff's office, alerting them about the three escapees, and heard back that they had received a previous alert from Stringer's office with detailed descriptions and had been keeping sharp eyes out for them. We next sent a wire to Appaloosa to see if there had been any new details regarding the prison break or if there was any new information regarding the man that had fled from the shootout at Meserole's saloon and learned there was nothing new to report on either front. Last, we tried to contact the prison, but still there was no connection.

Virgil and I walked to the Rawlings Hotel. It was the nicest hotel and the oldest, sort of like the Boston House in Appaloosa but bigger, and with a larger saloon. We booked us each a room, then settled in to the bar, where an older Negro fella was playing the piano. The place was fairly empty. There was a corner table with some men in suits sitting with a few saloon ladies, and at the far end of the bar sat two other dapper-looking older fellows having a lively liquor-fueled discussion.

"Two whiskeys," I said.

"And let me have one of those cigars you have there," Virgil said to the bartender as he pointed to an open box behind the bar.

"You bet," said the barkeep.

He poured us each a whiskey, then removed a cigar from the box.

He clipped the end with a brass tip cutter and handed it to Virgil. Then he struck a fat match, cupped his hand over the flame, and held it out over the bar. After Virgil got the cigar going good, the bartender shook the flame out and moved on down the rail.

We drank some whiskey and listened to the piano for

a little while, thinking about our options. Like the deputies had mentioned, the Montezuma was the largest hotel in the west, maybe in the whole United States. With more than four hundred rooms, built by railroad tycoons on the Gallinas Creek north of Las Vegas, Montezuma was a hot-springs destination for the wealthy who could afford the lavish accommodations.

"We, of course, could ride up there to Montezuma and not find them," I said.

Virgil nodded.

"Got to go someplace, though," I said.

"We do," Virgil said.

"If it's running," I said. "Maybe we take the train to Vegas. Be quicker."

Virgil nodded as he puffed on his cigar.

"Excuse me," I said to the bartender as he came walking by. "You wouldn't happen to have a train schedule back there, would you?"

The bartender turned and plucked out a printed schedule from an upright menu box and handed it over the bar to me.

"Much appreciated," I said.

"What you see there is pretty much what you get," the bartender said. "Amazes me how they can stay on time . . . The way of the world, I guess."

He walked off as I read the schedule.

"Leaves here at seven," I said. "Arrives Vegas, two in the afternoon."

"Take us the whole day and then some if we were to ride," Virgil said.

"The way of the world," I said.

33

Late in the evening, Driggs watched the princess *sleeping as he dressed. He had been curious about her pretty teeth, her pearly white teeth that pushed forward ever so slightly. He thought the little overbite was a sensuous part of her appeal. She was in every way a beautiful woman, and her teeth, with that slight protrusion, made her even more alluring. He had wondered before if it was because she had sucked her thumb as a child. Now, however, he was sure as he watched her with her thumb tucked softly into her mouth as she slept.* Baby, *he thought. He looked at her softness and youth and saw that even now, she was still not much more than a child, only a third his age. But she was by no means young in her actions and feelings. He took a swig from the bottle, then sat and rolled a few cigarettes as he gazed at her sucking her thumb. She was an old soul, he knew.*

Driggs removed a pillowcase from one of the pillows as he watched the princess. He wondered about her being dead and what it would feel like if she were dead and gone. He folded the pillowcase and put it in his pocket, then opened the door and closed it behind him as he left the room.

When he came down the stairs, he stopped in the saloon and ordered a whiskey from Wallis.

"Same as before?" Wallis said.

Driggs nodded.

"Your best," Driggs said.

"Coming right up."

Wallis pulled the bottle from the top shelf and poured Driggs a drink.

"There ya go, that's the Kentucky Gold, best I got, and it's just for you."

"Thank you, kind sir," Driggs said.

"You bet," Wallis said, then went to replace the bottle on the shelf.

"This time I wouldn't put that away just yet," Driggs said with a grin.

Wallis smiled in return and set the bottle back on the bar.

"It is there for your consumption, my friend," Wallis said.

"Thank you."

"Are you enjoying your stay here in Appaloosa?" Wallis said as he put his big hands on the bar in front of him.

"I am," Driggs said.

"Good, good," Wallis said. "Been seeing you come and go."

"You have?"

"Coming and going," Wallis said with a warm smile. "Going and coming, I trust the Boston House is treating you favorably."

"Everything has been dandy," Driggs said.

"What brings you to Appaloosa?" Wallis said.

"Oh, I've come to do some rearranging of sorts," Driggs said. "Readjustment of assets, so to speak."

"Banking is a bit over my head," Wallis said. "They get

mad at me here when I don't add my bar numbers correctly. Which is often, I might add. No pun intended."

Driggs smiled.

"Money in the wrong hands can become a very dangerous commodity," Driggs said.

"Well," Wallis said with a chuckle, "I knew there was a reason that I can't hang on to it and don't have any."

Driggs laughed and Wallis moved on down the bar.

After a few more shots of whiskey, Driggs paid up, then moved on and out into the night. He had always liked the dark better than the light. He felt more comfortable in the dark, maybe because he could move about, to some degree, unseen.

It was well past midnight and there was hardly anyone on the streets, and he appreciated that. He liked the loneliness the evening brought. He knew where he was going this evening. He'd made this trip twice before, but those ventures were strictly for reconnaissance, so now he knew exactly what he would encounter. Tonight, however, was different. Tonight his plan was to get closer than he'd been before, much closer.

He had just one stop to make first and he knew this stop would take only a moment. It was a place he'd read about in the newspaper and had already checked out in his reconnaissance runs before tonight. He knew where he was going and exactly what he was looking for. This stop was not in a nice part of town. In fact, it was in the worst part of town, near the tracks on the far south side. When he found the building he was looking for he made sure no one was around to see him as he slipped along the side of the building to the back. Within a few moments he was on the inside. It was dark and he lit a match so he could find his way, find what he was looking for, and then he saw them. He studied them, then settled on one. A nice big one. He removed the pillowcase from his pocket, then carefully snatched the big one, then *stuffed it in the pillowcase and quickly headed to his final destination.*

He walked the back alleys as he crossed to the far side of town on the northeast. This was the nicest part of Appaloosa, with the biggest homes, and when he got to the home of his choice he stood across the street in the shadows and watched the place for a while. It was a beautiful three-story Victorian, with a front porch that spanned from one side of the house to the other. He found a few trees across the way that clustered together on a slight berm where he could sit. He lit a cigarette. Somewhere in the distance he heard a dog barking nonstop. He wondered what it could be barking at. Was he agitated because he was locked up, locked out, or locked in, or was he barking at an intruder, a thief, or was he just barking at the moon? He finished the cigarette, then lit another and after a while the dog tired and very slowly stopped barking. Driggs finished his cigarette, then calmly walked across the street to the house. He set the pillowcase at his feet, then pulled his picking tools from his pocket. In the dark, under the overhang of the front porch, he quietly picked the lock, scooped up the pillowcase, and silently entered.

34

By the following morning it had stopped raining in Yaqui, but there was still heavy cloud cover that kept the sun from showing through and drying up some of the wetness.

After a quick breakfast of eggs and ham, Virgil and I loaded our horses and boarded the train for Las Vegas. We left the young deputies, Hart and Flower, in Yaqui. They were both eager lawmen and good at their jobs, but Virgil figured both to be more of a liability than an asset for the job at hand.

The train ride from Yaqui to Las Vegas was a pleasant journey, and by midday the clouds had separated some and the sun offered up a welcoming appearance.

When we arrived in Las Vegas the sun was out and the wet landscape was drying up quickly. We did not bother to enter the streets of the town so that we could make it to the Montezuma by dark. We mounted up at the depot and rode straightaway to the hotel, and arrived about an hour before dark.

The hotel was a spectacular structure. Virgil and I had been to the hotel before, just after it was built, but had not seen the place in years. It was elaborately constructed with stone blocks and fancy woodwork inside and out and from top to bottom. The entrance of the hotel had a dome and spire that was more than five stories high. There were three restaurants, a number of bars, and hot-springs bathhouses built on the back side of the hotel, where guests soaked away their aches and pains. It was by far the nicest, most lavish hotel in the entire western expanse.

We were not sure just how long we would be in the Montezuma, so we did not stable our horses but left them saddled and looked after by the stable hands. We asked the hands if they had noticed three men come in that stood out in the manner of being less put together than what they'd expect of doctors and such. All of the stable hands said they'd not seen anyone who met that description.

We entered the hotel at just about sunset, as the evening light came through the celestial stained-glass windows high above the central atrium, scattering a kaleidoscope of colorful rays in every direction.

The central area under the atrium dome was filled with separate seating areas where numerous well-dressed guests sat visiting and sipping tea. The sound of the cups on saucers and the voices echoing under the great expanse resonated with an odd loudness that was the opposite of pleasant.

"You feeling what I'm feeling?" I said.

"We stick out like a sore thumb."

"Yep."

"Don't see anybody staring at us yet, though."

"Not as of yet, no," Virgil said. "I don't, either."

"Matter of time."

"Well, there is one thing for certain," I said. "If they're here, in this place of all places on high, there is a good chance they'd have to have got some clothes."

Virgil nodded.

"You'd think," he said.

"But then you have to think, how the fuck would three dumb-ass no-good hardened criminals even have an inkling of an idea how to function in an environment like this in the first place, clothes or no clothes."

"Ravenscroft is a lowlife and mean," Virgil said. "And no good, but he was a town member before he got to killing people and got his ass in a sling."

I nodded a little, thinking about that.

"Well, without some refinement they'd stick out like a cete of badgers amongst this gaggle of geese."

"They would," Virgil said.

"Hell," I said. "The idea of them just walking across this polished floor would be enough to cause concern."

We just stood and watched and listened for a moment before we made a move.

"Since we got no real idea of what to do exactly," I said, "or where to go, I figure we check out the most obvious possibilities first."

Virgil nodded.

"Whiskey," Virgil said.

"Yep," I said. "Don't think we'd find them among this bunch sipping tea."

"No," Virgil said. "I don't, either."

Virgil looked over to the front desk.

"Maybe we have a visit with the man in charge first," Virgil said. "Gotta be a man in charge."

We walked toward the long, wide desk, where a well dressed woman and two men wearing matching vests were helping a handful of guests.

The woman was the first to look to us, and she came

over to where we were standing. She was a nice-looking dark-haired woman with even darker eyes. She walked with her shoulders back and her head held high, as if she were in charge.

"Good evening, gentlemen, and welcome to the Montezuma Hotel. How can I be of service?"

I smiled and I tipped my hat, then Virgil ever so slightly showed his badge as he said quietly, "I'm Marshal Virgil Cole. This is Deputy Marshal Hitch and we would like to have a talk with the person in charge of this outfit."

Her eyes worked back and forth between us, and then she nodded. She walked out from around the counter and smiled.

"Right this way," she said.

We followed her as she walked across the polished floor toward a set of double doors off the main atrium. Above the doors was a sign: STATE ROOM. She stopped just before the door and turned to us.

"I'm not allowed inside," she said as she opened the door, "but you will find Mr. Havenhurst sitting back there on the side of the bar, having his dinner."

"Thank you," Virgil said.

"My pleasure," she said.

I smiled at her and entered behind Virgil, and the door closed after me.

It was a dark room with a low ceiling, and it was full of cigar smoke. Scattered throughout were a lot of men sitting on stuffed wingback chairs and couches. At the far end of the room there was a long bar with a mirror that extended the length of the bar, making the room appear to be twice its size. Virgil and I weaved between the tables and chairs and walked up to the bar. We were met by a heavyset bartender with arms the size of hams. He had slicked-back graying hair and was stuffed into a formal black suit with a white starched shirt and a silk tie.

"May I help you?" he said in a deep voice.

Then we saw him, a tall, slender man with white hair. He was sitting off to the side of the bar with a napkin tucked over the collar of his shirt, sipping soup from a large spoon.

"Mr. Havenhurst?" Virgil said.

He lowered his spoon into the soup bowl and shifted his eyes between Virgil and me.

"Yes?" he said.

Virgil and I moved down the bar toward him and Virgil showed his badge.

"I'm Marshal Virgil Cole and this here is Deputy Marshal Everett Hitch and we are looking for three men. We believe they could be here at your hotel."

"I see," he said. "And I assume these men you are looking for are wanted men?"

"They are," Virgil said.

"We will do what we can to assist you."

"Pardon me," the big heavyset bartender said, interrupting as he held up his hand like a schoolboy, then looked to Mr. Havenhurst.

"Sir, I believe I know exactly who they are looking for."

35

"Who is it, Tony?" Havenhurst said.

"At least I think I know, or I suspect."

"Go on," Virgil said.

"Well, they were in here last night and again this afternoon," he said. "Last night they were okay. I thought them to be odd men, though. Not the kind of men that come in here, anyway. I've had three presidents in here. But today they were drunk, and I don't put up with drunks. Not in the State Bar. This is a respectable establishment I run here."

"Know where they are?"

"Not at the moment I don't, but I told them they needed to leave," he said. "Told them they'd had too much, that they needed to sober up. I told them if they sobered up that I would let them come back, but not until then."

"What'd they look like?" I said.

"All about forty, I'd say. Wearing fairly nice clothes, nothing too fancy. Two were pretty skinny and the third was bigger, strong-like, bald, had a crooked nose."

I looked to Virgil and Virgil looked to Havenhurst and nodded.

"That's them," Virgil said. "That's for certain the men we're looking for."

"This is the first I have heard of these men," Havenhurst said. "I know you wired last night inquiring, and I'm sorry, but we had no way of knowing. But it seems now we do."

"Does," Virgil said.

Havenhurst removed the napkin stuffed into his collar, folded it, set it on the bar, and said, "How can we help you?"

Virgil looked to me and I looked to Havenhurst.

"I know you have other bars and saloons here," I said. "Where are they located?"

"Across the atrium there is the Aztec Billiard Room and on the second floor there is another, the Canary Lounge. A small, more intimate place where women are allowed, a romantic couples place, mostly."

"You got whores that work here?" Virgil said.

"I do not," Havenhurst said in a defensive tone of voice.

"None around here? No whores?" Virgil said, looking back and forth between the bartender and Havenhurst. "You mean there is no place here where men can get some comfort from a woman friend?"

"Not really," the bartender said.

"Not really, meaning yes or no?" I said.

The bartender looked to Havenhurst.

"We just need to know where to look," I said.

"If there is a place here where ladies sell their goods," Virgil said. "Just let us know."

"There are a few ladies who work here," Havenhurst said reluctantly. "They live elsewhere, not on the premises, but do service the guests on occasion."

"And how would a guest know about this service?"

The bartender looked to Havenhurst, then back to us.

"Through me and the other barkeeps," Tony said.

"They didn't ask you, did they," I said. "About where to get some company?"

"No," he said. "But they could have asked the others."

"And the women come to the rooms?" I said.

Tony nodded.

"They do."

"Do the men visit them outside of the hotel," I said, "at another location?"

"No."

"And how do you get in touch with the whores?" Virgil said. "To let them know they have a paying client?"

"We have a runner."

"How many whores in all are there?"

"Five to seven," Tony said. "Unless things get real busy, then they bring in some friends from Las Vegas."

"Good," Virgil said.

"Good?" Havenhurst said.

Virgil nodded.

"The work we do, Mr. Havenhurst, is a matter of de . . . de . . . what's the word I'm looking for, Everett?"

"Deduction."

Virgil nodded.

"That's right," Virgil said, "deduction. You understand that, don't you, Mr. Havenhurst?"

"It's just that I run a respectable business here."

"Well, I know you got a tall steeple up top, but you ain't operating no church here, Mr. Havenhurst . . . Presidents, doctors, escaped convicts all need to get a little pussy now and again, just how it is. It's nothing personal, we just need to know the lay of the land, that's all."

36

Havenhurst walked with us across the atrium toward the Aztec Billiard Room.

"We've been fortunate not to have much trouble here, thank God," Havenhurst said as we walked. "For a time I had two security guards on full-time. They were retired deputies from Las Vegas law enforcement, but after a period of complete calm I let them go. They are on call, though, so to speak. They live near here, should trouble arise, but thankfully I've not had to request their services. That is until now, so I can certainly send for them if you'd like."

"Everett and me will be okay," Virgil said as we arrived at the doors of the billiard room.

We stopped shy of entering and Virgil turned to Havenhurst.

"You should remain out here, though, Mr. Havenhurst. Never know how things might go down and I would not want you to get summed up on the wrong end of some kind of weapon wielded by a goddamn escaped prisoner who has no intention of being locked up again."

"Yes, yes . . . I understand, Marshal . . . Please know, I do my best to run a tidy ship here, so hopefully when and if you do find the men you are looking for you can settle this with decorum."

Virgil looked at me and nodded a little.

"We will do our best," I said as Virgil and I both pulled our Colts. "Decorum is our business."

We both checked the chambered loads, and with our Colts close to our sides I opened the door and followed Virgil inside. As the door closed behind me Virgil leaned toward me and said, "Decorum?"

"Good behavior," I said as we both scanned the stately dark billiard room for our three men.

There looked to be twenty, maybe thirty, people in the wide room with ten billiard tables, and it appeared there was a game happening at each table.

"Full house," I said.

"Is."

Like the previous saloon, this place was full of cigar smoke, but unlike the previous place, this room was noisy with the sounds of pool balls, laughter, and game commentary.

"No one looking at us," I said.

After continued perusal Virgil shook his head.

"Don't see 'em."

"No," I said. "Don't, either."

Virgil slid his revolver back into its holster and I did the same. Then we walked slowly toward the bar, all the while keeping a sharp eye out for the three, but as we strolled and neared the bar we saw no sign of them.

We stood toward the right end of the bar, and within a short amount of time the bartender came walking over.

"Evening, gents," he said.

He looked like he might be the brother of the bartender across the way at the State Room, except he was bigger and not as heavy.

Virgil showed his badge and I turned my back to the bar so as to keep an eye on the room.

"We are marshals," Virgil said, "and we are looking for three men. We know they have been in the hotel as late as this afternoon. We just had a conversation with Mr. Havenhurst and Tony across the way. Havenhurst is just outside the door here. Havenhurst and Tony have shared with us how the whores are lined up for your guests. So now we need a few answers to a few questions."

The big man looked back and forth between Virgil and me, and before Virgil could continue, he said, "I know exactly who you are talking about."

I turned and looked to him.

"And they were liquored up," he said. "Two darkheaded guys with scraggly beards and hair and a bigger guy, bald, strong-looking."

Virgil glanced to me.

"That's them," he said.

"You can find them at the bathhouse. The far end bathhouse, number sixty-three. It's a place where some of the girls go with the guests. It's an option, instead of the rooms. They paid for three gals, and bathhouse sixty-three . . . They had the money."

We wasted no time, and with Havenhurst leading the way we quickly made our way to the bathhouses.

Bathhouse 63 was situated just off the wide, tree-lined creek behind the hotel. The hot waters from the hot springs offered up rising vapors that gave the whole setting a mysterious foggy atmosphere.

"What is on the far side of the bathhouse?" Virgil said. "The side we can't see?"

"On the opposite side of the structure there is an opening with a deck. The hot waters follow a channel to a pool in front of each bathhouse. They are all situated the same way. Sixty-three is no exception."

"Thank you, Mr. Havenhurst," Virgil said.

"What would you like me to do?" he said.

"Nothing you can do right now," Virgil said. "You should go back inside and wait. And make sure no one comes this way. Later, there might be some need to clean up a bit, but we won't know what is what until we have a chance to get in there and assess the situation."

37

There was a path lit by gaslights on poles that led down to bathhouse 63 and there was a door to the bathhouse, but it was closed. Virgil and I skirted off the path and moved up to the building from the dark. As we neared we could see light and could hear voices coming from within. The window that faced us was small and covered with a curtain. There was a window in the door, but it, too, was covered with a curtain.

"Let's go off that way a ways," Virgil said quietly, "and come back from the dark on the far side where we have a better idea of what is what."

We moved off in the dark and crossed the steaming creek, down some into the woods, then came back to where we had the bathhouse in view. Sure enough, we knew right away we had the men we were after when we saw Ravenscroft.

He was sitting in a pool of steaming hot water with a woman under his arm. Behind him on the side of the pool we could see a pair of holstered pistols with the bullet belt wrapped around them.

The bathhouse behind was without a wall on this side that faced us, so we could see the other two men, also with women.

One couple was sitting up in a bed and the other twosome was lounging on pillows on the floor next to the bed, and everyone was naked.

Looking at six naked people in this open-sided bathhouse with the steam rising up conjured thoughts of what a scene might have looked like in the empire of Rome.

"What do you want to do," I said quietly.

Virgil thought for a moment.

"If by chance one or some of them can get on the run, I think one of us needs to be on the path side that heads back to the hotel."

I nodded.

"Then," he said, "we let them know they are surrounded and see who feels like throwing their hands up."

"'Bout it," I said.

"I'll go back around to the path," Virgil said. "You come in from this side. Once I get up to the path and get ready I will let them know we have them corralled. You can then voice from this side to surrender and let's see what they do."

"Okay," I said.

Virgil looked to me. I could barely see him but could see enough to see him nod a bit.

"All right, then," he said. "Here we go."

Virgil moved off, backing up into the woods, then moving upstream a ways, then crossed the creek. From where I was nested I could see him clearly as he came up the back of the creek and into the lighted path that led back up to the hotel.

I pulled my Colt and started to ease a bit closer toward the bathhouse and found a good-sided tree to take cover behind. I was watching the three men intently as I waited on Virgil's voice to interrupt their playtime. I wondered what they would do. I figured they'd react just like Skillman, Wythe, and Dekalb had reacted in Vadito, that they'd most likely stand and fight, and I knew the answer to that wonderment was a few seconds away, and then I heard Virgil.

"You are surrounded. Give yourselves up."

The three naked men all went for a gun. The man that was sitting in the pillows was the fastest. He was up and on the move, too.

"Don't do it," I shouted. "Don't move!"

But that did not stop them. The man in the bed took off, naked, with pistol in hand and ran out the door.

"Stop!" Virgil shouted.

Ravenscroft and the other man fired wildly in my direction and the three naked women screamed as they dove for cover.

Ravenscroft was gunning with both of his pistols.

I heard Virgil fire and saw the flash of his Colt and then one of the naked men came falling backward through the door and stumbled, then fell into the pool as Ravenscroft and the other man kept firing blindly in my direction.

I remained behind the tree, out of the line of fire, but could see the men.

Then Ravenscroft took off running into the creek. He was slanting away from me, and as he ran he fired both guns toward me. I took steady aim and squeezed off a shot.

"Arrggg," he said as he arched his back. "Goddamn."

But he kept firing and I shot again. This bullet hit him again and spun him around. Then he moved toward me and fired one more time but could not keep his feet under him. He stumbled forward and fell face-first into the foggy creek.

"Stop," I heard Virgil say.

Then I saw through the rising steam of the creek the flash of the last gunman as he tried to shoot Virgil as he ran in the opposite direction up the creek. Next I saw Virgil's shot and the man went down.

Virgil and I waited before either of us moved. I could see clearly the two men Virgil had shot, and neither was moving. Virgil and I waited a long time. It was an important time to just wait and make sure the three men who were not interested in returning to prison were in no real condition to do so if in fact they changed their minds.

38

Driggs and his princess ventured away from the *Boston House and made their way around Appaloosa, eventually ending up on Vandervoort Avenue. It was a beautiful day as they strolled up the wide street lined with brick buildings.*

When they saw Allie and Margie in the window they stopped and watched them as the ladies fitted a dress on a mannequin. Allie looked up and smiled. Driggs tipped his hat and his princess smiled. Then Allie stepped down from the window display and opened the door.

"What a lovely dress," the princess said.

"Well, I'm pleased you like it," Allie said. "It came all the way from Boston."

"We'll take it," Driggs said.

"Oh, honey," the princess said. "Really?"

Even though it was her money, she was thrilled to know he wanted her to have the dress.

"Well, my gosh," Allie said. "I'm not even open for business yet."

He smiled at Allie, a disarming smile.

"Does that matter?" he said.

"Well . . . um," Allie said. "I guess not."

"Do you think it will fit?" the princess said.

Margie stepped into the doorway and smiled to the couple. Allie looked back to her.

"They want to buy the dress," she said with a smile.

"Well," Margie said, taking over with the assured sass of a salesperson who knows her business, "I suppose we just fit this fabulous dress on this exquisite young woman instead of the not-so-exquisite wooden woman."

Margie looked to the dress in the window and to the woman.

"We will have to take it in a little," Margie said. "But that should not be a problem."

Margie stood back, and with a bow and a sweep of her hand toward the open shop door she said, "After you."

Driggs and his princess entered Allie's shop and in a matter of moments his beautiful lady was standing in front of the mirror admiring the low-cut dress. Driggs sat with his hat in his lap in a chair off to the side behind her, looking at her reflection in the mirror.

"Actually, it fits pretty well," Margie said. "Don't you think, Allie?"

"I do," she said.

"Do you like it, love?" Driggs said.

She turned from the mirror, nodded, smiled, leaned down, and kissed him on the mouth. It was not just a peck. It was a wet kiss that caused Allie to blush a little.

"I love it," the princess said.

"Okay, then," Allie said. "We just need to take it in a little here and there."

"It should be done soon," Margie said with a beaming smile. "We are so happy you stopped in."

"My first customer," Allie said.

Driggs's princess stepped behind the dressing screen to change.

"So this is your shop?" Driggs said, looking at Allie.

"It is."

"You must be Mrs. French?"

"I am."

"Mr. French is a lucky man," Driggs said.

"Oh . . . well. I'm a widow, I'm afraid . . . my late husband, Mr. French, passed away many years ago."

"But she is well looked after," Margie said with an exuberant nod. "Isn't that so, Allie?"

Driggs looked Allie up and down a little.

"Well," he said. "I'm sure she is."

"He's quite a man," Margie said with a grin.

"Well, he'd have to be," Driggs said.

"And he's a federal lawman, no less," Margie said. "A United States Marshal."

"Well, how about that," he said.

"Yes," Allie said with a smile.

"Living here in Appaloosa?"

"We do," Allie said.

"Marshal Virgil Cole," Margie said.

"Virgil Cole?" he said. "I think I have heard about him."

"Yes," Allie said. "He's . . . he's a fine man."

Margie moved behind the curtain to help Driggs's lady change dresses, leaving Allie with Driggs.

Driggs stood and moved toward Allie a little.

"So it looks like you will be opening soon?" he said.

"Hopefully this weekend," she said. "Saturday will be my official opening."

"How was it that this came to be?" Driggs said. "This dress shop?"

Driggs folded his arms and leaned his shoulder against the wall, looking at Allie.

"Oh, well. I just felt the need to have something of my own," she said.

"Oh, you have something of your own," he said.

Allie blushed a little, feeling a bit self-conscious.

"So who owns this building?"

"Oh, well . . . Mr. Vandervoort owns the whole block and most everyone rents from him."

"Vandervoort?"

"Yes. A wonderful man."

"Does he live here?" he said. "In Appaloosa?"

"Yes," she said. "Are you interested in renting, perhaps?"

Driggs moved a bit closer to Allie.

"No," he said. "Not really. We are just passing through."

"Oh," Allie said.

"But one never knows," Driggs said.

"Well, he's not hard to find," Allie said. "He is, however, out of town at the moment."

"I see," he said.

"And thank God," she said.

"Why thank God?" Driggs said.

"Oh, well . . . he might have had a heart attack if he were here," she said. "Or worse?"

"Why?"

"Oddest thing," Allie said. "His new bride, perhaps the most gracious woman in all of Appaloosa, I might add, woke up to find a rattlesnake in her bed."

"My God, is she all right?"

"Yes, thank goodness, she wasn't bitten. But can you imagine? In bed, of all places?"

"A snake in the bed?" he said.

"A rattlesnake," she said. "It was on her pillow. Can you imagine?"

"No," he said. "I can't imagine."

39

The three men we shot at the Montezuma bathhouses turned out were in fact Timothy Eckford, Willard Calyer, and Charlie Ravenscroft.

After the shootout, I pulled Ravenscroft from the creek where he had fallen. When I dragged him up on the deck of the steam pool, he moved slightly. He was bleeding profusely from the two bullets he received. My first shot hit him on the side just under his arm and the second was in the chest, but for a moment he breathed some and opened his eyes. He had that frightened expression, that look I'd seen many times before: the countenance of a man who knows he's dying. Ravenscroft stared at me with a curious look on his face. Then he smiled a little and said, "Everett Hitch."

"It is, Charlie," I said to him.

"I'll be go to hell," he said, and then he did just that, he went straight to hell, and the incident in the steamy bathhouse ended.

*   *   *

We left Montezuma early the following morning and took the train back to Yaqui to collect Skillman and Dobbin and return them to Cibola.

We wasted little time in Yaqui. We remained there only long enough to determine details from the deputies in the sheriff's office that let us know Sheriff Stringer and his posse had yet to come back with Ed Degraw and that the wire service to Cibola was still inexplicably out of service.

We rode the whole second half of the day with Skillman and Dobbin in tow. We camped that night, broke camp an hour before sunrise, and arrived at the prison the following day just before noon.

As we neared the prison, two guards looked out of a wide opening of a stone building that sat on a rise a few hundred yards before the prison's entrance. As we got a bit closer they came out to the road to meet us. Virgil moved his lapel and showed his badge. One of the guards, an older, stern-looking man with a gray beard, stood back as if he were leery. The other guard was a barrel-bodied, redheaded fellow carrying a Sharps fifty-caliber. He nodded as he walked closer to us.

"And you are?" he said.

"I'm Marshal Cole. This is Deputy Marshal Hitch. And these fellas here are two of the men who escaped."

He looked to Skillman and Dobbin, then said, "Welcome back."

"Telegraph lines working now?" I said.

The younger guard turned to the older guard and the older guard shook his head.

"Don't think so," the young guard said. "We haven't been inside today."

The older guard came a bit closer and said, "Where did you catch these two?"

Virgil looked to Skillman and Dobbin, then back to me.

"One in Vadito," I said. "One in Yaqui."

"And the others?" he said.

"So far, the others were not as lucky as these two here," I said.

The older man eyed Skillman and Dobbin for a moment.

"Thought you fellas could get away with this?" he said.

Dobbin just glared and Skillman did not look up as the guard moved a bit toward them. He shook his head, then looked to Virgil.

"We can get you to the warden," he said.

"Sure he'll be appreciative 'bout this," the younger guard said. "He's not in the yard, though. He's up at his house."

He pointed to a cluster of buildings on a rise about a quarter of a mile away.

"Need to get these two back inside first," the older guard said. "No prisoners are allowed near the quarters."

"That's what we brought them back for," I said.

"After you," Virgil said.

The older guard nodded to the younger.

"Go ahead," he said.

The young guard moved quickly for a hefty fellow as he opened the gate of a small corral and led out a stocky, short bay horse. He slid his rifle into a scabbard, tightened the cinch, then stepped up easily into the saddle.

"This way," he said.

The older man watched us for a moment, then moved back toward the building as the big man led us toward the prison. After a moment he slowed and the three of us rode abreast.

"How did you find them?" he said.

Virgil said nothing. Virgil never did say much of anything when it came to answering questions.

"I'm Mickey, by the way, Mickey Dodd."

"Well, one thing just led to another, Mickey," I said. "'Bout all I can tell you."

He nodded, then looked back to Skillman and Dobbin.

"I've been working here since the place opened, twelve years ago. Since that time we had just one escape and he was caught the following day, but this . . . well, my God, this is just . . . hell, crazy as all hell is the only thing you can say for it."

"How many people are there here?" Virgil said.

"Inmates or workers?"

"Both."

"Well, we are overcrowded here. 'Bout three hundred inmates and ten to fifteen workers; most are guards, and of course there is support staff, too, cooks, cleaners, and such."

I looked back to Skillman.

"Our prisoners have been tight-lipped and offered up nothing about how this happened, really. What do you know about how these men got out?"

"We don't know nothing, either . . . Least I don't."

He pointed up to the warden's place and shook his head.

"Warden Flushing has not really been out since this happened," Mickey said. "Think he's taken this hard. Kenneth Tillary is his chief assistant and he's the one who has been handling things."

"And you don't know anything about the escape?"

"Nope, it was late, sometime in the middle of the night, and I was not there, I was on day shift. But Mr. Smith back there, he's the outside boss, he was there and he didn't see or hear anything. Fact of the matter is, at least from what I know, no one saw anything. All I know is Benny and Chuck, two guards inside, were killed. That is all I know. I kind of thought the warden would have gathered us and at least offered up something, said something by now, but he has not. I guess he can't believe it, I don't know. Hell of a deal, though . . . it's like they just vanished."

40

The warden's assistant, Kenneth Tillary, met us inside the prison walls. He was a thin, older, sunbaked man with silver hair and wise blue eyes behind thick spectacles. He was pleasant enough as he collected Skillman and Dobbin. For the moment he treated the men kindly, as if they had never escaped. He avoided asking about the other escaped men and remained focused on reprocessing Skillman and Dobbin. After a short but formal explanation of what would happen to the men once the circuit judge came through, he instructed two guards to return the two men to their cells. Virgil and I watched as the escapees were quickly hustled away. Skillman looked back to Virgil.

"They've both suffered wounds," I said.

The guards that were moving them off acted as if they did not hear me or did not give a shit.

"Why don't you fellas come into my office," Tillary said, then looked to Mickey. "I'll take care of the marshals from here."

"I was gonna take them up—"

Tillary interrupted, "Thank you, Mickey, that will be all."

Mickey looked at us, nodded and said, "Good to meet you." Then took off on the bay horse. A couple guards pushed the gates open and Mickey galloped off back to the entry station as the doors were closed behind him.

We walked with Tillary across the compound and toward the northwest corner office.

"Is your telegraph back in service?" I said.

Tillary stopped at the bottom of the office steps, turned to Virgil and me, and shook his head.

"Don't have no service," he said as he looked up to the office. "I'll show you."

We walked up the stairs to the prison office perched atop the corner of the prison wall. The office had wide pulley-operated batwing windows on each side that were open and offered a view in every direction. On the north side of the office there was a bank of pigeon cages full of carrier birds that were perched on crap-covered branches and feeding troughs. There were also a number of pigeons perched here and there around the office. A few were on a ceiling beam and a few walked about on the floor. They scattered as Tillary walked to a corner pine desk.

"This is where the key and sounder and batteries used to be," he said. "As you can see, they are no longer there."

"Don't make much sense for them to go to the trouble to do that on their way out," I said.

Tillary nodded.

"There is a good deal regarding what happened here that don't make much sense . . . Please sit."

Tillary took a seat behind a center room desk and Virgil and I sat on two stiff-backed chairs opposite of him.

"Where is the warden?" Virgil said.

"He is up at his house," Tillary said with a pained

looked on his face, "and I will escort you there subsequently, but I think it important we go over some details. Some of what you know and some of what I know."

Virgil nodded.

"Here is what I know," Tillary said. "This escape happened sometime in the night and the following morning both of the guards who were on duty were found dead and nine inmates were out of their cells and gone from the prison yard. The stables were opened and a buckboard and all of the horses were taken."

"The guard Mickey had a bay he just rode up here on."

"Oh, yes," he said. "I meant to say all the horses that were in the stable. We had fenced others that were out, the escapees just took those from the stable."

"You said nine men got out? It was reported to us that there was eight," I said.

"Who reported that?"

I looked to Virgil.

"Dobbin. He was the first one apprehended," I said.

"Well," he said. "Dobbin is mistaken or lying."

"He told Sheriff Stringer there were eight of them that got out, that is the information Stringer reported to us."

"At first I thought that, too, actually, that there were eight gone," Tillary said. "But one other had escaped from the Tomb."

"Tomb?" I said.

"Solitary confinement."

"How did he get out of solitary confinement?"

"How the hell he got out I have no idea . . . no . . . no . . . let me rephrase that, I know perfectly well how he got out. He got out just like the others got out, with a key."

"How'd they get a key?" Virgil said.

Tillary shook his head slowly from side to side.

"We don't know," he said. "No earthly idea."

. I pulled the list of names from my pocket.

"Here are the list of names that were reported to us along with their descriptions. Ben Wythe, Boyd Dekalb, Ed Degraw, Timothy Eckford, Willard Calyer, Charlie Ravenscroft, Richard Skillman, and Bernard Dobbin."

Tillary nodded, got out of his chair, and walked to the open southeast window and looked down into the yard. He gave a loud whistle, then called out to a guard, "Bring Dobbin up here."

Tillary turned, walked back, and sat behind his desk again.

"Those that you just read were eight of the men from Murderers Row," Tillary said.

"Two of those, Dobbin and Skillman, are of course back with you," I said. "Five are dead and the eighth or ninth man might be dead or captured by now, we don't know. One man was being pursued by a posse that is being led by Sheriff Stringer out of Yaqui."

Tillary nodded.

"We originally believed that man to be Ed Degraw," I said. "But I suppose he could be the other man who you said escaped from the confinement cell."

Tillary nodded.

"That was Donnie Lonnigan," he said.

"Donnie Lonnigan?" I said.

"Yes," he said.

Virgil cut his eyes to me.

"Know him?" he said.

I met Virgil's eye, shaking my head a little.

"The Don Lonnigan I knew fought with me when I was soldiering, but he was lost in action. That was a long time ago in a fight with Lakota and Cheyenne on the Platt River."

41

"Lonnigan or Degraw, either one of them," Tillary said as he picked up his pipe from a pipe tray on he desk, "they are scary trouble. Both are damn sure a force to be reckoned with . . . The hell of the thing is those two men thoroughly despise each other."

He struck a match and lit his pipe. He puffed it until it glowed, then waved the match, dropped it in the ashtray, and stood up. "In their own separate ways, those two were the absolute worst we had to offer here . . . They caused all of us, including the warden, fits."

Tillary walked past the pigeon cages and looked out the window toward the warden's home atop the rise in the distance. He puffed on his pipe some as he looked off, then turned back to us.

"That being said, ever since this has happened the warden has seemed to have slipped off the deep end, I'm afraid."

"How so," I said.

Tillary shook his head.

"He's pretty much stayed up there in the house with his wife. When he has come down here he's been inebriated. Last time I told him he needed to stay away. I told him I did not want the other guards to see him like that, told him it was not good for the morale of all. I said he should rest and take care of his wife and come back when he was sober, feeling well again, and up for the job. I sent word to his wife to let me know if there was anything at all she needed . . . poor thing. He's just a mess."

Tillary looked back to the house on the hill.

"I shouldn't really comment on this," Tillary said. "But the young couple should not be out here, and though he has proved himself to be a capable warden at times, I feel this remote place and the demands of this job are a little too much for him."

"How long you been here?" Virgil said. "Working at this prison?"

"Since the beginning," he said.

"How is it that you are not warden and some younger man holds the position?"

Tillary smiled.

"Good question."

"Bad answer," Virgil said.

"Warden Scholes Flushing the Third," Tillary said, "is the son of Territorial Lieutenant Governor Scholes Flushing the Second is the reason why."

"Good answer," Virgil said.

"The Flushings are one of the wealthiest families in the Territory," Tillary said. "All thanks to General Scholes Flushing the First, a southerner who amassed a fortune on a cotton plantation before the war. I think the lieutenant governor positioned young Scholes here so to give him some character, and I'm not certain that was the best row to hoe. This place gives one character, but it also takes some character, if you know what I am saying."

We heard footsteps coming up the office stairs. It was Dobbin, wearing a pair of handcuffs and accompanied by one of the stern guards who had whisked him away earlier. Dobbin looked to be in pain but was keeping his head up. I could tell Dobbin was the type of young man who would never let you think you were ever getting the better of him. But he jerked his arm from the guard's grip as they came to attention just inside the office door. The guard grabbed for him.

"That's okay," Tillary said to the guard.

The guard instantly refrained his need to manhandle Dobbin and stood back a little.

"Got some questions for you, Mr. Dobbin," Tillary said. "I know you feel you have been forthcoming and whatnot, but I don't think you have provided a clear picture of what you know and what happened."

"What do you want to know?" he said.

"You provided Sheriff Stringer with information that there were eight of you who escaped," Tillary said.

"That's right. The sheriff said he would see to it that my cooperation would be recognized by the good judge, and I told the sheriff all I knew."

"Why did you lie?"

"I didn't lie," he said defensively.

"Why did you fail to include Donnie Lonnigan?"

"Donnie Lonnigan? I didn't include Lonnigan because Lonnigan was not with us, that's why."

"Then where is he?"

Dobbin shook his head.

"Hell. I ain't got no idea."

"Why would you protect Lonnigan?"

Dobbin looked completely confused and his eyes darted among Tillary, Virgil, and me.

"I ain't protecting nobody," he said.

"Give us an account of the escape," Virgil said.

"Well, I told Sheriff Stringer all of what happened," he said.

"Just go again," Virgil said.

"All I know is I was sound asleep. I was in the same cell with the blackie, Dekalb, and Old Man Wythe, and Dekalb nudged me and told me to get up—that we were leaving. It was dark and we filed out in single file. Eight of us, all from compound C. We went to the stable. Them others got saddle horses and Dekalb, Wythe, Skillman, and me ended up in the buckboard. I figured there was no use in arguing with the likes of Degraw and Ravenscroft 'bout who gets a saddle horse and who don't. So we took off. Them with the horses went one way and we went the other and there was no sign of Donnie Lonnigan."

42

Tillary mounted up on a tall gray mare and Virgil and I followed him out the prison gates and rode slowly up the winding road to the warden's house. When we approached the home, which was situated behind a low rock wall surrounding the property, Tillary stopped and turned back to us.

"Maybe give me a minute, let me go in and let him know you are here," he said.

Virgil glanced to me, then nodded to Tillary.

"Sure," he said.

We rode on up to the house and stopped at a hitching post next to a well and dismounted. We tied off and Tillary walked up toward the house. The home was a well-built large adobe with a wide porch. There was a nice-sized barn on the west side behind the house and a few other outbuildings to the east.

Tillary knocked on the door, and when he did we heard a gunshot from inside the house. Tillary dropped quickly to one knee, then moved at a low crawl away from the door.

Virgil and I pulled our Colts and dropped for cover behind the rock wall. I could see Tillary clearly from where we were crouched. He pulled the Smith & Wesson service revolver he had on his hip and stood with his back to the wall between the front door and the window.

We waited for a long moment, then Tillary called out, "Scholes!"

He waited for a reply, but there was nothing.

"Scholes," he called again.

Then.

"Mrs. Flushing?" Tillary said. "Can you hear me?"

Tillary looked to us and shook his head a little.

"Scholes," he called again. "Mrs. Flushing!"

Again nothing, only silence, and Tillary looked to us and raised his palms upward.

"We have help here, from territorial marshals, they're here with me now," Tillary said.

We waited for a long while, but there was no sound or sign from anyone.

"Not feeling real good about this here, gentlemen," Tillary said as he moved out a bit and looked to the front door. He stood there just looking at the door, then turned to us and shook his head. He looked back to the door again, then eased off the porch and moved slowly back toward the well.

Virgil and I stood up slowly from our crouched positions when Tillary got close. He glanced back to us and shook his head as he put his revolver back in its holster.

"I'm thinking the worst here," he said.

"When were you last up here?" Virgil said.

"Been a while," he said as he remained looking at the front door.

"You been up here since the breakout?" Virgil said.

He shook his head.

"No," he said. "No reason, really."

We all remained looking at the house.

Tillary was shaking as he removed his hat and wiped his sweat-covered forehead with the back of his shirt-sleeve.

"The poor crazy fucker," Tillary said, then looked to us. "I'm kicking myself very hard in the ass right now. If we get in there and see he's done something bad, killed her and himself, I will be forever regretful, I can tell you that."

"Don't have another choice," I said, "but to get in there and see what is what."

"We don't," Virgil said.

We took cautious time getting into the house. I entered in the back and Virgil and Tillary came in from the front, and I was the first to see the blood.

"Back here," I said.

Virgil and Tillary came walking into the dining area just off the kitchen where I stood looking at the young man sitting at the end of the long, thick wood table. His pistol was still clutched in his hand. He'd shot himself in the temple and blood was splattered across the wall and a painting of Jesus behind him. In front of him on the table was a pair of binoculars, a half-empty bottle of whiskey, a letter, and a pen. Next to the letter there was a silver-framed wedding tintype of the young warden with his new bride in wedding clothes, and it, too, was splattered with blood.

When Tillary saw him sitting at the head of the table, he took a step back.

"Oh . . . dear God. I should have prevented this," he said. "You see her?"

I shook my head.

"Gentlemen," he said. "Please. Help me, let's look."

Virgil looked to me and nodded a little.

Then as Tillary and Virgil started to move I looked to the note left on the table and said, "Don't bother."

43

"She's not here," I said.

Tillary turned and looked at me.

"What?" he said. "Where? Where is she?"

" 'She left me,' " I said, then looked to Virgil and Tillary. "Those are the first words here on this letter."

I glanced at the body of the letter, which included some writing on the back.

"Lot here," I said. "It's for you, Mr. Tillary. It's addressed to you."

"She left him?" Tillary said in disbelief.

"That's what it says," I said.

Tillary shook his head a little. He walked slowly over to me and I handed the letter to him.

"I understand it's addressed to you personally," Virgil said, "but it'd be a good idea we know what's written there."

Tillary nodded.

"Of course," he said.

His hands were shaking as he held the letter at arm's

length and started to read, " 'Dear Mr. Tillary. She left me. She is not coming back. It was my fault.' "

Tillary looked up to Virgil and me and shook his head a little.

"Dear God," he said, then continued to read the letter. " 'First off, please know, I have appreciated your patience with me. In some ways you were more of a father figure to me than my own father ever was. I have the utmost respect for you. I learned a great deal from you and would have liked nothing more than to make you proud of me. Regardless, I should have seen this coming with Eleanor and done something about it, but I had no earthly idea something of this magnitude, this drastic, could have happened. Nonetheless, it is now too late. I knew it would be only a matter of time before authorities would be here and I knew any day, you or someone would be coming to the house and paying me a visit. The fact of the matter is, I can't face the truth of this, sir. It is unbearable and humiliating beyond compare.' "

Tillary was having a hard time with his sight, his emotions, and his shaking hands. He handed the letter to me.

"Would you mind?" he said. "I'm sorry."

I took the letter and continued.

"Let's see . . ." I said. " 'Therefore I feel it imperative that I provide some underlying detail of this dishonoring dismay. I am nothing but ashamed of myself. I simply could not face my family over this spectacle. I think you know mistakes and weakness have plagued the better part of my life. I thought by taking on this remote job and marrying Eleanor, a woman of stature, of principle, would prove to my father that once and for all I was a solid man with promise who was standing on firm footing. It was, however, only a short amount of time after marrying Eleanor that I realized there was no way in hell I would hang on to her. At first she could not see through me, see my weakness. In the beginning she was blinded by my pedigree and unfortunate good looks. Good looks that I got from my father, no less, but her fascination with me quickly faded. I am only my father's son and nothing more. She never let on in public, to you or any-one else, that she was disillusioned. At least I don't think she did, but here, behind closed doors, it was another matter. I masked my consumption of alcohol as much as I could, but I'm certain it's no shock to you that I have drunk myself to sleep every night for the last year.' "

I looked up to Tillary. He met my eye, then looked to Virgil and nodded a little.

" 'This next bit of information,' " I read, " 'however, most certainly will come as a shock to you and most, Mr. Tillary: Eleanor was responsible for the men escaping from prison.' "

Tillary swiveled his head like he'd been slapped.

"What?" he said.

I stopped reading and looked to Virgil and Tillary staring at me.

"My God," Tillary said. "What? That's insane. Non-sense . . . What in God's name is he talking about? I'm sorry . . . Please continue."

Tillary, looking as if he was about to pass out, dropped into a chair next to the wall as I continued to read.

" 'She also took all the money. Twenty-five thousand dollars I had in my safe. She took my best guns and two of my finest horses, but most important, she took the last bits and pieces of my heart and certainly my pride . . . The following is what I believe was the sequence of events.' "

I stopped reading out loud and read a bit to myself. Then I looked to Virgil and shook my head some.

" 'I was passed out when this happened. I believe she got my key and released Donnie Lonnigan from the Tomb.' "

"Donnie Lonnigan," Tillary said. "My God. Seriously?"

I nodded, looking at Tillary.

"Fucking Donnie Lonnigan!" he said, shaking his head.

I continued to read. "'I am not certain how the other men from compound C escaped, but she let Lonnigan out, set him free, of that I am sure. The events that followed I am, however, unsure about, but I knew in my pitiful heart that she was enamored and in love with Donnie Lonnigan. Last, please tell my family that I love them and that I thank them for all they have done for me and that I am truly sorry, Sincerely, Scholes Flushing the Third.'"

I looked to Tillary, then to Virgil.

"Good God," Tillary said.

44

Tillary was hit hard by this news. He said nothing as he gathered some rags and went about the task of cleaning up the mess that Scholes Flushing had made of himself. After Tillary cleaned the blood off of Scholes's face and hands, we helped him get Scholes into a fresh shirt, then laid him out on the long table and covered his body with a bedsheet.

"I'll get some of the men to gather him and we'll get him back to his family right away," Tillary said, then shook his head in disbelief. "They will be devastated."

"You have any idea about his wife," Virgil said. "About her having a liking for the inmate?"

"In hindsight," Tillary said, "maybe."

"How so?"

Tillary shook his head.

"I'd say I don't believe it. But the fact of the matter is I do believe it, or better said, it seems as though I have to believe it."

"Why do you say that?" Virgil said.

"She started a Bible study program for the inmates. Giving them Bibles and so on."

"What do you mean by 'so on'?"

"She would meet with them and talk with them about God."

Virgil looked to me and shook his head a little.

"Where?" he said.

"How?" I said. "Not in their cells?"

"Oh, no, outside of their cells, always escorted by a guard," he said. "She was convinced, or convinced her husband, anyway, that there was need in the men's lives for rehabilitation."

"She preach to them?" I said.

"No. She would just talk with them. On Sundays a preacher comes through. Not all Sundays, but some. He comes and preaches to the men in the yard."

"All the men?"

He shook his head.

"Those that are interested in listening."

"And Mrs. Flushing was part of the service?"

"Mrs. Flushing would lead the hymns."

"This Lonnigan was allowed to partake?"

"Much to my dismay. Him and others. Believe me, it was something that I was dead set against, but she influenced Scholes and he did what she wanted. She had that way about her."

"What way, exactly?"

Tillary shook his head.

"There is something about Eleanor. She has that thing that makes men weak . . . especially Scholes, and she so . . . she gave off that air, you know?"

Tillary stared at the floor for a moment like he was lost in thought.

Virgil looked to me.

"Air?" I said.

"Oh, hell . . . I don't know. Look, I liked her very much, and I looked at her like a daughter, really, and Scholes like a son, but her interest in God seemed, hell, I don't know, less than genuine. She seemed more interested in getting attention from men, and she got a lot of it."

"But you did or did not see the connection or relationship with Lonnigan," I said.

"Not really, no . . . I didn't. The thing is, when Scholes was in the yard and on duty I was not around. We alternated. On numerous occasions, however, when I returned I would find Lonnigan in the Tomb yet again and Scholes's explanation was always the same. He had it coming. I asked the other guards and they told me that they had no idea why, but that they did what they were told to do."

Tillary picked up the wedding tintype of Scholes and Eleanor and looked at it sadly.

"I thought she was here at the house," Tillary said, shaking his head. "All these days since the escape I had no idea something like this had happened. I thought she was up here."

Tillary set the tintype back on the table and moved to the open back door and looked out across the expanse. He leaned against the doorjamb.

"The thought never crossed my mind and Scholes let on nothing other than, well . . . like I mentioned," Tillary said, turning back to us. "The few times I laid eyes on him he was a drunken mess and now I know why . . ."

Virgil picked up the tintype and looked at it closely. He studied it for a moment, then looked to Tillary.

"This woman here," Virgil said. "This is her, Mr. Tillary. This is Mrs. Flushing?"

"Yes," he said with a nod. "That's Eleanor and Scholes, that is their wedding photograph."

Virgil looked at the tintype again for a long moment.

"Everett," he said, then removed his eyes from the tintype. "The woman here in the photo, Eleanor Flushing. She look familiar?"

Virgil handed me the tintype and I looked closely at the woman.

45

I looked from the tintype to Virgil, then back to the tintype.

"I'll be goddamned," I said.

"What?" Tillary said.

"He took Lonnigan's name," I said.

Virgil looked to Tillary.

"What?" Tillary said. "Who?"

"Man I knew," I said.

"You got a photograph of Donnie Lonnigan?"

"No," Tillary said.

"Describe him," I said.

After Tillary gave a detailed description of Donnie Lonnigan, Virgil looked to me.

"Damn sure sounds like him," Virgil said. "The fella you knew, that we saw."

"I'll be damned," I said.

Tillary looked back and forth between Virgil and me with a frown on his face.

"What?" he said. "What are you talking about?"

"We believe we have seen him," Virgil said.

"Four days after the breakout," I said.

"With her?" Tillary said with a confused look on his face.

I nodded.

"Where?"

"Appaloosa," I said.

"Better than a good chance that it is her, Eleanor," Virgil said. "And him, Lonnigan."

"Appaloosa?" Tillary said.

Virgil nodded.

"Who took Lonnigan's name?" Tillary said, narrowing his eyes.

"Someone I knew a long time ago."

I looked to Virgil.

"Why Appaloosa?" I said.

Virgil shook his head a little.

"Gotta be some reason," Virgil said. "Otherwise he might just stay hiding."

"You sure?" Tillary said. "Appaloosa is a hell of a long way from here."

Virgil looked to me.

"Damn straight," I said. "Two names I know coming up from long ago seems better than a good chance."

Virgil nodded and looked to Tillary.

"Where is the closest depot?"

"San Cristóbal," he said. "Due west, 'bout seventy miles."

"Getting out of here and getting to Appaloosa," I said, "without a care in the world, looking like a refined, distinguished couple. Seems kind of bold and excessive, but who would ever consider them a convict and his accomplice."

Virgil nodded.

"It is far enough away to start anew, though," I said.

"Scholes said they took his best horses," Virgil said.

"San Cristóbal's a big place," I said. "They rode there, bought fineries, sold the horses, or loaded the horses and left, took the train to Appaloosa."

Virgil nodded.

"Then again," I said. "This could all be a bunch of something made out of nothing."

Virgil looked to me like he didn't believe that notion any more than the conviction I used in saying it, but he obliged the moment for consideration.

"The woman we saw was for certain older than this photograph of her in her wedding gown, though," Virgil said.

"How long ago was it they were married?" I said.

"Four, maybe five years," Tillary said.

"So let me understand. In Appaloosa?" Tillary said. "You believe you saw Eleanor with him, with Lonnigan."

"His name is not Lonnigan," I said.

"What is his name?"

"Gus Driggs. Augustus Noble Driggs," I said.

"You ever hear that name?" Virgil said.

"No," Tillary said.

"Well," Virgil said. "Not uncommon for criminals to change their names."

"No," Tillary said with a scoff.

"Especially when it's a name of someone they know from their past that no longer existed," I said.

"Hell, no telling who is really who when it comes to the incarcerated."

I nodded.

"We've damn sure seen that," I said. "And I believe we are seeing it now."

Virgil nodded.

"Hell," Tillary said, "half the time the crimes that criminals are accused of are lesser crimes than they committed while going by their given name. Crimes they want to be distant of. So they are more than willing to be someone else if they can get away with it."

"No telling what kind of life Driggs lived after I last saw him. Most likely not one without plenty of dead in his wake."

46

"We fought together," I said. "Like I mentioned, it was a long time ago, during the Indian Wars. Lonnigan, too. Lonnigan was lost in action, never found him or his body. The same thing happened to him that happened to a number of soldiers during those times. They ended up just gone."

"Driggs and Lonnigan obviously knew each other?" Virgil said.

"They did," I said.

"And Driggs?"

"Driggs's situation was a far sight 'nother matter altogether. He was let go of his rank and command for killing. He'd be sent on a mission to round up Indians and they'd end up dead. Happened more than once. He enjoyed the killing. He was mad as hell when he was let go. He thought the other officers, including me, had turned him in. Fact of the matter was, the general knew all too well who Driggs was. He figured it'd be only a matter of time before his killing spree would end by getting himself killed. I kind of thought that'd be the case, too. I will say he was smart, graduated top of his class."

Tillary nodded.

"Lonnigan was a smart fella," he said. "No doubt about that, what so ever. Spent most of his time reading."

Virgil looked to Tillary.

"How long was Lonnigan, or Driggs, locked up here in Cibola?" Virgil said.

"He'd been here for four years but locked up for eight altogether. He was transferred here. He came in here in need of an operation. He was first sent to San Cristóbal for the surgery, then was transferred to here. The first six weeks here he spent most of the time chained to a bunk in the infirmary. Most likely where he met and developed a relationship with Eleanor. Though I don't know that for certain, but that could very well be the case. If what Scholes believed to be true is in fact a reality."

"What was he locked up for at the other prison?" Virgil said.

"Murder and robbery."

"You got a file on him?"

"We do on Donnie Lonnigan," Tillary said. "Providing Lonnigan and this Driggs you are talking about are one and the same, as you say. I can most likely tell you what you want to know, though. Know most every inmate's history or the ostensible criminal history that led them to incarceration."

"Tell me about him."

"Well, Donnie Lonnigan is a powerful sonofabitch. Once he recovered fully after the surgery he became one of the most revered men here . . . Didn't liked being locked up, though. Most of the men get used to it, but Lonnigan never did . . . *Revered* might not be the right word. *Feared* is the right word. Kept to himself, would spend most of his time exercising or reading books or newspapers. We let them read whatever we have to read—newspapers, books, and so forth. We encouraged reading here, a good distraction. The other inmates were scared of him . . . well, all but Ed Degraw. The other one you are after. Degraw is not afraid of anybody. Both Degraw and Lonnigan, or Driggs, or whoever the hell he is, are both kind of hell on earth, I guess you could say. Each in their own way. Degraw is a beast. He's been in and out of prison since he was old enough to walk, robbed banks, dynamited rail-car safes, burnt down an entire village, then killed an old couple with his bare hands, that's what got him locked up last. He's ruthless, like a pissed-off griz, as fierce and as scary as one, too. Lonnigan has a powerful way about him that works through his mind as well. Degraw and Lonnigan were in the same cell together for a time and we had to separate them, thought they might kill each other . . . In hindsight I suppose that would have been the best thing to happen to them."

"Where was Lonnigan first locked up," Virgil said. "Where did he transfer from?"

"Mexico," Tillary said. "He was in prison in Mexico City. Cibola is the closest stateside facility to Mexico. Well, here and El Paso, but he ended up here."

"Who'd Lonnigan murder?" Virgil said. "Who'd he rob?"

"He had been convicted of murdering three people during a robbery that involved other robbers besides him. Apparently it was a big heist worth millions of dollars in cash, gold, and jewelry that was never found."

I looked to Virgil, then to Tillary.

"Millions?" Virgil said.

"Hell of a deal," Tillary said. "The robbery took place on a Spanish ship coming to Mexico. My understanding, the gold, jewels, and cash that was aboard the ship was intended as a gift from the Queen of Spain that was to be delivered to the president of Mexico. Lonnigan and his gang somehow got on the ship before it made port and absconded with the loot. But Lonnigan got shot during the heist, three times in the back, and was caught. Prior to serving his time here he was at the previous facility, in Mexico. Apparently he recovered there okay, but then later on he was in need of a second surgery to remove a piece of lead so he got himself transferred here."

"The others got away?" I said.

Tillary nodded.

"He was the only one caught," Tillary said.

"Who shot him?"

"The Federales said that he was shot by his own men, his fellow bandits, but you know how the Federales are. Certainly can't go by what they report. They most likely did it, shot him, blamed the others, and took off with the gold, jewelry, and cash themselves."

Virgil nodded a little as he thought about what Tillary said.

"Know if Lonnigan ever talked to the law about the other men," Virgil said. "Offer up information in respect to the others he was in cahoots with?"

"In an effort to make sentencing easier on himself?" Tillary said.

Virgil nodded.

"Not that I know of," Tillary said. "He never said much. Hard to get a word out of him most times."

"And none of the others were ever caught?" Virgil said.

"Don't think so," Tillary said.

"You ever hear names, who they might be, how many?" I said. "Not that names 'mount to a hill of beans when it comes to robbers and killers, but do you know any details?"

"I do not," Tillary said.

"He was tried and convicted in Mexico?" Virgil said.

Tillary nodded.

"Yes," he said.

Virgil looked to me and shook his head some.

"Be better than a good idea for us to follow the path," I said. "Get ourselves to San Cristóbal and catch the train back to Appaloosa."

47

Tillary stood out front of the warden's home as we mounted up for San Cristóbal.

"I appreciate you fellas being here," Tillary said. "Not sure how I'd've handled this without you."

"Sure you would have managed," I said.

"At least you got a few back," he said.

"Was not without some consequences," I said.

"No, I know," he said. "Maybe the governor will let me keep my job. Though, after this, I'm not all that certain I want to keep the goddamn job."

"I understand that," I said.

Tillary smiled, I think for the very first time.

"You do?" Tillary said. "You mean there is something better than being out here on the Hot Box on the Hubs of Hell?"

"There might be," I said.

"I think those two young people had no business being out here," Tillary said. "The goddamn devil himself got to them."

Virgil said nothing as he looked off, watching a tornado of dust skitter across the flat land in front of the house.

"I should have new telegraph equipment soon, so please let me know what happens," Tillary said.

"Will do," Virgil said.

"What will happen to her?" he said.

Virgil shook his head.

"Hard to say."

"Shame," Tillary said.

"Is," Virgil said.

"She's in serious trouble," Tillary said.

"That much we know," Virgil said. "But what is truth and what is not truth in that letter and her involvement is hard to say."

"I guess that will be up to a judge to determine," Tillary said. "If she is lucky enough to get to that. As far as Lonnigan/Driggs is concerned, I don't give a damn."

Virgil nodded a bit.

"I think Scholes was most likely accurate in his account of her, I'm afraid."

"Most likely," Virgil said.

"I'd say 'Poor girl,' but I guess I should not," Tillary said. "If it is true, she damn sure has to be held accountable."

Virgil turned his horse toward the road.

"Hope we can catch up with them," Virgil said. "And follow the process of the law . . . We will let you know."

Tillary nodded some as he took a few steps back.

Virgil said, "Mr. Tillary." Then tipped his hat and started off down the road.

"Sorry for your loss here, Mr. Tillary," I said. "Take care."

"Thank you," he said. "You boys be safe."

"Do our best," I said.

I caught up to Virgil and we rode side by side for a bit. I looked back to Tillary standing in front of the warden's house, then looked to Virgil.

"One thing I did not mention about Driggs," I said.

Virgil looked to me.

"I didn't want to say it in front of him back there, but Driggs was also involved with a woman, kind of the same situation. A woman who belonged to someone else, way back when."

"He's got a pattern," Virgil said.

"That woman was our CO's wife," I said.

"That's why he was let go," Virgil said. "Relieved of duty."

"No. The reason was for killing Indians, for his ruthlessness."

"Don't imagine it helped him none, fucking the boss's wife," Virgil said.

"No, it didn't, but what happened was, later, after Driggs was let go, she was found dead."

Virgil looked at me.

"He did it?"

"I don't know. He was nowhere to be found."

"But you think Driggs did it?"

"Not for sure, I would not have put it past him, but our CO was blamed for it."

"Maybe the CO did it," Virgil said.

"Could have, I guess."

"Damn sure had a motive," Virgil said.

"He did."

"Convicted?" Virgil said.

"No," I said. "But it ruined his career, his life."

"Seems nothing but bad swarmed around this goddamn Driggs," Virgil said.

"And then some," I said.

We rode for a moment and said nothing, then Virgil looked at me.

"What we saw," he said, "them two walking into the Boston House seemed just like two proper face cards of the same suit."

"They did," I said.

"Cards is goddamn tricky, though," Virgil said.

"Driggs is goddamn tricky," I said. "That's a fact. They could be long gone, out of Appaloosa by now."

"Then again, maybe there was a reason for them going to Appaloosa?" Virgil said.

"Figure we should wire Chastain to let him know he has one of the escaped convicts right under his nose?" I said.

I could tell Virgil was thinking about that, but he didn't say anything as we rode.

"Don't think Chastain should be fucking with Driggs, Virgil," I said.

"No," Virgil said. "I thought the same thing."

"I suppose the one exception would be if Chastain found out that Driggs and Eleanor were still there and if they tried to leave town, then and only then should they stop them."

Virgil nodded.

"Then again, Chastain would have to identify who we are talking about."

"Not sure that is a good idea, either," Virgil said.

48

Driggs had grown very comfortable with the surroundings of Appaloosa and was venturing out freely. He had no care in the world and was not worried about who he might bump into. He was ready for whomever, whatever, whenever, but was—as always—in no hurry.

The day had been a hot one and the two of them, Driggs and the woman, stayed in the cool room, in the bed. After some twisting, digging, triggering, and ruling, Driggs got up and took a long pull of whiskey. He looked out the window, watching the good folks of Appaloosa going this way and that. He liked to watch out the window, the unsuspecting masses, those who had no idea just what the fuck was going on. He was growing fond of the city and its unsuspecting citizens.

He'd grown accustomed to the hotel room routine, too. Like the days previous when he got out of bed after he was done, he looked at her—like he was looking at her now—sprawled out and covered with sweat. He liked that. She was in every way ripe, and he enjoyed that about his prin-

cess, but most important, he admired her for her guileless fervor.

"Want me cleaned up?" she said in a purring voice.

He just stared at her and said nothing.

"You like me clean," she said.

He remained silent, just looking at her.

"What about when I'm dirty?"

He smiled.

"But you like me clean and smelling like a rose, don't you?" she said with a sly smile. "Don't you?"

He smiled again, with his eyes now, boring into her.

"Wash me?" she said.

Driggs took another pull off the whiskey, looked out the window for a moment, then moved to the bed. He stood over her, looking down on her. Then he scooped up her naked body and held her, just looking at her. Then he turned, walked with her in his arms, and gently placed her in the bathtub in the corner. He slid his fingers through her sweaty hair, gathered a handful of her thick mane, and leaned her head back so he could have a good look at her eyes, but said nothing. He just looked at her and she just looked back at him.

"You make me hungry," she said.

"I know," he said.

Driggs pulled back her hair some more, stretching her long, sensuous neck. He caressed her neck, then . . . laid his princess slowly back in the tub.

"Rain . . ." she said, with the anticipation of a little girl.

She closed her eyes. Driggs stared at her, then reached up and pulled the cord. The cord opened a valve allowing the rooftop tank water to shower over her body. She sat up straight when the cool water hit her hot body.

"Oh," she said.

Then she relaxed and let the water pour over her head.

"*My God, that feels good,*" *she said.*

After a decent amount of water rained down, Driggs pulled the valve closed, got the rose-scented soap, and began to lather her body. He slowly washed her, every inch of her: her sharp shoulders, her narrow back, and her long legs. She lay back, enjoying his gentle touch. Then he opened the valve again and rinsed her. After, she stepped out of the tub and he finished by toweling her dry. Then he popped his princess with a sharp slap on her butt—signaling that her bath was complete.

She turned to him, looking up at him. He leaned down and kissed her.

"*My turn,*" *she said.* "*To clean you.*"

Driggs smiled. He took a drink, then moved over and stepped his big frame into the tub and lowered into the soapy water. Then she reciprocated, and just as Driggs had washed her, she washed his hard body, scrubbing him clean.

"*What are we going to do?*" *she said.*

He looked to her and smiled.

"*We're doing it.*"

"*Are we going to stay in Appaloosa forever?*"

"*Forever?*" *he said.* "*That's an eternity, isn't it?*"

"*It is,*" *she said.*

"*No,*" *he said.* "*Not forever, not for an eternity.*"

"*Once your business is done here,*" *she said,* "*maybe we could go someplace back east, someplace more civilized.*"

She lingered over the bullet holes in his back.

"*Tell me,*" *she said.*

"*What?*"

"*I want to know about these,*" *she said.* "*About who shot you and why.*"

He just looked at her and said nothing.

"*Don't you want to tell me about these?*" *she said as she circled the washcloth gently over the scars.* "*'Bout what happened?*"

Driggs looked back to her, smiled.

"You know what I'd rather do?" he said.

"What?"

Driggs reached over and grabbed the straight-edged razor lying next to the tub . . .

49

She looked to the razor and recoiled.

He smiled.

"I'd like you to shave me," he said. "I see my whiskers have left you a little raw in places."

After he was shaved, cleaned, and toweled, he rolled a cigarette. Then he sat on the bed, struck a match, and lit the tip. He took a few good puffs, then leaned back against the headboard. He smoked and watched her dry her hair as she patted it smooth between thin white cotton towels.

"We're clean," she said with a giggle as she sat on the edge of the bed. "We're clean."

Driggs just looked at her. He marveled at her delicate features and at the fluidity of her movement. He wondered about her fight and her will to live, her will to survive—what it would be like to strangle her.

Later, in the late afternoon, *Driggs strolled with her up Vandervoort Avenue and stopped into Allie's shop to pick up the altered dress he'd purchased.*

Allie and Margie were excited to see the couple. Once in the shop, Driggs sat like the perfect gentleman he purported to be as Allie and Margie led his beautiful princess behind the screen and helped her out of one dress and into the brand-new one.

Driggs looked around the room as he waited. He was as calm as could be, but there was a small fire beginning to burn somewhere deep inside him. He could not deny that. He was accustomed to the fire, though, it was his friend, perhaps his only real friend. Oh, she tried and she believed— like the others before her—that she was endeared. And on one hand the princess was most assuredly endeared, she was in the lap of care and consideration, but on the other hand she was dangerously far from it. She was more endangered than endeared.

His eyes wandered around the shop. There were delicate hats with lace and a few hanging dresses up front near the windows. There were photographs from catalogs arranged in managed clusters and tacked to the walls. Shelves stacked with horsehair, wire, and netting covered the back wall next to the screened dressing area.

He looked up to the beams, then trained his eyes toward the front of the building, to the entrance made from brand-new bricks that were laid in a handsome arch over the door. He thought about the design and the integrity and the craftsmanship of the arch. Slowly he turned and looked at himself in the mirror. He stared at his handsome self, long and hard. Then he smiled and nodded to the reflection of the man in the mirror. It was like he was acknowledging an old pal or perhaps a new acquaintance. He stared at the man for a long moment. His reverie was broken momentarily when he heard the women giggle, but then Driggs was brought right back into looking at the man in the mirror staring back at him. Driggs continued staring at himself, then said out loud, "The anticipation is killing me . . ."

"Patience," the princess said from behind the dressing screen.

She then poked her head around the corner of the screen and said with a smile, "Good things are worth waiting for, my dear." He could see the ribbon edging of her cotton camisole draped around her slender collar bone.

Then, like a turtle, her head disappeared back behind the screen, leaving Driggs only to smile at the man in the mirror smiling back at him.

Then she stepped out wearing a yellow silk organza dress with a deep and revealing décolletage and moved in front of the mirror. The dress's hem was trimmed in deep plum brocade with sewn seed pearls that rustled as the princess crossed the shop.

Driggs whistled and said, "Look at you."

"A perfect fit," Margie said.

"You look like a princess in that dress," Allie said.

"Looks like? Why, she is a princess," Driggs said, then winked at Allie.

Allie blushed as the presumptive princess turned to Driggs.

"Do you like, really?" she said.

"Very much," he said.

"You're not just saying that?"

"Come here," he said.

She walked to him, taking delicate steps, almost childlike steps, lifting her skirt to reveal several layers of laced and embroidered petticoats underneath, and stopped in front of him. He reached up with his muscled arm, slid his strong fingers behind her dainty neck, and pulled her to him.

"Look at me," he said with a smile. "I never say anything I don't mean. You of all people should know that."

"Thank you," she said.

He remained holding her by the back of her head. She bit her lip a little as he stared at her for a steady moment.

Margie looked to Allie.

"Well," Allie said. "We are so delighted . . . our first customer. Thank you."

Driggs released the princess's neck and sat back in the chair, looking at her.

"Turn around," he said.

She turned, then he smiled and looked to Allie.

"Exquisite."

"She is," Allie said.

"Would you like to change back to your dress or do you prefer to wear this now?" Margie said. "You look so truly lovely, it'd be almost a crime not to wear it out."

The princess looked to Driggs.

"I think you should wear it another time, dear," he said. "For a special occasion."

"Agreed," she said.

"Won't you need matching gloves and this perfect little thing?" said Margie, picking out a small beaded purse from the display counter at the back.

"Oh, my, what is that?" said the princess.

"It's a reticule," said Margie. "To keep your handkerchief and perfume, of course."

"Of course," said Allie. "It completes the ensemble."

Driggs turned his head slowly and looked to Allie. His eyes wandered down below her waist, then slowly moved up to her eyes.

"Good," he said. "We're in agreement. Let us complete the ensemble."

Allie's lips quivered into a smile.

50

The ride Virgil and I took was hot and dry, and it took the better part of two days to get to San Cristóbal. We arrived in the city just prior to sunset and our first stop was at the Western Union office. We wired Sheriff Chastain straightaway in Appaloosa to let him know about the situation regarding the escapee Driggs and the warden's wife.

In the telegram, Virgil sternly instructed Chastain to make certain all law enforcement stayed clear of the Boston House. Virgil next gave Chastain a detailed description of Driggs and Eleanor. He ordered Chastain to personally be on the lookout for the pair but to make damn certain the couple did not notice him. He instructed Chastain to be very careful and that if he did identify Driggs and Eleanor to avoid any and all confrontation with them. Virgil commanded him not to inquire with any of the Boston House staff regarding the guest. He stated he did not want any employees to draw unnecessary attention to themselves. He also instructed Chastain to make no attempt to arrest the couple, unless they attempted to depart Appaloosa—and, most important, to exercise extreme caution.

The operator in Appaloosa was Willoughby and he let us know he would deliver the message to the sheriff and that we should expect a reply within the hour.

Virgil and I had spent some time in San Cristóbal a few years back dealing with a bank robbery, and were familiar with the stately community. San Cristóbal now supported a turntable for the Santa Fe and the Transcontinental. The rail direction table that handled twice the amount of travel was something San Cristóbal didn't have when we were previously in the town. But it was obvious that with that addition, San Cristóbal was a good size bigger than it used to be.

Virgil and I bought tickets for the train to Appaloosa that would depart the following morning. We stabled our horses at the livery and checked into the hotel. It was the same hotel we stayed at when we were previously in San Cristóbal, the Holly House. We got some food and drank a beer, then walked back to the Western Union office.

The operator saw us through the window as we walked up the boardwalk to the office and opened the door to greet us. He was an overgrown young man with a wide face and rosy cheeks.

"Good timing, just got a reply," the operator said excitedly. "Just this instant it came in."

He held out the note.

"Everett," Virgil said, nodding to the note.

I took the note from the operator, read it quickly, then looked to Virgil.

"We got a problem," I said.

"Driggs?"

I shook my head.

"The other one," I said. "Degraw."

"What about him?"

"Sheriff Stringer and his posse tracked Degraw and cornered him in a mine just outside of Bridgewater. It says here that the posse attempted to apprehend Degraw in the mine when Degraw or somebody dynamited the shaft. The fate of the posse and Degraw himself remains uncertain."

"That from Chastain?"

"Is," I said. "He says this information was received here in Appaloosa from Bridgewater."

"Who in Bridgewater?"

"Doesn't say, just states the telegram was intended for us, the U.S. Marshals. Signed the Bridgewater Emergency Department."

"Say anything about Sheriff Stringer?"

"No," I said.

"Goddamn," Virgil said, shaking his head.

We responded to Chastain, trying to gather more details about Stringer, and his reply told us that the telegram simply originated from the Bridgewater Emergency Department. There were no additional details regarding Stringer or his posse.

Virgil told Chastain to stay put and we contacted Bridgewater. Within a short time the sounder clicked and Bridgewater wrote back.

The operator copied the note, then handed it to me.

I read it and looked to Virgil.

"They don't have any more information to offer other than they believe the posse and the escapee they were after were all trapped in the shaft. There is no sign of Sheriff Stringer. They all could be alive and they all could be dead. At this point and time they do not know. This, too, signed the Bridgewater Emergency Department."

The sounder clicked and the rosy-faced operator copied the next incoming telegram, then turned again to me with the note.

"Chastain says he understands your orders regarding Driggs and the woman. Says he will stick to your directions exactly as you detailed them. He will only make moves to arrest Driggs and the woman if in fact the two of them are indeed still there and make an attempt to depart Appaloosa."

Virgil shook his head and looked to the floor.

"Seeing how there is no telling what is happening with Driggs, if he is even still in Appaloosa," I said, "we might want to get to Bridgewater first . . . don't you imagine?"

Virgil nodded, then looked up to the operator.

"You got a territorial map?" he said.

"Yes, sir."

The operator retrieved a rolled-up map from atop a cabinet and handed it to Virgil. We rolled it out on the desk. Virgil pointed to the spot.

"We could get there before day's end tomorrow," I said. "Take the train to Phoenix Junction and ride on from there."

Virgil nodded.

51

In the morning we loaded the horses and took the train from San Cristóbal up to Phoenix Junction. There we saddled up and rode from the Junction directly to Bridgewater. The ride was an easy one, but it took up the afternoon and we arrived close to sunset.

We had made arrangements to meet with the Bridgewater Emergency Department. We had determined after a few more telegrams that the emergency department was comprised of local off-shift miners from the area. When there was a problem they banded together to deal with whatever arose within the mining community.

When we arrived we were met by a group of miners gathered around a long table inside the general store. One of the miners, a smaller older fella sitting at the head of the table, introduced himself.

"Name's Cotton Horton," he said. "I'm the off-shift foreman here."

Cotton went around the table and introduced the

other men. Then he pointed to a spot on a map he had laid out on the table in front of him.

"This is number forty-two," Cotton said. "This is where the explosion occurred."

"How is it you know the posse and the Yaqui sheriff, Stringer, were inside?" Virgil said.

Cotton looked to a younger man with dark hair and bright silvery-blue eyes. "This is Jeff. Tell 'em what happened."

"We were coming out of one of the lower shafts," Jeff said as he pointed one of his big, rough hands toward the north, "and me and another fella, Bobby, we was on the road coming back to town when we run into a big mean sonofabitch wanting to know how to get to forty-two."

"Why forty-two?" I said.

"It cuts across the mountain all the way to the other side," Jeff said. "Pretty straight shot . . . well, it used to be, till it got closed up."

"How is it he knew to look for forty-two?" I said.

"That I couldn't tell you," Jeff said.

"Thing is," Cotton said, "forty-two is not active, has not been active for a long time, but we have used it for storage as well as a thoroughfare to the other side."

"A tunnel across," Jeff said.

"Who all uses it?"

"Just us," Jeff said, then looked to Cotton.

Cotton nodded.

"We let a few locals use it from time to time to pass through. Otherwise it's a long way around."

"And this fella, the mean sonofabitch you are talking about, he went into forty-two."

"Far as I know," Jeff said.

"What about the posse," Virgil said. "How do you know they were here, you see them?"

Jeff nodded.

"The posse came through 'bout a half-hour after," Jeff said. "They asked me if I had seen the man and I told them I did and I told them about forty-two and they hurried up the road after him."

"And you know for a fact they went inside of forty-two?" I said. "Did you or someone follow them there?"

"No," Jeff said. "But they did."

"How do you know for certain the posse and the escapee were caught inside. Did someone else actually see them enter and not come out?" I said.

"We did not see them go in but after the blast, after Bobby and me heard the explosion we hurried up there and . . . the horses were there but none of the men, I'm afraid."

"We can take burros through and we do, so do the other few locals I was talking about, but no horse can get through there. It's the biggest widest shaft we have and the only one that goes to the other side, but it's damn sure not tall enough for a horse."

Virgil looked to me and shook his head slightly.

"We got their horses here," Cotton said. "We gathered them up and they are in the corral across the way here . . . Anyway, we don't know what happened, we did not see it, but there are horses here, and a shaft that has damn sure been dynamited."

"Tillary told us Degraw had blown shit up before," I said.

Virgil nodded.

"Train safes," Virgil said.

"So he's no stranger to this sort of thing," I said.

"Have you or anyone else gone to the other side of the mountain?" Virgil said.

"No. Hell, that's a long way around the mountain," Cotton said. "And there is no reason for none of us to get mixed up in poking our nose into some escaped convicts' business. Like to do what we can to help the good men of the law, but I hope you understand our business is hard enough. The last thing we need to do is confront some convict, or convicts. But the fact of the matter is, it's hard to say if him or any of the lawmen are even alive."

"How many saddle horses did you find at the mine?" Virgil said.

"Six altogether," Cotton said.

Virgil looked to me and I nodded.

"Stringer's horse, his three deputies, and Locky his Kiowa tracker, that's five horses," I said. "Then Ed Degraw . . . that's it, that's six."

Virgil leaned over to look at the mining map.

"How deep," Virgil said. "How far back was this explosion?"

"Right at the portal," Cotton said. "At least that is what it appears to be, but we won't know for certain. That is all we can see."

Jeff nodded in agreement.

"No telling how deep," he said.

"Assuming it was the escaped man that blew the shaft up," I said, "where would he have found the dynamite to do this?"

Cotton pointed.

"On the main road up top we have a storage facility up there, near forty-two. He broke in there."

"How much was removed?" I said. "Do you know?"

"Not exactly," Cotton said.

"Don't think he got that much," Jeff said.

"There were no complete cases taken, that we know," Cotton said.

"But he got enough to do what he did," Jeff said.

The other miners around the table nodded.

Virgil looked to his watch.

"What can we do?" he said.

"Open it back up," Cotton said.

Jeff nodded.

"Need to dynamite the shaft back open," he said.

"How long, you figure?" Virgil said.

"Not sure how much it's blocked, won't know till we know," Cotton said. "We will eventually have to, no matter what. Like I said, it is a passage to other mines that we have on the other side. So we'll have to do it sooner than later."

He looked to his hands resting on the table, then looked back to Virgil and me and said, "We would have done it by now . . . but like I said, we don't have any idea what might happen. For all we know there is nothing but trouble on the other side. Fact is, Jeff had no real evidence the men they saw were who they said they were."

Jeff nodded.

"It was early and it happened kind of quick," Jeff said. "Them men following the other fella kind of gave me and Bobby a start, and they just hurried on . . . and, well, Bobby and me we didn't ever see no badges. I don't know, like I said, happened fast and they moved on and so I just told Cotton here what we saw, what happened."

Cotton nodded.

"I told Jeff and Bobby I needed to contact authorities, let this be what it is, a matter of law, and now that you are here we will do what we can to help you open forty-two back up."

"Can we be ready to do that at sunup?"

Cotton looked to the other miners and they nodded.

"Sure," Cotton said. "But we can do it now, too."

Virgil looked to me.

"Tonight?" I said.

"Sure," Cotton said. "We work in darkness . . . It's what we do."

52

Driggs insisted Allie and Margie join the princess and him for dinner at the Boston House. Allie felt some apprehension and Driggs sensed it. He possessed a keen sense for others' dispositions. He felt half the time that he knew what someone was thinking. He sensed Allie was titillated by his presence, his manliness, and it unnerved her. Made her more vulnerable and uncomfortable. Margie, on the other hand, seemed to be more dubious of him. That, too, he sensed. He was uncertain just why exactly; he had been careful not to show all his cards. He was good at that, too, that was his trademark, doling out only what was necessary for the given situation. Driggs looked at Margie the same way he looked at his princess and Allie, and at all women. He knew the effect of his attention, it was constant, but Margie was almost indifferent.

"Thank you, but I really must get home," Margie said.

"Nonsense," the princess said. "Please."

Margie looked to Allie.

"Allie?" she said. "There are a few important things that need attending to before the grand opening."

Allie smiled, a slightly nervous smile while Driggs's eyes bored into her. "Thank you, Margie. But I think we've all done enough for one day." Then she nodded some as she looked up to Driggs.

"All right," Allie said. "We'll join you, but I must warn you that I eat a great deal."

"That's what I like," Driggs said as he opened the door of Allie's shop. "A beautiful woman with an appetite."

It was just past sunset as Allie locked up the shop and the four of them strolled up Vandervoort Avenue.

"All these bricks," Driggs said.

"Yes," Allie said. "New York in the making."

"How did all this come about?" he said. "Why did this Vandervoort fellow decide on bringing his business here to Appaloosa?"

"Well, I am not sure," Allie said. "You'd have to ask him."

"Perhaps I will."

"Never thought we'd be walking down a street—an avenue, no less," Allie said. "Right here in Appaloosa."

Driggs stopped walking and looked up at the carved stone above the stately office constructed in the center of the avenue.

"Vandervoort," Driggs read on the stone above the office.

Then Driggs looked up the block, then down the opposite direction, taking it all in.

"It's quite the accomplishment," he said.

"It is," Allie said. "Mr. Vandervoort came to Appaloosa a few years back, and, well, he has singlehandedly changed the face of this place."

"Where did he come from?"

"New York, I believe," Allie said.

"Well, of course, I should have guessed," he said, looking around at the buildings. "Well, I'll be . . ."

He looked to Allie.

"Have you been?"

"New York?" Allie said.

"Yes," he said.

"Why, no," Allie said. "I have not."

Driggs looked to Margie.

"How about you?" Driggs said.

"No," she said. "I'm just a simple girl from Nebraska."

"No?" he said.

"Yes," she said.

"Yet you have the sophistication of a young woman of culture and taste," he said.

"That's nice of you to recognize my developed interest," she said. "But rest assured I'm as Midwest as a girl can be."

"What city do you come from?"

"Lincoln," she said.

"Ah, a wonderful city," he said. "Are you familiar with the Hanrahans?"

"No," she said. "I am not."

"Wonderful family, the Hanrahans," he said. "You must have been in the square in the Haymarket named after the great Henry Hanrahan?"

"The square?" said Margie. "Yes, how could I have forgotten? With the wisteria-covered gazebos? So beautiful in the springtime."

"No one could forget those . . . And you, Mrs. French, where do you come from?" said Driggs.

"Oh," Allie said. "I'm from a little bit of everywhere."

"And how about you," Margie said. "Where are you from?"

Margie stopped walking and looked to the three, who stopped and looked back to her.

"After all this time," Margie said. "We have yet to be properly introduced."

Driggs removed his hat.

"How rude of me," he said. "I have a tendency of going about my day as if I'm in another world. I do apologize."

He looked to the princess. "This is Mrs. Gloria Bedford, and I'm Lucas Bedford."

"Mrs. Bedford," Margie said. "Mr. Bedford . . . Margie Witherspoon. It's a pleasure."

"The pleasure is all ours," he said. "I assure you. And the promise of more to come."

53

Driggs considered the dinner a success and enjoyable for the women. He could be entertaining and charming when he needed to. He'd learned that from his father, and during all those years at West Point. Those lessons have finally paid off, he thought. West Point taught him discipline. His father taught him the importance of intelligence. He remembered his father telling him: Intelligence was made for men like us, men who are destined for greatness.

After dinner the women and Driggs sat at the corner table and sipped tea. Through the evening, Driggs learned a lot about dressmaking from Margie and Allie. Mainly Margie.

"For a young lady out of Nebraska," Driggs said, "you sure know your business when it comes to fabric and patterns and stitches."

"Yes," the princess said. "She sure does."

Allie reached over and took Margie's hand.

"I'm lucky," Allie said. "To have such a good seamstress, friend, and confidante."

"Confidante," Driggs said. "Why, that is wonderful to have a place to share your darkest secrets . . ."

"Well, yes, it is," Allie said with a nod.

Driggs studied Margie, then said, "How did you two meet?"

"Oh," Margie said. "How was it, exactly? I saw her, Allie, at the shop and one thing led to another."

"Yes," Allie said. "That's right, and I'm very glad."

"I see," he said. "So you are new friends?"

"Yes," Margie said.

"And you are new to Appaloosa?"

"Why, yes," Margie said. "I arrived here on family business and stayed."

"And how long have you been in town?"

"Oh," Margie said. "Just weeks, really, but I like it here and I intend to stay. At least till Allie gets tired of me."

"Oh, poppycock," Allie said. "Listen to you."

"And you?" Margie said. "What brings the two of you to Appaloosa, Mr. Bedford?"

Driggs looks at Margie for an extended moment, then said, "I, too, have some family business here."

Allie and Margie waited for some more words, but Driggs left it at that as the clock on the dining room wall rolled around to the hour prior to midnight and started to chime.

"Well, it has been a lovely evening," Margie said, looking at the clock. "Thank you, Mr. Bedford, Mrs. Bedford, but I'm afraid it is after my curfew."

"Are you sure?" he said. "How about a nice brandy to close out the evening?"

"No," Margie said as she stood. "Again, thank you for a very enjoyable evening."

"Well," Driggs said as he slid back his chair and got to his feet. "Let me see you home."

"That's quite all right," she said. "I'm just across the way."

"Are you sure?" he said with a warm smile.

"Yes," she said as she looked to Allie. *"I will see you tomorrow . . . I have some business to attend to in the morning, but I can come by in the early afternoon."*

"Okay, dear," Allie said, then looked to Driggs and his princess. *"I, too, should be going."*

"Oh, please," the princess said. *"I've had yet to enjoy myself as I have this evening. A few more moments of your time won't be too much of an imposition, will it?"*

"Well," Allie said. *"I suppose I could sit for a moment or two longer."*

Allie looked to Margie.

"I'll see you in the afternoon, dear," Allie said.

Margie smiled, curtseyed a bit, then walked away and out the front door.

"What a lovely woman," the princess said.

"She is," Allie said.

"Indeed she is," Driggs said. *"Indeed she is."*

Driggs laid his napkin on the table and scooted back his chair. He leaned in, looking at Allie and his princess, then said, *"Please excuse me for a few, if you would be so kind, I need to check on my elephant . . ."*

The princess laughed and Allie smiled.

"I shall return subsequently."

Driggs left the parlor restaurant and walked through double doors into the Boston House Saloon. He weaved his way between the crowded tables to the side door of the saloon. He looked out over the top of the saloon doors. He looked to his left, then to his right. Then he saw her, a tiny glimpse of Margie as she rounded the corner.

He stepped out onto the porch and moved toward the hotel entrance to where he could see her walking away. He watched as she crossed the street and then he saw her turn. He stepped out and walked down the hotel steps and moved *under the awnings of the boardwalk and walked until he had a view of the street she turned on. Then he saw her again. She was halfway down the block. He watched her as she entered a boardinghouse with a sign above the door that read* Rooms for Rent by the Day. *He walked on the opposite side of the street and moved toward the boardinghouse, where he had a good view. Then he saw a light come on in a second-floor window.*

Driggs stood there under the awning and pulled a rolled cigarette from his pocket. He struck a match on the post and lit the cigarette as he watched shadows moving about in the room. He waited until he got a clear glimpse of Margie moving to fully close the draperies, then turned and walked back to the hotel.

When he returned to the table, Allie and the princess, Mrs. Bedford, were having a discussion with their noses inches apart.

"Am I interrupting?" he said.

They looked to him.

"Looked as if you two were about to kiss," he said. "Did I miss something?"

"Don't be silly," the princess said. "I was marveling at Mrs. French's eyes."

"I have a flaw," Allie said.

"Don't we all," Driggs said, holding up a bottle of champagne that he'd been hiding behind his back. "I figure we should have a toast. A celebration to Mrs. French."

"Oh," she said, looking at the champagne. "I really shouldn't."

"Nonsense," Driggs said as he sat.

"Me?" Allie said. "Why ever toast me?"

"For your new dress shop, of course, and for us being your first customers."

"Well, that's very kind of you," Allie said, blushing.

"I figure it is the least we can do," Driggs said as he removed the cork cover. "I mean, seeing how your husband is away chasing bad men."

"Oh," Allie said. "We are not married."

Driggs put his thumbs to each side of the cork.

"Living in sin," he said, looking at Allie as the cork exploded in dramatic fashion. "I like that."

54

Before we took off to shaft number forty-two we wired once more to Appaloosa to check with Chastain regarding the lookout of Driggs.

We waited for the response, then Chastain replied that he had nothing to report. He stayed clear of the hotel but kept the entrance in sight from a long distance, but said he did not see anyone matching the description we provided him of Driggs and the warden's wife.

Virgil and I followed Cotton and a handful of his men riding in a buckboard up a winding road to the location of number forty-two. The moon was out, but it was a little under half full and there was slight cloud cover, so it was dark as we traveled up. A few of the men in the buckboard carried lanterns, so the path up to the mine was easy to follow. It was a good half-hour ride out of Bridgewater, and the moment we arrived the men bailed out of the buckboard and got to work.

Cotton turned the buckboard around and pulled next to Virgil and me.

"Follow me. We'll go around to the other side of the bluff. Leave our animals over there, away from the blast."

Virgil and I did as Cotton said, and once we got the horses tied we walked back around the bluff with Cotton to where the men were setting the explosives.

"There's the entrance of forty-two," Cotton said. "You can see the rails disappearing into the middle of it where it's covered up from the blast. We're setting small explosives at the entrance by the rails. We'll blast away at the cover-up. We have to do this a little bit at a time, just like we do when we're building a shaft. Otherwise we could bring the whole damn mountain crumbling down over the entrance, and we don't want that."

"How far to the other side?" Virgil said.

"Oh, 'bout an eighth of a mile," Cotton said.

"And how far is it to the other side of the mountain?" Virgil said.

"Long damn way," Cotton said. "There is no short way over, take half a day to ride over there from here."

"How long will it take to go at this a bit at a time," I said.

"Hard to say. Depending on how much we need to shore up, or if we have to shore up. My guess is the blast that closed it up happened just inside the portal collar-set, which is sturdy as hell, so I'm thinking the blast just brought in the rock behind that . . . we'll know soon."

The first blast was ready within a matter of minutes. Cotton's men had moved back toward where Virgil and I were standing. Cotton lit the fuse on the dynamite, then walked back over to where we were, just behind the edge of the bluff. The explosion sounded kind of muffled from where we were standing, but the light from the blast lit up the pine trees surrounding us like a lightning strike. Then the men moved back to the shaft and got to work on preparing a second blast.

"Why this?" Virgil said.

I looked to Virgil. He was staring off, looking out into the dark, then looked at me.

"Why up here?"

"I know," I said.

"Leave your horse here and enter this here shaft," he said.

"Don't make a lot of sense."

"Not really," Virgil said.

"You think maybe Degraw lured them?"

"Crossed my mind," Virgil said.

"But then if Degraw did that, he wouldn't have left the horses."

"No, I know," Virgil said.

"We could just get going and ride around to the other side?" I said.

"Let's see what happens here first," he said.

"Sounds right," I said.

Virgil looked off for a moment, thinking.

"Stringer has been family to us, Everett."

"He has," I said.

"Damn good hand," Virgil said.

I just looked at Virgil but didn't say anything for a moment, then he said, "He helped us with Bragg way back when."

"That he did," I said.

"These are some bad hombres we've come across," Virgil said.

"Damn right they are," I said.

"Five dead, two back behind the walls," he said.

"According to Tillary, these last two are the worst," I said. "And according to me, the one of the two that I know, Tillary's account is correct."

"Driggs might be long gone," Virgil said.

"Degraw, too," I said.

"I know," Virgil said. "Here we go."

I followed Virgil's look to the miners walking toward us and Cotton lit the fuse for the second blast.

55

By the time they finished off the champagne, the *three of them were the only ones remaining in the dining room. The princess had worked up a case of the hiccups and was unsteady as they stood to leave. Allie, on the other hand, was a seasoned drinker. Though she, too, was feeling the effects of the bubbly, she was far better off than the princess, who stabilized herself on Allie's shoulder as they moved away from the table.*

"Sorry," the princess said with a hiccup. "Oh, gosh . . . listen to me, I'm so, so sorry."

"Oh," Allie said. "There is nothing to be sorry about. I've been there plenty of times, believe you me."

The princess laughed, then stumbled slightly as Driggs came to her side.

"I've got you, dear," he said.

"Gosh," she said. "Thank you."

"Let's get you upstairs, princess," he said.

He looked to Allie.

"Will you be okay?" he said.

"Oh," Allie said. "I'm fine."

"Are you sure?" he said.

"Let us walk . . . walk you home," the princess said.

"No, my goodness," Allie said. "I'm fine."

Driggs laughed at the princess. "You're not walking anyplace except up those stairs and into bed."

"My favorite place," she said.

Driggs looked to Allie.

"I'm happy to walk you," Driggs said.

"I'm good," Allie said.

"It's late and dark and she should not be on her own," the princess said with a hiccup.

"I just need to get her in the bed upstairs," Driggs said with a smile.

"That's okay," Allie said.

"Might you help me here," he said. "Get her settled and allow me to walk with you, Mrs. French."

"Oh . . . well . . ." Allie said. "I . . ."

"Most certainly," the princess said with a slur.

Allie looked around as if someone, somewhere, was watching her, then she took the princess by her arm opposite Driggs.

"Let's go, dear," Allie said, looking first to Driggs, then toward the stairs.

Driggs and Allie helped the princess up the stairs as lively gambling and drinking sounds drifted through the closed double doors that led to the crowded saloon. The noise echoed into the silent dining room and up the staircase to the second floor as they assisted the princess. They were on each side of her as they navigated her down the hall to the room. Driggs opened the door. Then Allie helped him lead her to the bed where she timbered over with a smile.

"Do you mind," he said, "helping to get her into her nightclothes?"

Allie was doing her best not to act like a trapped animal

and Driggs could sense it. Her face was flushed and she was flustered, but she focused on helping the princess. He stepped back and watched her as she took charge of helping the younger woman out of her dress. He could tell she was not shy about the situation. It occurred to him as he watched her help the princess that she had done this before, she was accustomed to situations outside the prudish realm of normalcy.

"Thank you," the princess said.

Once Allie got the princess into a dressing gown and under the covers, she turned to Driggs. He was sitting in a chair, just watching her.

"There she is," Allie said. "Snug as a bug in a rug."

"Shall we get you home?" he said as he got to his feet.

"Really, I'm fine," she said.

Driggs opened the door.

"That's obvious," he said. "After you."

Allie looked at him for a moment, then walked out the open door with Driggs following her.

Once they were out of the Boston House and walking down the boardwalk toward Allie's home, Driggs could tell she was a little more at ease. They walked for a bit without talking, then Driggs looked at Allie and smiled, and she smiled.

"Your friend Margie," he said. "She said she was in town on family business."

"Yes," Allie said.

"What kind of business?"

"Oh, gosh," Allie said. "Has something to do with her late uncle's estate."

"That where she resides?" he said. "With her family, here?"

"Oh," she said. "Well, I don't know . . . I suppose. Why?"

"Oh, just curious about creatures," he said.

"That's wonderful," she said. "To care . . ."

"Well, it's just my nature," he said. "And I care about you, too."

"That's nice. Thank you."

Driggs pulled a rolled cigarette from his pocket.

"Care for a cigarette?"

"Oh, no, thank you."

Driggs paused next to a post to strike a match and light the cigarette. Allie stopped, stood with him. Then they moved on as he shook the match and flicked it away into the street.

"Care for a puff?" he said.

"No, thank you."

He stopped. She slowed and looked back.

"Oh, here," he said. "Have a taste. This is fine Virginia tobacco."

He moved close to her and held it out for her. She looked at it for a moment.

"Go ahead," he said. "Not going to kill you."

56

It took the whole evening and twenty-eight consecutive blasts to get through the rubble that filled up the portal of forty-two and enclosed Degraw and Sheriff's Stringer's posse.

It was just past midnight when Cotton and the miners finally broke through an opening and into the shaft. The rock fall had filled the portal completely, more so than what Cotton had figured on. Once there was an opening that was large enough for us to enter into we waited for a short amount of time. We did not want to enter into the opening right away; we waited to see if there was any sign from anyone within.

We called out into the opening for Stringer and his deputies, to see if by chance we could get some kind of response, but got nothing. We called, too, for the escapee, Ed Degraw, to surrender but again—and not surprisingly—we heard nothing.

"Time we have a look-see," Virgil said.

I nodded.

"Might be a good idea," Cotton said, "that you let us enter first to make certain everything is safe."

Virgil shook his head.

"Given the devil of the sonofabitch we are after, that the posse was after," Virgil said. "Think it'd be good to let us ease in there with you."

"Your call," Cotton said.

"What do you figure, Everett?"

"After all night of blasting to get into this, I'd say there's not going to be a reception party waiting for us, but you never know."

"No telling what we may find," Virgil said.

"Okay," Cotton said.

"We just take it real slow," Virgil said.

The three of us each took a lantern and climbed over the rubble and entered the shaft. We crawled over rock for a good fifteen feet before we got to where we could see the rails on the shaft floor, tapering off into the darkness.

Once we were inside and past where the blast had brought down rock there was nothing to be seen other than crates of supplies and stacked pillar beams lining the tunnel walls.

"Smell dead," Virgil said.

Cotton nodded.

"That's not completely uncommon in these mines," Cotton said. "We find all kinds of animals in these shafts. For one reason or another they die in these tunnels . . . crawl in wounded, or chased and eaten, coyotes, mountain lions, happens."

Virgil held up his lantern some looking off into the dark.

"What do you want to do now?" Cotton said.

"Are there no other shoots off this tunnel?" I said.

"No," Cotton said. "There used to be when this was

active, but they are closed up now, not been opened for a long time."

Virgil held up the lamp in his hand and looked back at the mound of rock behind us, then turned and looked down the rails leading in the opposite direction.

"Only one thing to do," he said.

Cotton nodded.

"Okay," he said. "Before we go any farther, let me make sure these pillars are solid."

Cotton held up his lantern and looked closely at the top of the beams, making sure that they were snugged securely under the crossbeams. He moved into the shaft some ten feet, checking them out on both sides of the tunnel, then turned back to us and nodded.

"Looks okay," he said. "Come on ahead."

We walked on through the tunnel toward Cotton. Then he turned when we got to him and the three of us moved into the shaft toward the other side of the mountain.

We walked without talking for a long ways. Then, almost ghostlike, I thought I saw something ahead of us and I moved to the sidewall behind a pillar. Virgil and Cotton followed my lead and got next to me with their backs to the wall.

"You see something?" I whispered.

"No," Virgil said.

"Thought I did," I said. "Thought I saw something, some movement."

I peeked out and looked around the pillar, then moved back.

"What is it, Everett?"

"Somebody," I said very quietly.

Then we heard some sound. It was a voice, but it was quiet and hard to make out clearly. Especially difficult to hear what was being said, but it was unmistakably a voice we were hearing.

I leaned out and looked past the pillar again, but now I saw nothing. Then I saw movement again. There was someone there in the darkness. They were slowly moving toward us between the rails. I was still protected behind the pillar but was peeking out around the side of it so I could see. Virgil was still next to me and Cotton was next to him.

"What is it, Everett?" he said. "What do you see?"

I raised the lantern up so the light would have a farther reach, and then I saw who it was.

"It's the Indian," I said. "Stringer's Kiowa tracker . . . Locky."

Virgil moved out from behind the pillar to have a look and Cotton did the same.

Locky moved slowly toward us, barely staying on his feet. His face was covered in blood.

We walked toward him. He was mumbling in Kiowa as he stumbled between the tracks. The whites of his eyes showed through his bloody face. When he saw that it was Virgil and me, he fell to his knees and said in a raspy voice, "Madre María . . ."

57

When Driggs and Allie got close to her house she *stopped and turned to him.*

"Thank you," she said.

"This is you?" he said as he kept moving toward the house.

"It is."

Driggs sensed Allie wanted to call it a night right here, but he continued moving toward the gate as he looked to the house. Driggs knew the difference between want and desire.

"A white picket fence, no less," he said.

Allie hesitated to follow as she looked around a bit, then lingered after him as he continued toward the house. Driggs stopped at the gate and gazed up at the house for a long moment. When Allie moved up he turned to her a little, then looked back to the house.

"Lovely home," he said.

"Thank you," she said as she looked toward the house, then glanced to him. "I appreciate you seeing me home safely."

"My pleasure."

He lifted the gate latch.

"After you," he said.

Allie stuttered a bit as she said with a nervous laugh, "Oh, I can see my way from here."

"I'm taking you all the way," he said as he removed his hat and pointed toward the front door.

Allie looked at him without moving, then back at the house, and moved up the rock path toward the door. She could feel Driggs's formidable presence just behind her as she climbed the steps to the dark porch.

When she got to the door she paused slightly, then turned. He was still holding his hat in his hand.

"You've been so kind," she said as she retrieved the door key from her clutch.

"I aim to please," he said.

"Well, then," she said as she held out her hand. "Again, thank you for a lovely evening."

He took her hand and held it, then brought it up to his lips and kissed it. He then pulled her gently toward him. He leaned and kissed her on the cheek . . . and just as quickly as he had pulled her out of her world and into his, he released her.

"You are okay from here on, I take it?" he said.

"Yes, yes, of course," she said as she turned and fumbled, trying to get the key into the lock.

"Allow me," he said.

Driggs took the key from her and slid it into the hole, turned it, and opened the door. It swung into the room slowly and freely as it offered a long, eerie creak.

She looked up to him and smiled. Then he held up the key. She reached for it, but he held it back slightly.

"Do you want me to come inside?" he said. "Make sure everything feels right?"

"No, I believe I can make it from here, and if I can't, then I guess they might as well put me under."

"Let's not go that far," he said with a laugh.

She stepped inside and turned to him. He put his hat to his chest, bowed, and said, "Good night . . . and sweet dreams."

"Good night," she said and closed the door.

He put on his hat, turned, and walked down the steps. He opened the gate, shut it behind him, and moved off. Then he looked back just as he passed behind the adjacent building for one last look at the house. He could see Allie's silhouette as she looked out the front door.

As Driggs moved on, he thought about what it might have been like if he'd gone ahead and got inside that house and did what it was that he did so well. But there were more pressing things churning up now, far more important happenings for him to be concerned with. The fire that he'd felt earlier when he was looking at himself in the mirror in Allie's dress shop was getting hotter by the hour. He was beginning to feel the full heat all over his body now. It was no longer just in his loins but was spreading like a wildfire through his body.

"Fear not," he said quietly as he walked on. "I am the first and the last. I am the one that lives. I was dead but behold I am alive for evermore. And I hold the keys of hell and death. I saw heaven open and I behold a white horse and he who sat upon him was called faithful and true. And in righteousness he doth judge and make war. This is the second death. And the great dragon was cast out, that old serpent called the Devil and Satan which deceived the world was cast down to earth. Behold I come quickly, my reward is with me to give every man according to his deed. I am the Alpha and Omega, the beginning and the end, the first and the last."

Back in the room, *Driggs drank some whiskey and smoked cigarettes as he thought about the evening, about*

Margie, about the princess, about what he needed to do, and about Allie. He liked her, the way she moved, the way she smelled. Once everything was said and done he figured he'd take good care of her, like he knew she needed, wanted . . . but currently he had those more significant thoughts that were occupying his head.

Around three in the morning he crawled into bed, and when he did the princess stirred and for the next few hours he toiled and procured before his mind eased and he eventually drifted off to sleep.

58

Locky was caked in dried blood and new blood and very badly wounded. It was obvious by his appearance that he was suffering from injuries caused by an explosion. His shirt and trousers were ripped and he was bleeding from cuts and scrapes along one entire side of his body.

Virgil, Cotton, and I quickly gathered up the young Indian tracker and carried him back toward the mine's portal.

"Snap to, fellas," Cotton called out across the stack of rubble to the men outside. "I need four of you, now. We have a badly injured man in here."

Cotton looked back to us then called out again, "Let's everyone be alert here, might be more to come. Get our medical supplies ready, everything, no telling what we might need."

Within moments, there were four miners including Jeff crawling over the rocks to get to us.

Locky was weak and seemed close to death but kept

talking as if he desperately needed to be heard. His garbled words were a mixture of Spanish and Kiowa. He kept trying to point to the opposite end of the shaft as we laid him down near the mine entrance.

"Can you understand anything that he is saying, Everett?"

Locky held my arm tight. His eyes were wide as he stared at me, speaking intently. His words were jumbled and it was difficult to make out the language combinations.

"No," I said. "Not really . . ."

Then Locky spoke clearly.

"*Querido Dios el único . . .*" he said through his clenched teeth as he was fighting off pain. "*Diablo escapado.*"

"Escaped?" Virgil said. "That much I got."

I nodded.

Then Locky said, "*Sorprendido de explosión . . . mucho sorprendido.*"

"Surprised by explosion," I said.

The miners wasted no time getting to us.

"Get him out," Cotton said. "Do what you can to keep him alive."

Locky squeezed my arm and with eyes wide he mumbled a string of Kiowa then ended with, "*Esperó Diablo . . . para nosotros . . . todos . . . todos.*"

I looked to Virgil.

"The Devil waited for them . . ."

The four men lifted Locky and started making their way out. Virgil, Cotton, and I moved on to the opposite end of the tunnel. We could hear Locky mumbling as we moved away. After a moment the only sound we could hear was the sound of our own footsteps.

Judging by the sight of Locky, I was not feeling good about what we might find at the opposite end of the shaft.

We walked past where we found Locky and the smell of death intensified with each step.

Then Cotton stopped.

"It's closed off on the east end for certain," Cotton said. "There is usually a breeze. Didn't say nothing before about that, wasn't real sure. I thought the air was just stacking and not coming through because there is such a small opening at the portal but there should be, would be, moving air through here . . . And the dead smell I was talking about? Well, this is not that, not what I was talking about, this is something much worse."

We walked on a ways, then we came across loose rock scattered about the shaft floor. As we continued walking there was more and more rubble and the smell got stronger and stronger.

"That is where the opening was," Cotton said. "He closed off both ends."

Then Cotton stopped, raised his lantern some, and pointed.

"My God," Cotton said.

Lodged in a crevasse of the rock wall was the bloody chunk of a posse member's head. There was bone, hair, beard, and a single ear visible.

Virgil looked to me and shook his head.

"He got them to this opening, then somehow blew them up," Virgil said.

We walked on a ways, and as we did we began to see more and more blood and pieces of the dead men. Two bodies we came across were badly mangled but still intact. They'd been blown back and wedged, upright, one man atop the other between a pillar and the wall. Virgil, Cotton, and I moved closer to the rubble with our lanterns raised. When we got next to the blockage at the tunnel's end there was an arm sticking out of the rocks still clutching a pistol.

"My God," Cotton said again.

The portal on this east end of the shaft was lower but wider than the opening on the west. It was at least twenty feet across. Virgil moved off to his left and I went toward the right. Within a moment I spotted something that put a lump in my throat.

"Virgil," I said.

He looked to me as I leaned down, picked up Sheriff Stringer's badge, and held it up for Virgil to see.

59

Locky was the only survivor from the blast that closed off the east end of forty-two and killed Sheriff Stringer and three of his deputies. The Kiowa tracker was taken down to the village of Bridgewater in the buckboard and taken into the care of Cotton's wife and daughters. It was hard to understand just how he could have come out of that blast in one piece, but he did. According to Cotton's wife, who was the resident self-made town doctor with a background of medicine and helping miners, Locky would survive.

Virgil and I took a short rest, got some food, then rode out of Bridgewater for the east side of forty-two. We rode south on the road and just as the sun was coming up we found the pass over the mountain; the trail switchbacked going up on the west side, as well as traversing down on the east side.

Once we arrived at the eastern portal there was no one in sight and no immediate evidence that provided us any details as to the direction of Ed Degraw.

There was a spectacular view of the valley below from where we sat our horses for a long moment.

"Unless the sonofabitch found a burro on the other side that we don't know about," I said, "he had to walk away from here."

We both looked down at the ground and moved our horses away from one another to see if we might find any evidence of track. There was a flat piece of land around the portal and we moved a little bit at a time around the perimeter.

"Nothing over here," I said. "Nothing obvious, anyway."

Virgil shook his head.

"Here neither."

We rode back toward one another and stopped directly in front of the portal entrance.

"One thing is," Virgil said. "He more than likely figures there's no one left to be on his ass."

"No," I said. "He shouldn't."

"Which way would you go?" Virgil said.

I turned my horse around and faced the same way Virgil was facing, again looking out at the open vista below. I looked around for a moment and pointed the direction that looked like the natural fall and the easiest walking.

"There," I said. "Toward that meadow with those spring flowers."

Virgil nodded.

"Looks inviting," he said.

"Pretty fertile over here," I said. "Much more so than the other side."

"Is," Virgil said.

"Awful nice country to have a monster like this nogood fucker moving around in."

"That, too," Virgil said.

"He'll stay with the green as long as there is green," I said.

We rode for an hour down through the pines, fremonts, spruce, and hackberry. There was a decent-sized brook that came from the mountains behind us that we crossed back and forth a few times. Virgil rode up a hill to a clearing just above the water, and when he got to the top he held up his hand and stopped. I stayed in the stream, where my horse was drinking.

"What?" I said.

"Smoke," he said, pointing.

I moved up out of the creek and rode up next to him. I could see a narrow line of smoke rising up in the distance.

"Half-mile, maybe," Virgil said.

I pulled out my scope and took a look.

"Can't see anything, really," I said. "The source is behind a rise in the foreground."

We were at a slight elevation above the smoke's source and it was clear that it was rising up in the cradle of the belt of green that followed the water.

"Reckon we best have a look," Virgil said.

Virgil rode on and I followed right behind him. We traveled within the creek's green belt, and when we got close to the source of the smoke we dismounted. We tied our horses, readied our Winchesters, and continued on by foot.

When we got close we slipped down to the creek's edge and eased our way through the low-growing grasses and thickets until we could see the smoke's source.

"Good goddamn," Virgil said.

Even from the distance away we could tell we were looking at the leftovers of a group of wagon settlers who had been slaughtered. We saw no one moving about, but we could see bodies on the ground as we neared.

Once we had the whole scene in clear view, it was obvious to us that we were most certainly witnessing the bloody and brutal craftsmanship of the notorious Ed Degraw.

We walked slowly and cautiously into the camp to find two men, a woman, and a boy all dead on the ground.

We heard something flutter in the bushes. Virgil and I both turned quickly with our rifles to see that it was one of their chickens. We watched the chicken walk among the dead for a moment.

"A no-good sight," Virgil said.

"It is," I said.

Each person had been shot more than once. From the way the woman was lying with her legs spread and her nakedness showing from her waist down, it was obvious the miserable no-good took the time to rape her.

"The Kiowa was right," I said. "Diablo."

"He damn sure is," Virgil said.

"Look," I said.

Across the creek there were two mules grazing.

"They had at least four animals pulling the wagon," I said. "Could have had more."

"'Spect Degraw took one, maybe two," Virgil said.

"That he did," I said.

Virgil looked at the dead boy and shook his head.

"Damn sure no longer on foot," I said.

Virgil nodded.

"No, he's not," he said.

60

Driggs was generally an early riser, but he woke *up much later than usual, perhaps because he was awake most of the night taking care of business, but also because it was so dark outside. Driggs lay in bed, looking out the window. He heard a low roll of thunder. He looked over to the princess, who was still sound asleep. He watched her for a long moment, then he looked to his pocket watch on the nightstand.*

"One-thirty in the afternoon," Driggs whispered. Then he said even quieter, as if he were humoring himself, "One-thirty in the fucking afternoon . . ."

Driggs anticipated that the rest of the day would be good and he would accomplish much of what he was looking forward to achieving. This was the day he'd been waiting for. He was not yet going to complete what he came here to do, not today, but this was the beginning of the end. He was in fact A-okay with the time of day. Though he had no comparison, he considered time was always on the side of the living.

He started the day like most of the recent free daytime beginnings he'd spent, with a refreshing tip or two of fine whiskey and a cigarette. He would not get to see the morning regulars he normally watched, but that was okay. He would get to see a whole other group. He thought perhaps he would get to witness the non-workers who went this way and that carrying out their self-important duties and responsibilities and obligations.

When he moved to the window he was pleased with just how incredibly dark the day was. He marveled at the stark contrast of colors between the beiges and browns and whites of the buildings lining the street and the foreboding dark gray blanket that covered Appaloosa. It was not raining, but that seemed inevitable. The dark had a weight to it, as if it could produce a tornado that might just tear all of Appaloosa off the earth. The darkness, the encroaching doom, did not prevent the civilized from going about their business, but it did prevent them from moving slowly. Most everyone moved at a brisk pace.

One of the first people he saw was Margie. She was rushing down the street, hurrying—most likely—to Allie's place. Driggs thought it interesting that she was one of the last people he'd seen the night before and now she was one of the first he'd laid eyes on. It must mean something.

She was elegant in a form-fitting cream-colored dress with the high bustle that was the newest fashion. She was almost an aberration, a bright and shiny nymph with wings fluttering through the dark void. He thought about knocking on the window to get her attention but since it was so dark out and she was in a hurry, and he was naked and sporting his usual morning tumescence, he refrained.

A rumbling thunder shook the glass of the window and reverberated through the floor of the hotel.

He took one of his rolled cigarettes from the dresser, struck a match, and inhaled the first intoxicating cloud that in-

stantly stimulated his sleepy head. He took a second shot of whiskey, and when he had the bottle tipped back something caught his eye out the window. He nonchalantly turned away from the window and moved back into the shadows of the room. Then he moved to the second window toward the foot of the bed. This window was covered with curtains. There was an opening between the curtains. When he peeked out, he was slightly surprised by what he saw.

Down Main Street there was a two-story structure under construction. It was not one of the new brick buildings. It was a well-built wooden structure that had yet to be painted. Driggs thought it might be a small hotel or a boardinghouse. There were three windows on the second floor, and in the center window stood a man. He appeared to be looking out toward the Boston House. Driggs watched him for a moment. "I'll be goddamned," Driggs said.

He knew he was not visible to the man, but he didn't want to take a chance. Driggs was not completely certain the man he saw was actually even looking at him, not directly. But Driggs thought it odd a man standing at the window, looking out like that, and above all, Driggs was cautious. He took a pull off his cigarette, then leaned in and looked out through the curtains again.

"Good morning," the princess said.

Driggs turned from the window and looked to her.

"What's out there?" she said.

"What's not?"

She giggled.

"That's what I adore about you."

"What's that?" Driggs said.

"Your outlook."

"The bright side," he said with a smile.

"But it's so dark," she said.

"That it is," he said.

"Something interesting out there in the dark, I hope?"

"*The coming and going . . .*"

"*Rain?*"

"*Not yet.*"

"*How glorious,*" she said.

She rubbed the sleep from her eyes as she sat up in bed.

"*What will the dark day bring?*"

"*What would you like for it to bring?*"

"*What I like is this right here,*" she said, stretching out her body across the bed.

"*Good,*" he said.

"*I don't remember much of last night,*" she said.

"*No?*"

"*No.*"

"*You don't remember Allie putting you to bed?*"

She squinted her eyes some.

"*I do,*" she said. "*Oh . . . My gosh . . . She put me to bed.*"

"*She did.*"

"*She undressed me?*"

"*She did.*"

"*Goodness,*" she said.

"*She enjoyed it.*"

"*What?*"

"*She did,*" he said.

"*She's lovely,*" the princess said.

"*She is,*" he said.

The princess yawned and stretched her arms above her head.

"*Oh . . . my head hurts,*" she said as she lay back.

"*I'll dress and go out to the drugstore and get you something.*"

She looked down at his nakedness and smiled a coy, sleepy smile.

"*I'm looking at what I need,*" she said, meeting his eyes.

61

After Driggs finished plowing and seeding, the *princess fell instantly back into a deep sleep and he got dressed. The darkness looming out the window seemed even heavier now, but it had yet to produce any rain. As he slipped on his trousers he glanced out the open window toward the building down the way. He thought perhaps he saw the man in the second-story window again but was not certain. If in fact there was a man in the window looking at him, Driggs was careful not to look directly at him. He also made a point of displaying himself, moving by the open window as he put on his shirt and tucked it into his trousers. Then he peeked out the curtains of the other window and was pleased to see there was no one in the window of the building under construction down the way, and no one looking out toward the Boston House. Good, Driggs thought. Last thing he needed was to have someone on to him. When he turned to leave, Driggs looked back one last time and he saw the man move into the window again, looking toward the Boston House. "I'll be damned. There he is again," Driggs thought as he took a step back from the crack between the curtains. "Can't be looking at me."*

Driggs leaned in and peeked back out. The man was right there, in the window, looking out. Then Driggs saw him raise a pair of binoculars. "Who the fuck is that?" he thought as he moved back away from the curtains. "Who could be on to me? The fucking law? How? If it is the law, why have they not come after me, tried to arrest me?" Driggs was not completely certain if he were the one that was being watched. Regardless, he needed to move now, make certain that if he was the one, the object of the surveillance, he could not let anything get in the way of what he needed to do, what he came to Appaloosa to accomplish. What was more than breath to him.

Driggs displayed himself again in front of the open window as he put on his long frock coat and hat. Then he crossed to the door and left the room.

He exited the Boston House and stood on the front steps looking out at the darkness. He casually lit a cigarette and spoke to a few folks on the hotel porch offering how-do-you-do's, but did not look up to the building with the man in the window.

He crossed the street and headed in the direction of the man in the window. He strolled leisurely, allowing the man to have a good view of him. Then he crossed the street directly in front of the building. Driggs had his hands on Colt revolvers in each pocket. He was, if anything, ready. He was looking at everything and nothing, casually. But he wondered: Are they coming for me? Are they surrounding me?

When he got to the boardwalk on the opposite side, thunder rumbled loudly and it began to rain. Driggs stood under the boardwalk awning and watched it rain. He did not look in the direction of the man in the window. Instead he walked away, passing a few businesses before entering Dale's Drugstore.

He closed the door behind him and moved to the counter, positioning himself near the front window. He took a quick nonchalant glance up and out the front window of the shop to see if the man was looking down toward the drugstore—and he was. I'll be goddamned, *Driggs thought.*

"Coming down now," Mr. Dale exclaimed as he stepped out from behind the counter.

Driggs looked back to him.

"Just a matter of time," Driggs said.

Mr. Dale moved toward the front of the store next to Driggs and looked out at the rain.

"Felt this coming on all morning," Mr. Dale said.

"What have you got for a morning throb that has come about from an evening of a bit too much?"

"I'll fix you right up," Mr. Dale said.

Driggs moved back to the counter and Mr. Dale gathered up a small can of bicarbonate of soda and Dr. Corby's Hangover Cure.

"These should do the job," Mr. Dale said.

Driggs paid and they said their good-byes, then Driggs started to leave but stopped.

"Say . . . would you mind if I left out the rear door, save me the headache of having to walk all the way around the block with the rain?"

"By all means . . ." Mr. Dale said with a smile as he opened the back door. "Just take both of those, drink plenty of water, get a nap, and you'll be good to go for tonight . . . hurry before this rain gets stronger or you're gonna get yourself all wet."

"Thank you," Driggs said, then stepped out the door and into the rain.

Driggs moved at a quick pace down the alley. When he was certain he was out of sight of the building on the corner where the man spied from the upstairs window, he walked between two buildings and back up to the street. Then he crossed the street, went through a narrow opening between two dwellings, then moved back up the alley toward the building. The rain started to come down hard as Driggs walked toward the building where the spy was perched in the second-story window. He had no idea what to expect. Was there a goddamn posse there waiting for him? Regardless, this was it; he could not risk being the hunted. Not now, not after all he'd done and all he'd yet to do.

When he came upon the back of the building, he stepped up out of the rain onto the building's rear steps that were covered by a small overhang. The top half of the back door had a window and Driggs could see inside that the hall went straight through the structure all the way to the front door. Toward the end and before the front door there was a set of stairs.

The door was not yet fitted with hardware and was secured with only a rope. Driggs quickly pulled it loose and entered without hesitation. The noise of the rain provided him the cover to get inside quietly. Once inside he closed the door but remained still. Halfway down the hall there was what appeared to be a closet under the stairs, but was not fitted with a door. Driggs moved quietly the few steps up the hall and into the opening. He knew the man would not wait too much longer for him to walk out of the drugstore.

Driggs knew human nature and he knew damn well the man would not be comfortable with losing Driggs that easy. Now Driggs knew for sure that it was indeed him that the man was interested in and Driggs was not going to have any of it.

It was dark where Driggs was standing inside the little

*alcove closet off the hall, but a bright flash of lightning out-
side briefly made the dark interior light up and when it did
Driggs spied some loose lumber leaning up against the closet
wall. He picked up a solid piece of hardwood that was about
three feet long and fit perfectly in his hand like a club.*

62

Virgil and I circled, looking around the settlers' campsite, until we picked up the tracks of Ed Degraw.

"Looks like he took two horses," I said.

Virgil looked at the tracks on the ground, then looked up in the direction of where the tracks were headed.

"He damn sure don't think there is anyone left looking for him," I said.

"Don't seem," Virgil said.

"Not just walking off like this," I said. "Taking two animals, not moving too fast."

Degraw made no attempt to hide his direction. The tracks we discovered were on the road. It was a well-traveled, deep-rutted wagon road, and the only other fresh tracks were those the settlers had left coming from the opposite direction. Degraw stole just the one horse he was now riding and was traveling northeast toward dark clouds that covered the landscape before us.

"That don't look inviting," I said.

"Sure don't," Virgil said.

Inside the dark there was a flash of silver.

"Been a bunch of it of late," I said.

"More than," Virgil said.

"That time of year," I said.

"Is."

"Damn sure don't feel like a bright and uplifting spring, though, does it?"

"Damn sure don't, Everett."

We rode silently for a moment.

"Hard to believe all them got blown up like that," I said.

Virgil nodded but did not respond.

"Stringer was a damn good hand," I said.

"He was," Virgil said. "And those boys of his, too."

"All them hands working with him damn sure looked up to him," I said.

"Just these two men to go, though."

"The worst two," I said.

"Ain't that how it goes," Virgil said.

"I should have stepped back when I thought that was him," I said. "When we saw him."

"That was then," Virgil said.

"Chastain not seeing Driggs yet there in Appaloosa might mean that the sonofabitch has more then likely moved on."

"Very well could be," Virgil said.

"Rolling stone," I said.

"He's brazen," Virgil said.

"He is," I said.

"Smart," Virgil said.

"Sure wooed the woman," I said. "Made it so he got out . . . took some conniving."

"And then some," Virgil said.

"Taking the warden's money, horses, guns. Then Driggs outfitting himself in fancy clothes. The two of them acting like they are good to move about the country just as they please."

Virgil looked to me and shook his head.

"They're damn sure doing it," he said.

"The whole of the prison break leaves a lot to the unknowing," I said.

"He damn sure let out all the others so to make things easier on him," Virgil said.

"Why Degraw, I wonder?"

Virgil shook his head a little.

"Tillary said there was not any love lost between the two of them, Driggs and Degraw," I said.

"The fact that Degraw is one of the ones we are still chasing after is likely why Driggs made certain he was one of the ones that got let out," Virgil said. "Knowing the bastard would be someone to reckon with."

"He is at that."

"I don't know exactly just where we are," I said. "But if we keep in this direction we should eventually get back to the Transcontinental line."

Virgil nodded.

"We'll have to contend with that though first," I said, nodding to the dark clouds across the horizon in front of us.

"Lookie here," Virgil said, then stopped his horse.

Ahead of us was a small cluster of buildings.

Virgil turned off the road through some brush and I followed. Once we were off the road a ways we stopped and dismounted.

We tied our horses, grabbed our Winchesters, and moved through the thickets toward the buildings. When we got to an opening where we had a good view of the buildings we saw clearly that it was a small supply store with a few outbuildings and corrals. There was a ridge beam that stuck out over the front porch of the store, where a man was hanging from a rope around his neck. There was blood caked around his crotch and his trousers were down around his ankles.

63

Driggs remained standing in the small closet under the stairs of the empty building. After a short time Driggs heard the distinct sound of chair legs scraping on the floor upstairs. Then he heard footsteps moving around and within a moment they came walking down the stairs. He waited as the footfalls got to the bottom of the steps then eased out of the closet and raised the piece of lumber, ready to strike.

When the man took the last step from the stairs to the floor, he instantly sensed Driggs's presence and went for his pistol, but Driggs struck first, swinging the hardwood like an ax, striking the man with a powerful blow to his throat. The man fell back on the steps. Driggs quickly put his boot to the man's chest and pinned his head against the last step and the wall.

It was just light enough for Driggs to make out the man's face. He was the older fellow with the bowler hat who had been in Meserole's the night his lanky partner was shot and killed.

Driggs picked up the man's pistol, tucked it under his belt, then grabbed the man by a fistful of shirt and jerked him up on his feet. Driggs pressed the hardwood to the man's throat and stared at him.

"Hello, Uncle Dave," *Driggs said with a smile.*

"Don't . . . hurt . . . me."

"Hurt you?"

Driggs applied some pressure to the board he held across Dave's throat.

"Please," *Dave said, coughing.* "Jesus . . . please."

"He's not here," *Driggs said.*

"Stop," *Dave said.* "My God . . ."

"None of 'em are here, Uncle Dave. No Jesus, no God, no Holy Spirit. I'm the closest thing to God you will ever see, Uncle Dave."

Driggs backed off applying pressure. Dave's eyes were wide with fear as he gasped and coughed.

"Why did he put you to watching me?"

"He don't know you are here. Least if he does know he never let on to me. I just saw you, and I thought I'd seen a ghost . . . I just had to be sure that it was you."

"Don't lie to me. You know I'm here, so he knows I'm here, doesn't he?"

"Look, I saw you last night. Walking up the stairs. I was in the saloon late and was at the bar and I turned and I saw you walk by the door and go upstairs, and I thought, My God, that looked like Augustus. Then I went out front and I saw you turn on the lamp in your room upstairs. I knew the room and I figured I'd come this morning and see if what I saw was right."

"You're nothing but a lying fool."

"I'm telling you the truth."

"Truth? You know nothing of truth. You are just a low-life peon, Uncle Dave. Why are you watching me, Uncle Dave?"

"I . . . told you. I . . . just wanted to know for certain it was you . . ."

"Stop," Driggs said.

"What?"

"Why?"

"Fucking truth. I thought, no way could it be you," Dave said. "But then, I watched you . . . It's you."

"Who do you think I am?"

"What?"

"Who?"

"What? It's you, Gus. Look . . . I seen you, last night, and I . . . I . . ."

"You what?"

"Thought you was dead, Gus, I swear . . ."

"Thought wrong."

"I can't believe it . . . What the . . . ?" Dave said. "What the hell you doing here, Gus?"

"I could ask you the same thing, but that would be wasted verbiage on my part," Driggs said. "I know damn good and well what you are doing here."

"Don't . . . Don't hurt me, Gus, please . . ." Dave said.

"Hurt you? Now, why would I want to hurt you?"

"You know I was not the one."

"The one? What do you mean, 'the one'?"

Dave just stared at him, shaking his head hard from side to side.

"I was not the one that shot you."

"No?"

"I swear to God. You have to believe me."

"Why?"

"It's the truth."

"You've never told the truth in your life, Uncle Dave, so why do you think I have to believe you now?"

"He done it. It was him . . ."

"Don't need to tell me what I know."

"I'm not . . . . I mean . . ."

"You mean? You mean nothing, absolutely nothing. And here, I'm thinking you are the law looking on me."

"Law? No. Hell. I'm no law."

"You don't need to point that out, either, Uncle Dave. Still kissing ass. You have not so much as even been invited to sit and eat lunch with him, have you?"

Dave just stared at him.

"No, I wouldn't think so," Driggs said. "You're still leveraging for him. That's what you are doing. Making the little people like you pay to stay? Threatening to take over businesses. Or are you just polishing his boots? Getting young pussy for him? Sucking his dick when he wants you to?"

"What . . . what do you want from me . . . ?"

Driggs shook his head.

"Nothing."

Dave looked relieved, but then Driggs put pressure on the board he held across Uncle Dave's throat. Uncle Dave's eyes bulged as he stared at Driggs.

"This will be good for you, Uncle Dave," Driggs said. "It will be the best thing that has ever happened in your lifetime."

Uncle Dave tried to pull the board from his throat, but there was no stopping the force of Augustus Noble Driggs, not when he had his mind set, and his mind was—dead set.

64

The darkness of the clouds was not yet upon us, but we could feel the pressure. Virgil and I watched the store for a long moment before we made any move. In the corrals there were a handful of mules. In another pen there were some goats and pigs. Toward the back of the property was a long milk barn with a few cows behind the barn, but there was no one moving about.

When we finally walked out of the thickets and up to the store we found the scene was nothing more than another gruesome field of carnage left by Degraw. He killed three men. The older tall fella we cut down who had been strung up and hanging from the ridge beam had also been shot and castrated. And two other men, younger Negro fellas we found dead off the side of the porch. Both men had gunshot wounds to the head.

When we walked out the back door we saw another person. A skinny young Negro fella, he was standing in knee-high grass in front of the milk shed. He appeared to be looking directly toward us, but something seemed off about the way he was just standing there, staring at us. The milk shed backed up to a stand of hackberry trees that were currently covered with an anxious murder of crows. They were cawing and cackling as if they were a chorus of angry mourners.

The young man stood perfectly still, looking at us, and then he fell face-first and disappeared into the high grass in front of him.

When we got to him we discovered he had a long, bone-handled knife sticking out of his back. The wound had left a trail of blood that had traveled all the way down his backside to the lower portion of his legs. His face was turned to the side and he was trying to look up at us with his large eyes.

"Help me," he said.

He was a delicate and gentle-looking fella with smooth skin and almost feminine features.

I got on my knees next to him and leaned down, looking at him.

"We are here for you," I said.

He just looked at me with terrified, shifting eyes that were full of tears.

"Just be very still," I said. "Close your eyes."

He was beyond frightened and his eyes started moving nervously, but he did as I instructed and closed his eyes. I looked up at Virgil, then to the knife in the young man's back. I held out my hand, then got a hold of the knife, pulled it from his back, and when I did the young man screamed out in pain as his eyes bolted open.

Virgil retrieved a wheelbarrow that was leaning up against the milk shed.

"We are gonna get you out of the grass and inside the store," Virgil said.

"You just do your very best to breathe," I said. "And though I know it's hard, just try to remain as calm as you can . . . Okay?"

He bit his lip and nodded.

Virgil looked to me. We got on each side of the young man, lifted him out of the grass and into the bed of the wheelbarrow. Then I positioned myself between the handles, lifted the wheelbarrow, and swiftly moved him toward the store.

Once we had him inside we placed him on his stomach across a table that we covered with a blanket. I cut open his shirt and saw that he had been stabbed twice. We scoured the store for medicinal supplies, coming up with alcohol and bandages, but he was bleeding badly and for now all we could do was clean and keep pressure on the wound.

Virgil leaned down and looked at him closely.

"We are gonna do what we can to get you outta here," Virgil said. "But you just need to stay strong."

The young man nodded.

"Okay," he said. "Okay . . ."

"How long ago did this happen?" Virgil said.

He shook his head a little.

"Two, three hours, maybe."

"How many of you were here at the store?" Virgil said.

"Mr. Gibson, he own the place, and my papa he worked for him, my cousin, too."

"That it?" Virgil said. "That is all the folks that were here?"

"Yes sir," he said. "But no more, they . . . they been killed."

He started crying.

I looked to Virgil. He followed my look to the blood

that was continuing to flow from the wound. I shook my head and looked back to Virgil.

"Maybe it will help if we sit him up," I said.

Virgil nodded.

"We are gonna have you sit up here, okay," I said.

He nodded and Virgil helped me turn the young man to his side and sit up.

"Stay strong," Virgil said.

The young man nodded as he stared at Virgil.

"What is your name, son?" Virgil said.

"Gracie," he said.

"Well, Gracie," Virgil said. "We are gonna do everything we can to help you here, young man."

"Thank you, sir."

Then he just looked at Virgil and me and shook his head and said, "Why this happen?"

"No reason," Virgil said.

"Crazy man just came in here. He told my daddy and my cousin to hang Mr. Gibson or he'd have Mr. Gibson hang them."

Virgil looked to me but did not say anything.

"That's what happened?" I said.

"No, he shot my daddy and cousin, just shot them in the head, then shot Mr. Gibson in the stomach. Then he strung up Mr. Gibson while he was alive. Then he cut off his . . . privates."

Gracie stopped talking. He looked down, then looked back up to us.

"He . . . he cornholed me . . . before he stabbed me," he said. "He did that to me . . . Made the lady watch."

"What lady?" Virgil said.

"She was no lady, no woman," he said weakly as tears fell from his eyes. "Not really, she was a girl, younger than me . . . I'm fifteen."

"Goddamn," I said.

Virgil shook his head.

"Settlers' girl."

I nodded.

"What's the closest town to here?" Virgil said.

"Twenty miles, up the road here, there is Rose Rock," he said.

65

Driggs went upstairs to the center room where *Uncle Dave had been keeping watch. There were cigar ends and rib bones on the floor, a canteen, a few empty bottles of beer, and the pair of binoculars. Driggs looked out through the binoculars to his room up the street. He peered at the window, thinking he might catch a glimpse of the princess, but saw nothing. Then he collected all the stuff—the bones, bottles, cigar ends, canteen, and binoculars. When he got back downstairs he dumped the stuff and Uncle Dave's body into a hinged opening he discovered that led to the building's substructure.*

When he was done he scanned the room, making sure everything was in order, then moved toward the front of the building and looked out the window. Then as he watched the rain pour from the porch overhang, he heard a deep voice behind him. "Got a gun to the back of your head. Get your hands up."

Driggs froze. He did not turn and he did not raise his hands.

"*Who are you?*"

"*I am the sheriff of Appaloosa,*" he said. "*Name's Chastain. Got a Colt pointed at the back of your head. Now I need you to raise your hands . . . right now.*"

Driggs did as he was told.

"*As high as they will go,*" Chastain said. "*Straight up in the goddamn air and do not turn around. You don't do as I say I will not hesitate to put a bullet in your head.*"

Driggs raised his arms higher. Then he started to turn.

"*Don't you fucking move,*" Chastain said. "*Don't you think about fucking moving unless I say so.*"

"*What seems to be the problem?*" Driggs said, as he remained looking out the front window of the building with his hands held above his head.

"*Problem?*"

"*Yes,*" Driggs said.

"*One of my smallest problems with you, and it ain't the first one, or the biggest one, I might add, is you thinking you is sneaky, going through the goddamn drugstore like you did, trying to lose me.*"

Driggs started to lower his hands some.

"*Fucking up and high, goddamn it,*" Chastain said.

Driggs did as he was told, and once he had his hands back up high, Chastain said, "Turn around, slow-like."

Driggs turned very slowly and faced Chastain.

"*What the fuck you doing in this building?*" Chastain said.

"*Just stepped in to get out of the rain,*" Driggs said.

"*Fuck you,*" Chastain said.

"*The truth, Officer.*"

"*I know who you are,*" Chastain said. "*So you can spare the horseshit.*"

"*I don't know what you are talking about,*" Driggs said.

"*I followed your ass, tracked you in the mud all the way to right here, you see.*"

"*You followed me?*" Driggs said.

"*You goddamn right I did,*" Chastain said. "*Footprint by footprint.*"

"*Why?*"

"*You are under arrest,*" Chastain said.

"*For what?*"

Chastain took a pair of cuffs from his pocket and tossed them to Driggs. The cuffs hit Driggs's chest and fell to the floor.

"*Put those on.*"

"*Why,*" Driggs said. "*What for?*"

"*You are under arrest for escaping Cibola for one, and I'm sure when it is all said and done there will be a whole bunch of other shit that you will be charged with.*"

"*You have the wrong man,*" Driggs said.

"*Put them on,*" Chastain said. "*Put the cuffs on, now.*"

"*Okay, just know I'm here to cooperate,*" Driggs said. "*So just take it easy . . . but you have made a grave mistake, I'm afraid. I'm not who you think I am.*"

"*Do like I tell you,*" Chastain said as he moved toward him with his Colt pointed at his head. "*I won't ask again, and believe me, I got no problem in putting a bullet in your goddamn fucking head. Put them on, now.*"

"*Okay,*" Driggs said.

Driggs lowered his hands.

"*Very fucking easy as you go,*" Chastain said. "*You so much as flinch, make any kind of goddamn move otherwise than getting them cuffs on, you will be a dead man.*"

"*Okay, Sheriff,*" Driggs said. "*Okay . . . please just take it easy . .*"

Driggs leaned down and picked up the cuffs. He secured one side of the cuffs to one wrist and then clicked the other side closed.

"*There,*" Driggs said. "*Are you happy?*"

"*Let's go,*" Chastain said.

Driggs smiled and looked to the doors.

"Front door or back door?"

"Same way you came in."

"As you wish," Driggs said. "But you are making a big mistake, I assure you."

"Just move," Chastain said.

Driggs walked toward the rear door. Chastain followed with his Colt pointed at his back. The door had swung back closed after Chastain's entrance. When Driggs got to the door, he turned ever so slightly to Chastain.

"Shall I open it?" Driggs said. "Or do you prefer to open it? I don't want you to be impetuous."

"Just open it very easy," Chastain said. "Easy all the way to the jail and you won't have a problem. You don't and you will be dead."

"Yes," Driggs said. "As you have reiterated."

Driggs reached for the door and as he pulled it open he swiftly removed Uncle Dave's pistol from under his belt, swiveled his hands around his side without turning back toward Chastain, and pulled the trigger. The bullet caught a piece of Chastain's side just as Chastain pulled the trigger of his Colt. His bullet just missed Driggs's head as it splintered the doorjamb. Driggs spun around on Chastain, but Chastain's body slammed him into the door before Driggs could fire again. The impact with the door made Driggs lose control of the pistol. Driggs spun around with his boot outright and flipped the sheriff off his feet. Chastain got off a second shot but the fall made the bullet go wild. Driggs got his hands on Chastain's Colt.

Driggs tried to wrestle the pistol out of Chastain's hand and, even though Chastain had received a shot to the side, he was every bit as strong and as powerful as Driggs. Driggs was now on top of Chastain and he slammed Chastain's pistol free. Chastain managed to turn his body and reach for the fallen pistol, but Driggs got his cuffed hands over

Chastain's head. With the chain between the cuffs around Chastain's neck, Driggs pulled hard. Chastain reached behind him, trying to get ahold of Driggs, but Driggs maintained control. Driggs put his knee to Chastain's back as he pulled the cuffs tighter and tighter around Chastain's neck. Chastain began to violently flail as Driggs choked him. Chastain spun around, kicking. He kicked a hole in the wall, spun, and kicked a hole in the door. He fought as he got to his knees, then he got to his feet, but Driggs kept choking him. Chastain kicked the glass out of the door, then spun around into the room with Driggs on his back. He dragged Driggs toward the front door, but before he got too close Driggs fell back with him. Chastain spun around, getting to his feet again, but Driggs was not about to let up. Chastain charged a wall and tried to dislodge Driggs, but to no avail.

"What'd I tell you," Driggs said. "What the fuck did I tell you? Huh? Nothing to say?"

Chastain stumbled, falling forward to the floor, as Driggs continued to pull hard. Then Chastain rose up and powered his strong legs in reverse and slammed Driggs hard into the wall.

But Driggs just pulled even harder on the cuffs. Chastain moved away from the wall and then powered back again, slamming into the wall, but Driggs did not let go. Chastain moved to the center of the room and turned, then turned again as Driggs choked him. Chastain dropped to his knees with Driggs still on his back. Chastain toppled forward onto his face and after a moment he gave up the fight as blood flowed from his neck and puddled onto the floor. Driggs looked around at Chastain's face as the last bit of life drained from his eyes.

"I told you that you were making a mistake . . . I goddamn told you."

66

Driggs moved to look out the front window for *other lawmen. He figured they had to be right there, ready to pounce on him. He did not see anyone. He rummaged through Chastain's pockets and found the keys to the cuffs. He unlocked the shackles, then dumped Chastain's body into the same opening where he discarded Uncle Dave.*

He looked out the broken glass of the back door but saw no one. He stepped out the door and just stood there for a moment, then moved down the steps into the alley.

The rain was still coming down hard and the alley had a good-sized creek running down the middle of it. Driggs moved to the opposite side of the alley and stood under the building's overhang. He looked left and right to make sure nobody saw him and he saw nobody. Then he slogged off down the alley the way he came.

Driggs thought that Chastain coming on his own was abnormal procedure for a city lawman. Driggs stopped and moved under an overhang out of the rain. He wondered if he was going to be confronted at any moment by other Appaloosa lawmen, but the only thing that came and continued to come was rain.

He fished a cigarette and match from his vest pocket. He lit the cigarette and just stood there for a moment letting his fast-moving blood slow down some. Driggs was never really riled and he was not riled now but he was intent on taking care of business. He knew himself well enough to know that this sort of stimulation was like opening valves and gates made for destruction.

He moved between two buildings and made his way back to the street. He crossed the street, passed through the alley behind the drugstore, then emerged out onto a street a block closer to the Boston House.

When he started up the boardwalk he walked right under the Room for Rent *sign where Margie boarded. He stopped, then took a step back and looked inside. There was no one in the small lobby. Then he walked to the side of the building and looked up to the window where he previously saw Margie when he'd followed her.*

"What the hell, now is as good a time as any." He knew she was away so he entered the boardinghouse. He stood still for a moment just inside the front door, thinking someone might come through a door that was just off the small lobby, but no one came. He walked up the steps to the second floor. Margie's door was locked. There were two other rooms on the floor. Just to be safe, he knocked on both of the doors to see if anyone was in, but no one came to either door.

He pulled his knife, working it between the door and jamb, and made his way easily into Margie's room. Inside Margie's room, he began to search. What exactly he was searching for he did not know, but for something that would hopefully tell him who Margie really was.

He suspected just who she might be, but he had to find out for certain. He could not just speculate. He'd read about women like her, but he needed to know for sure. He *needed to know just why she lied about Lincoln, Nebraska, and what she was doing there in Appaloosa. That lie she told meant only one thing to Driggs: she was hiding something, and Driggs was determined to find out just what that was.*

What a gloriously strange day, *Driggs thought, as he looked through Margie's personal items. Everything had changed, and it would be only a matter of time before Driggs could get to the bottom of his business.*

And there was nothing short of death that would keep him from doling out his vengeance. "If thine enemy hunger," Driggs thought, "feed him. If he's thirsty, give him drink, for in so doing thou shall heap coals of fire on his head. Dearly beloved, avenge not yourselves but rather give place for God's wrath. For it is written, vengeance is mine. I will repay, saith the Lord."

Driggs's excitement grew as he looked through Margie's personal belongings. Then Driggs found something that made him realize he was indeed keen, perceptive, and all-knowing. What he discovered in the bottom drawer under Margie's underclothes made his loins grow perfectly rigid.

67

The dark weather came upon us as Virgil and I loaded up young Gracie in a buckboard that we hitched up to two of Gibson's mules. Gracie was alive and hanging on but was very weak and going in and out of consciousness. We covered the bed of the buckboard with tarps, then tied our animals to the back and headed out for Red Rock.

"Good chance we could happen upon the sonofabitch Degraw up here in Red Rock," I said.

"Hope so," Virgil said.

"He damn sure didn't go back the way we came," I said.

"No . . ."

Virgil hawed the mules and popped the reins.

"He'll bed down someplace," Virgil said. "Likely Red Rock or thereabouts."

"He goddamn sure shows up wherever he wants and does whatever he wants."

"He does at that."

I turned and lifted the tarp to look at Gracie.

"Gracie?" I said.

He tilted his head a little and looked to me.

"You doing okay back there?" I said.

Gracie nodded a little. I watched him a moment then I turned back in my seat.

"Poor kid," I said.

Virgil looked to me as he worked the mules.

"We've come across some evil hombres in our time," I said. "But this one we are chasing now is as lowdown as any sonofabitch we've ever had to hunt."

"Sure he was beyond no good when he got to prison and being locked up just made him worse."

"Does that, don't it?"

"Does."

Virgil popped the reins and encouraged the mules to move on.

"Mad at it all," Virgil said. "Starts there . . . ends up real fucking close to hell."

"And now he's got some young girl," I said.

Virgil shook his head at the thought.

"Look forward to his demise," he said.

We checked on Gracie every few miles as we traveled. The first part of the trip was without rain, but eventually the dark clouds cracked and the rain fell. It was not coming down hard at first, but by the time we arrived in Red Rock it was coming down solid.

It was about two hours after dark when we came through the small but well-established lumber-mill village built up on the edge of Rio Blanco.

The only business open in Red Rock was an eatery saloon that was built near one of the mills on stilts close to the water's edge.

Before we entered we looked in the window, thinking there was a chance we just might see Degraw, but he was not there. We'd never laid eyes on him, but the descriptions we got gave us a very clear picture of the convict who had killed so many innocent people since his escape.

Inside we found the place kind of lively for a rainy night. In the corner there were some older lumbermen listening to fiddle music played by two old-timers.

Though we were standing there dripping wet, no one paid Virgil and me much attention when we entered. A short, round, red-faced woman wearing a checkered apron who came out of the kitchen drying her hands on a towel was the first person to greet us.

"Evening, fellas," she said.

Virgil showed his badge.

"I'm Marshal Virgil Cole. This is Marshal Everett Hitch."

"I'm Lucy."

"Need a few things," Virgil said.

She looked back and forth between us.

"Okay," she said.

"We are looking for a man that might have come in here sometime earlier," Virgil said. "With a young woman . . . a girl."

She shook her head.

"No," she said. "I've not seen any man with a girl . . . Sorry."

I glanced at Virgil.

"How about without a girl," I said.

Virgil nodded.

"Have you seen any strangers come through?" Virgil said. "Anyone at all?"

"Not in the last few days," Lucy said.

Virgil nodded.

"That being that," he said, "we could use some doctor help outside here. Pronto."

"We have a young man with us in a buckboard," I

said. "He's in pretty bad shape and in need of medical attention."

"You are in luck there," Lucy said as she looked to the men watching the fiddle players. "That's the most qualified man here in Red Rock right there. He's an ol' dentist who's a better vet, and even better doctor. Retired now for the most part, but he works on most anybody with whatever."

She moved toward him.

"Claude," she said.

Claude was a skinny, older fella wearing overalls. He turned and looked to us.

"Come here," she said.

Claude got up and ambled over to us.

"These men are lawmen and they need help."

The fiddlers stopped fiddling and the handful of fellas that'd been watching them fiddle turned and looked to us.

Then the woman barked orders at a few of the other men to help and we got Gracie moved inside. We laid him out on the most comfortable spot we could find. Then Claude looked to Virgil and shook his head some.

"I ain't never worked on no Niggra before," Claude said.

"Good news," Virgil said.

"What's that?" Claude said.

"Things have changed for you, Claude," Virgil said.

68

The fiddle players and their small audience cleared out of the eatery as Claude got to work on Gracie. He took immediate charge of the situation. He had Lucy put some water on to boil, then cleaned out the wounds in Gracie's back with soap and hot water. Gracie was already numb from the pain and barely made a sound as Claude scrubbed, then stitched up the openings. When Claude was done, Gracie fell instantly asleep.

"That is it for now," Claude said.

Claude watched the kid breathing for a moment. He put his hand to Gracie's head and left it there feeling his pulse at his temples. He touched his cheeks and the back of the boy's neck, then looked to us and nodded a little.

"He's very lucky," Claude said. "If either one of those wounds ended up a half-inch one way or another . . ."

Claude just shook his head, then looked to Virgil and me.

"He's gonna be okay," he said.

Virgil nodded.

Claude looked at Lucy.

"I'll stay here through the night," he said.

Virgil looked to me, then to Claude.

"Much appreciated."

"The fact me saying I never worked on no Niggra before had nothing to do with me not willing," Claude said. "I just never had the opportunity. In all my years, this here boy is my first."

Claude turned back to Gracie and rested his hand on his shoulder as he nodded a little.

"He's a strong boy," Claude said, then turned to Lucy. "How about a whiskey, Lucy?"

"You bet, Claude. Coming right up," she said, then looked to us. "Marshals?"

"Sure," we said.

Lucy poured us each a healthy glass of whiskey.

"Been a while since me and Everett have been through here," Virgil said. "Where would a man find a room 'round here, what's available?"

"You fellas are welcome to bunk down here if you like."

"More interested in where we might find the man we was looking for," Virgil said. "Where he might have ended up."

"Oh," Lucy said. "Well, there are no official hotels . . . Not yet, anyways. Growing every day and there's talk of one a'coming. For now there's just a few rooming houses up the street."

Virgil nodded but didn't say anything.

"There is a boardinghouse at the north end of town, but that stays pretty full with lumbermen. Each one of those places will have vacancy signs up if they got space."

"Saloons?"

"There's two small ones, Jim's and the other just says

Bar. Both of those are at the end just where the road goes back north."

"They open?" I said.

She nodded.

"Never closed."

Virgil nodded a little, thinking.

"Wire service here?" I said.

She shook her head.

"No, but the Transcontinental's not but eight miles up and the water-drop depot is right there where the road crosses the tracks. The section line operator is there, takes care of everything on the tracks and runs the section team and such. If he's not in when you get there, just wait awhile and he'll show up."

We took our whiskeys and stepped out onto the back porch of the eatery that looked out over the river.

"Ol' Claude at first seemed like someone you'd rather not have work on you under dire conditions," I said.

"Is."

Virgil glanced back to Claude sitting with Gracie, then moved to the rail and looked out toward the dark. We could hear the water moving over the rocks. The sound of the rushing water and the rain falling on the covered porch was loud.

"Still coming," Virgil said.

"Damn sure is," I said as I moved near the rail next to him.

"Been thinking 'bout that young girl he took," I said.

Virgil nodded but did not look at me.

"Me, too."

"I'd like to think some kind of good could exist for her," I said, "but . . ."

"I know," Virgil said.

"And that boy in there," I said, looking inside.

Virgil glanced back and shook his head.

"He'll not likely forget this . . . He'll carry those scars inside for all his born days," he said.

We stood there for a moment just listening to the rain and river as we sipped our whiskey.

"Something don't seem right," Virgil said.

"What are you thinking about?"

"Don't know."

He shook his head a little and looked to me but said nothing.

"Driggs?" I said.

Virgil thought, then nodded.

"No doubt we been after some real shits that got loose," he said. "And we got some kind of monster right here, right now, with this goddamn Degraw . . . but Driggs."

"We were talking there at the table when Rutledge came up, talked about his big party and mentioned the prison break," I said. "And Allie was concerned about the convicts ending up in Appaloosa."

"I know."

"That was a far notion from our minds at the time," I said.

"At the time," Virgil said.

"Not from Allie's," I said.

"Nope," he said.

"Rutledge said he heard about the break from a wire that came from his business partner in Yaqui," I said. "When he was ordering parts or some shit."

I could tell Virgil was thinking back on that night.

"I thought back on him, Rutledge," I said. "Saying that shit to us at the table . . . Don't think he was fishing, do you, about what we did and didn't know?"

"What do you think?"

"Don't know," I said. "Rutledge seems like a harmless blowhard, but hell if I know."

"He does," Virgil said.

We were silent for a moment as we thought about possibilities. "Wonder what else we ain't figured on?"

"Been thinking that, too," Virgil said. "Like Appaloosa."

I nodded.

"Why Appaloosa?" I said.

"Hard to say."

"It is," I said. "Appaloosa is not necessarily a place you'd pick on the map unless you had some business there."

"Or visiting someone," Virgil said.

"Who?" I said.

Virgil shook his head.

"Rutledge?" I said.

"Might well be," Virgil said.

"Got to be someone or some damn reason."

"There is," Virgil said.

"Or Driggs and the woman could be just passing through," I said.

Virgil shook his head.

"That don't seem right, though," he said. "Giving the fact him and the warden's wife is on the run."

"Course they're acting like they ain't."

"They are," Virgil said. "Or so it seems."

"Goddamn twisting past, present, and unclear future that has got Driggs to here," I said.

"That's a fact," Virgil said.

"Right from the beginning. The things Driggs did on the battlefield, the killing, the unnecessary killing . . . Who the hell knows, maybe he was responsible for the demise of our CO's wife way back when? Or better to the point, with all we know now, he damn sure most likely was. Hard to know what he did from that time on, when we were barely old enough to shave, up to the time he robs a fucking Spanish ship with a cache of money, gold, and jewelry. Gets himself shot up in the process. The other robbers get away. No one knows a damn thing about the money, gold, and jewelry. Gets locked up in Mexico, using the name Lonnigan, a fellow soldier who was lost in battle. For all I know Driggs maybe killed Lonnigan himself. Then he moved north to Cibola. Starts up spinning a web around the pretty warden's wife. Then lets out a band of murderers, breaks down the communications, makes off with the warden's money, guns, horses, and wife . . . Then . . . catches a goddamn train right back to the comforts of civilization."

Virgil and I thought about all that as we listened to the sounds of the rain and the rushing river. Then Virgil spoke slowly and precisely as he stared off in the dark.

"Driggs is on some kind of a hell-bent jamboree, Everett."

69

The last time Driggs had seen Uncle Dave was when they boarded the ship down in Mexico, and he was thankful he'd never have to see him again. And now, after killing Uncle Dave and Chastain, and then coming across the discovery in Margie's room, he felt rage running through his veins. It'd been a while since he had the feeling like he wanted to kill more. He'd not felt that back at the prison when he killed the two guards before he released the other inmates. But now he felt different as he stood in the shadows of the Town Hall and watched Allie and Margie.

It was hard for him to tell exactly what they were doing. It appeared to him they were perhaps sewing and cutting fabric. He could not make out exactly what it was, but he didn't really care. He was patient as he watched them. They were standing on opposite sides of a table toward the back of the shop, talking and laughing as they worked.

One thing Driggs could not understand but would get to the bottom of, one way or the other, was why Margie was working with Allie. Surely there was a better way to per-

form her duties than to cut and sew with Allie. Regardless, he was not about to let Margie or anyone else fuck up what he needed to do.

But as Driggs watched and waited it occurred to him that maybe, just maybe, Margie might be able to help him in some way. Maybe for the time being he could let her live. Not that he wanted to let her live. Not really. He was actually energized thinking about what he could do with her on her way out. Allie, too. Though Allie was outside of his bailiwick, of where he needed to focus his attention, he didn't really care. The simple fact that he titillated her made him want to work her into even more of a frenzy. But Driggs let that notion go. He let it go and moved on.

The rain continued through the day and into the evening. The whole of the afternoon Driggs spent with the princess. She had never experienced anything like what he delivered up on this stormy day. She had no idea where it came from, but she appreciated it, very much.

After, they came down and enjoyed an early dinner. Then they sat in the hotel parlor watching the rain out the window as they drank some brandy. Driggs had been quiet during the afternoon of sex and throughout dinner.

"I feel like I've died and gone to heaven," she said.

Driggs looked from the window to her and smiled.

"You do?"

"I do," she said.

"What makes you say that?"

"What do you think?"

"Tell me."

"You're an animal," she said as she pointed her toe and stroked his foot with her foot under the table.

"What kind of animal am I?"

"A wolf," she said with a smile.

"Wolves are carnivores," he said.

"So are you."

"You want me to eat you up?"

"You already have."

He shook his head.

"Not yet."

"No?"

"No," he said.

Tilda walked by the table and Driggs stopped her, then looked to the princess.

"Anything else, dear?"

She smiled and shook her head.

"I'm fine."

Driggs looked back to Tilda.

"I'll have one more brandy, and could you bring me an envelope, paper, and pen from the front desk."

"Most certainly," Tilda said, then moved off.

"Are you writing a letter?" the princess said.

"A short one," he said.

"What will it say?" she said with a smile.

"Just a few words," he said.

"Pray tell?"

He paused before he spoke.

"I am the first and the last. I am the one that lives. I was dead but behold I am alive for evermore . . ."

She stared at him for a long moment, then smiled.

"Yes, you are."

Driggs looked to the clock. It was eight and the chimes started.

"In fact, dear," he said. "Once I make certain the note is delivered, I will see you back upstairs."

"If I'm asleep," she said, "wake me up."

"You know I will."

Tilda came back to the table with the pen, paper, and envelope. The princess started to move out of her chair, but Driggs, like the gentleman he was, quickly got out of his chair to assist her.

She looked up to him and he kissed her.

"I won't be long," he said.

He watched her as she walked up the stairs. When she got to the landing she turned and blew him a kiss, then continued up. Driggs wrote the note, sealed it in an envelope, and delivered it to the front desk.

He dinged the bell. After a moment a chubby night manager came through the small door behind the counter.

"Do you have someone that could deliver a message for me?"

"Why, yes," the night manager said. "Where to?"

"The depot," Driggs said. "The incoming westbound train. It arrives at eight-thirty and this note needs to be delivered to one of the passengers. They won't be hard to find. They'll be coming off the first-class Pullman."

Driggs wrote the name on the front of the envelope and handed it to the night manager. The night manager looked at the name on the envelope and nodded.

"Indeed," he said, then called into the room behind the counter, "William."

A freckle-faced young man poked his head out.

"Take this note to the depot," the night manager said. "Make certain you get it there. He'll be coming off the first-class car. Can't miss him."

William took the note and read the name out loud as he put on his slicker.

"Mr. Vandervoort," he said with a chuckle. "No, he'd be hard to miss."

70

Virgil and I hunted all of Red Rock for Degraw and the girl but came up empty-handed. We rested in a dry barn behind the bunkhouse on the north end of town and in the morning just prior to sunup we checked on Gracie. He was asleep, but Claude was up drinking coffee when we stopped in.

"Morning," Claude said.

"Morning," we said.

"You find who you was looking for?" Claude said.

"Did not," I said.

"Sorry to hear," he said.

Virgil nodded to Gracie.

"How is he?"

Claude looked at Gracie.

"He's gonna be okay," Claude said.

"He has nobody left," I said. "Least where we found him he don't."

"Y'all moving on?"

"We are," I said.

"Know where to go to look for who you're looking for?"

"Don't," I said.

"I don't know how you do the work you do, but I'm glad you are doing it."

Claude shook his head a little.

"Once he's healed up good," Claude said, "I'll figure out what makes the best sense for him. If he doesn't have anybody else, I'll take care of him myself."

Virgil looked to me and nodded a little.

"Good," he said.

"My wife died this year," he said. "We never had any children of our own, and seeing how it's just me at the house now, there is no reason he can't stay there with me. Long as he don't mind the fact I can be a crabby ol' man now and again."

With that, Virgil and I said our thanks and good-byes and rode north toward the railway depot. The weather had cleared, leaving only mountains of white billowy clouds above and across the horizon.

As we approached the small depot we could see that the door was wide open. A few young section hands wearing greasy overalls were sitting on the porch. There were two long flatbeds parked around the depot hitched to mule teams that were loaded with railroad ties, rail sections, and tools. One of the fellas leaned his head in the door and said something to someone inside the depot and within a few seconds a heavyset man filled the doorframe. He stood watching us as we rode up and when we were close he moved out onto the porch to greet us. The hands were lounging for lunch, eating jerky and hardtack and drinking coffee.

"Howdy," the heavyset man said.

Virgil raised his hand friendly-like.

"Morning," I said.

"Y'all here to catch the train," he said.

"Well," I said, "that depends."

He stepped out a bit more as we stopped shy of the porch.

"Next train is northbound," he said. "It will be here in about three and a half hours."

Virgil pulled back his jacket, showed his badge, and introduced us.

"We been hunting a man," Virgil said. "Escaped convict out of Cibola."

The workers on the porch all kind of looked at each other, then to us.

"He may and may not have a young girl with him," Virgil said. "White child, fifteen or so."

"He's a big, broad-shouldered man," I said. "He's 'bout forty. Frizzy head of hair; wide, flat nose; pock-marked face."

"Nobody has caught a train outta here," the heavyset man said. "About two weeks back a man and woman come from Red Rock. But the man looked nothing like the man you described and the female was no girl."

"This man would have been through here like yesterday," I said.

The heavyset man shook his head, then looked to the young hands on the porch.

"Boys?" he said.

They all looked to us and said they'd not seen anybody matching the description of Degraw or a girl.

"There was a northbound that come through last night but I was not awake to see them, normally don't see the late-night and early-morning ones unless there is some maintenance scheduled or a passenger bought a ticket and is waiting. 'Pose there could have been a jump-on then. It does happen now and again. A south-bound came through at seven this morning, but nobody for sure boarded, ticket or no ticket."

"Boss," a small young hand with a mop of blond hair that covered his eyes said. "I did find this this morning."

He pulled a pink ribbon from his overalls and held it up for us to see.

71

The night previous Driggs followed the freckle-faced William to the depot to make certain the note was delivered. He stood in the shadows across the way where he had a good view of William waiting on the platform. When the train arrived, at almost eight thirty on the minute, Driggs watched as the passengers disembarked. He waited for what seemed an eternity but no one stepped off the Pullman. Then, as if he were a ghost, Vandervoort stepped off the train and out through the thick steam where he was met by William. William did as he was instructed; he delivered the sealed envelope with the note to Vernon Vandervoort. Then William hurried off.

Driggs watched expectantly but Vandervoort just put the letter in his pocket. Driggs was not necessarily pleased he did that but knew Vandervoort would get to it soon enough. Driggs watched Vandervoort as he spoke to the porter who was collecting his luggage and as he waited, he retrieved the envelope from his pocket, opened it, and stared at it. After a moment Vandervoort looked about with a curious expression on his face, then he stared back at the note.

Driggs knew that it would be just a matter of time before he would be seeing Mr. Vandervoort up close and personal.

Now Driggs was content *this beautiful afternoon reading the* Appaloosa Star Statesman *in the Boston House Saloon as he waited on the princess to come down for an early dinner. The feature article was about Thane Rutledge's celebration that was taking place the following night at the Vandervoort Town Hall. The event promised all of Appaloosa an evening of excitement and festivities that included lively entertainment, hors d'oeuvres, champagne, dancing, and a speech from Vandervoort himself.*

He was sitting in his favorite spot, next to the wall that separated the saloon from its gambling room. He was sipping fine whiskey, a new brand that Wallis had recommended. He was captivated by the lavish details of the party. He learned about the orchestra and the prominent speakers that would be in attendance including the guest of honor, Vandervoort himself. He was miffed to read about the ticket price for the event, more money than the average person of Appaloosa made in a day, but he knew better than most that that was the point of the event. Then, just to his right, he heard the saloon doors open.

"Hey, Wallis."

"Hey, Book," Wallis said.

"You seen Sheriff Chastain?"

"No, Book," Wallis said. "Have not."

Driggs did not turn immediately. He remained reading the article in the Statesman, *then after a moment he turned the page and casually looked over to Wallis and Book. The first thing he noticed was the shiny deputy badge pinned on Book's vest.*

"Been looking all over for him," Book said.

"Well, he's not been in here."

Book nodded and looked around the room. He made eye contact with Driggs. Driggs smiled and touched his brim. Book smiled, then looked back to Wallis.

"Well, if you do happen to see him, tell him Virgil has been trying to wire him."

"You check with the Cherokee gal?" Wallis said with a chuckle.

"First place I looked," Book said.

"He still seeing her?"

"Says he's not," Book said.

Wallis laughed.

"We believe that," he said.

"Sure we do," Book said.

Wallis and Book shared a laugh.

"If you happen to see him, tell him that we're looking for him, will ya?"

"You bet," Wallis said.

Driggs finished the last sip of his whiskey as Book walked out the door, then got up and walked to the bar.

"That was damn good," Driggs said as he set his glass in front of Wallis. "Believe I'll have another."

"You got it," Wallis said, then uncorked the bottle and poured.

Driggs laid his newspaper on the bar as he fished a few coins from his pocket and tossed them on the bar.

Wallis looked at the cover article.

"Big to-do tomorrow night?"

Driggs looked to the paper.

"You going?"

"Me?" Wallis said, scoffing. "Heck no. Too rich for my blood."

"Kind of the point, isn't it?"

"What's that?"

"That's the intention," Driggs said. "Throwing a party like that separates the rich from the poor. Puts folks in their place."

Driggs laughed and held up his hands.

"Hey, I don't by any means mean a damn thing by that comment, not saying you, me, or any other swinging dick does or does not belong, but I've seen enough of that sort of do-gooder bullshit in my time."

"You going?" Wallis said.

Driggs laughed.

"Why, of course."

72

Virgil and I sat our horses in front of the depot,
looking at the blond fella holding the pink ribbon that
was blowing sideways as it danced and twisted gently
with the breeze. The young hand got up off the porch
and walked over to Virgil and me. He handed the ribbon
to Virgil.

"Where'd you find this?" Virgil said.

"Just right up the way here," he said, pointing north.

Virgil handed me the ribbon.

"How far up the way?" Virgil said.

"Oh, 'bout a quarter mile."

"Just so you know, though," the heavyset boss said.
"This line is like every other line across this country, it's
littered with damn trash. Half the time that is what we
are doing, picking up trash. Not saying one way or the
other but we find all kinds of shit up and down these
damn tracks."

Virgil nodded, thinking. He looked to the ribbon in

my hand, then he looked up to the telegraph lines running next to the track.

"Telegraph working?" he said.

"It is," the heavyset man said.

"Like to send a wire," Virgil said.

"You bet," he said, then looked to one of the young fellas on the porch. "Fletcher?"

"Yes, sir," he said.

"Hump to," he said.

"Yes, sir."

Fletcher was a thin-faced young man, not more than sixteen. He wiped off his hands as he got to his feet.

"Come on in. Fletcher here is our operator. He'll tap out whatever you need . . . I'm Louis, by the way."

"Thank you, Louis," Virgil said.

"Hell, anything we can do, just say."

We sent a wire to Sheriff Chastain in Appaloosa and waited for a reply. We got a wire back in about fifteen minutes letting us know they were looking for Chastain and would have him wire back just as soon as he was located.

After an hour the sounder clicked and the message came in letting us know Chastain was nowhere to be found.

"Don't think he's shacked up again with that Cherokee he promised he was swore off, do you?" I said.

"Might," Virgil said. "I think he likes the fact that she don't talk much."

"What's not to like about that?" heavyset Louis said with a chuckle, then looked to Virgil and me as he moved to the door. "I'll be in the shed with the hands out behind us here, loading up for the afternoon fixes. Holler if you need me."

Virgil nodded and Louis stepped out the door.

"What do you figure?" I said.

Virgil thought for a moment as he looked to the rail map that was tacked to the wall.

"No telling where Degraw is," he said.

Virgil nodded to the map.

"Lot of land out there," he said.

"Is," I said.

"We could go this way and well, hell," Virgil said. "He could be that way."

"Could have jumped the night train," I said.

"Yep."

"Then again, he might not have," I said.

"Sure don't like the idea of this."

"The girl?"

"None of it," he said. "Especially the girl."

"No," I said. "Unless we find something that can tell us where to point no telling what to do or where to go from here . . . I don't want to give up, Virgil, but I don't think we have much choice at this point and time."

I got out of the corner chair I'd been sitting in and moved next to Virgil and looked at the map. After some time of looking and thinking, I turned to Virgil.

" 'Spect we should get on that train when it comes through," I said.

"I suspect so," he said.

With the exception of Fletcher and Louis, all the young hands loaded up in the flatbeds and headed back out to work on the rails as we waited for the train.

When the train arrived at the depot there was still no word back from Chastain but we let the Western Union office know that we would be back to Appaloosa by tomorrow night.

At four in the afternoon Virgil and I loaded our animals in the stock car, boarded the northbound train, and headed back to Appaloosa.

At the first water drop ten miles out we saw one of the

section-line flatbeds near the water tank. As the train slowed, a handful of the hands moved toward the train. The blond fella that found the ribbon was in front of the pack.

Virgil and I were standing on the third car porch as the engine slowed to a stop under the water drop. When the blond hand saw us he rushed over.

"I think we found the young girl you was looking for. She's over there in the flatbed," he said with a point. "She's dead. Looks like she was tossed off the train. Not sure if it was the fall that killed her or what. But she's naked and purty mangled up."

73

Driggs awoke the day of the party like he did every morning. He stood looking out the window watching the folks of Appaloosa going this way and that as he sipped some whiskey and lit a cigarette. Coming up the block was the man in the buggy being towed by the wide dun horse. Driggs watched as the man turned the corner in front of the hotel and moved on up the road.

Driggs turned back to the princess and watched her sleeping and thought about having her just get up and get dressed, pack up, and leave town. Go elsewhere, Frisco, Chicago, or Denver, but he had a job to do first, then they would go. He did not come all this way for nothing. He had some pertinent business to take care of and of course there was the party. He was looking forward to the party and dancing with the princess.

Driggs moved to the bureau, poured some water in the basin, and splashed his face. As he looked at himself in the mirror he thought it time for a haircut and shave. He wanted to look good for the party and for the princess.

Driggs dressed, kissed the sleeping princess, and left the room. He checked with the front desk for the best place to get a haircut and shave.

"That would be Mr. Blake," the desk clerk said. "Just two blocks up Main Street here."

Driggs tipped his hat and set out to Blake's Barber Shop. When he arrived he was surprised to see there wasn't a wait and Mr. Blake got him in the chair right away.

Mr. Blake laid the chair back and dropped a white face towel into a pot of boiling water. He let it soak in the hot water a minute, retrieved it with a pair of tongs, rolled the towel through the roller, then laid it gently over Driggs's face.

Just then Driggs heard a tap on the glass door.

"Ah . . . good morning, Mr. Blake."

"Oh . . . good morning, Mr. Vandervoort," he said.

"I thought I'd get here early enough to be your first," Vandervoort said. "But I see you have a customer, so I shall return."

"Okay, Mr. Vandervoort," Mr. Blake said. "Give me . . . oh, forty-five minutes."

"If someone comes before I return . . ."

"No problem, Mr. Vandervoort, you'll be next."

"Very good," he said. "Thank you . . ."

"You bet," Mr. Blake said. "By the way, how was your trip?"

"Hot and muggy, that New Orleans . . . I will tell you all about it when I return . . . Oh, that reminds me, I have a gift for you. A gift for my favorite young gentleman in all of Appaloosa."

"Why, thank you."

"Something very special for your shop here, from France. I think it will be a fine addition for your place of business, Mr. Blake."

"Why, thank you," said Blake.

"Soon as the crates are unloaded I'll see that it's delivered."

"Thank you."

"See you shortly, Mr. Blake."

After Vandervoort walked on, Driggs said from under the towel covering his face, "Heard a lot about that man."

"He's a special individual," Mr. Blake said.

"So I hear," Driggs said.

Driggs made certain Mr. Blake's grooming procedures were expeditious. The last thing he wanted to do was have a meaningless conversation with a barber in a barbershop.

On his return to the hotel he saw a crowd of people gathered around an ambulance in front of the building where he had the disagreements with Uncle Dave and Sheriff Chastain. When he passed he noticed Deputy Book, who'd asked Wallis if he knew where to find the sheriff and all Driggs could think about as he walked past was that the mystery was over.

The princess was standing in the tub, drying off with a towel, when Driggs entered.

"There you are," she said. "And look at you. You are so handsome. You got your hair cut."

"And a shave," he said.

"You look marvelous," she said.

"Tonight is the night," he said.

"The party?"

"Why, yes," he said with the excitement of a little boy. "The party."

His eyes were afire with anticipation and he actually paced a bit before he picked up the whiskey bottle from the nightstand and took a swig.

"And I want you in your new yellow dress."

"Oh, yes, darling," she said. "It's perfect."

"It is," he said.

He walked to her and scooped her up in his arms and laid her on the bed. He kissed her up and down her body and ended kissing her lips.

"This will be a good evening," he said. "A lavish engagement fit for a princess."

"Listen to you," she said.

"You will no doubt be the most beautiful of all," he said.

"Oh . . . kiss me some more."

74

Just after sunset Driggs hurried back to the Boston House with the orchid corsage he got from a Chinaman. He thought the ivory color would complement the princess's sterling blue eyes, dark hair, and new yellow dress. He bounded up the stairs to their room and when he entered someone was just inside, standing to the side of the door, and stuck a gun barrel to the side of his head. Driggs froze.

"Double-barrel," a deep voice said. "Fancy one. Took it off some Englishman religious fucking chap that was twice your size. He said it was a hunting gun. For grouse and pheasant and the like. Said it was given to him by someone that meant something to him or some shit. Funny thing was I didn't find no scatter bird loads for it. Just hard knocking double-ought buck is all I found. That's what this load is. Double-ought buck. Take your head off."

Driggs eyes turned.

"Easy, cocksucker," the voice said.

Driggs did not need to see who was holding the shotgun

to his head; he recognized the voice but looked anyway to see it was the hulking hayseed Ed Degraw.

"He used funny fucking words. He said things like 'chap' and 'jolly' and 'shit.' Until I stuck the gun up his ass and let go both barrels. You should have seen that. Fuck. The double-ought buck exploded out the top of his head. There was eyes and hair and brains and teeth and all kinds of innards all over the ceiling of the little chapel where it happened. I think he was the pastor or preacher or pope or whatever the fuck you call 'em."

Driggs just stared straight ahead. He was calm, poised, collected, and breathing easy.

"I know you are wondering how the fuck it is I found you, ain't you?" he said. "Fuck you, I'll tell you . . . Move your ass over there, to the corner, to that chair there, now."

Driggs moved fluidly and his eyes were steady as he walked slowly to the chair and sat.

Degraw kept the shotgun pointed at him with one hand as he removed an old newspaper article from his pocket with the other. He flipped it open. The paper was yellow and crumbly.

"You 'member this?" Degraw said. "From the Appaloosa Star Statesman? When we was locked up together you kept reading this goddamn article about the goddamn brick factory here in Appaloosa. That was damn near four fucking years ago and you kept reading it. I know it had to mean something to you. You 'member and I asked you why you kept looking at it and reading it and you said it was none of my goddamn business. But now look it here, it is my business, ain't it? You read it more than you ever read any of them other newspaper clippings. You read this all the fucking time. The goddamn Vandervoort Brick Factory in goddamn Appaloosa. Then when I get here I see half the town goddamn says that, Vandervoort. And then I think, I know you, Lonnigan. I know what a conniving shit you are

*and you are up to no good all the time. I knew you had
something here up your sleeve . . . You are a moneygrubber
cocksucker thief. So I figured I'd just come and get some of
what you was out to get . . . You ain't interested in sharing,
then I will just fucking turn you in or kill you. Both, I
would look forward to doing . . . I knew it'd be just a matter of time before I found you. I knew you had fucking
money and you'd live high. I know you. Know all about you.
What you did and how you got out. I figured it all out . . .
I did. I looked at all the other hotels first before this one. But
you know what? I would not have found you so easily if it
had not been for the little canary . . . the warden's wife."*

Driggs's eyes went to the left and then to the right.

*"You can imagine her surprise when it was me and not
you coming through the door."*

"Where is she?"

*"She looked really nice," he said. "Little canary. So do you.
You look like you're ready for a party . . . and, a goddamn
flower? Goddamn, Lonnigan, you're a regular dandy."*

"Where is she?"

Degraw rubbed his crotch.

"She was just as I imagined she'd be," he said.

"What'd you do?"

"What else?" Degraw said.

Driggs stared at him without an ounce of emotion.

Degraw grinned.

*"Have a look for yourself," he said as he nodded to the
armoire.*

*Driggs looked to the tall, mirrored wardrobe cabinet,
then looked back to Degraw.*

*"Go on," Degraw said, "I think you will like what you
see. You won't be disappointed."*

*Driggs rose out of the chair and walked to the cabinet.
He reached out and opened the door. He stared motionless
at what he found inside.*

"She was . . . good," Degraw said. "I knew that Bible bullshit she brought around was a bunch of bullshit. She was just like all the others, nothing but a fucking whore."

The princess was hanging inside the tall cabinet from a cord around her neck. Her eyes were wide open. Her purple tongue protruded from her lips. Her yellow dress was split all the way up the front, as was her body. She'd been split open from her crotch all the way to her chin with the straight razor that was lying at her feet.

Degraw leaned just a bit to get a closer look at Driggs's face.

"Is that a fucking tear?" Degraw said.

Driggs did not look at him.

"It is," Degraw said with a laugh. "I'll be goddamn. Donnie fucking Lonnigan . . ."

Driggs turned his head slowly and looked to Degraw. Tears were running down his cheeks.

Degraw laughed again, harder this time, and when he did Driggs quickly dropped and lunged just as Degraw pulled both triggers. The shotgun's double-barrel explosion was loud, but the shots missed. They went just over Driggs's head and blew through the top of the armoire door as Driggs's shoulder hit Degraw in his midsection, slamming him hard against the wall.

Driggs pulled on the gun but Degraw held it from him. Then Driggs grabbed Degraw by the hair and pulled hard, banging his head into the remaining jagged mirror of the armoire door, slicing Degraw across the face.

Driggs got Degraw in a headlock, then spun and charged toward the room door. The door shattered and splintered free from the doorjamb and fell into the hall followed by the big men. Driggs landed on top of Degraw and he twisted Degraw's head to the side. Degraw screamed in pain, as his neck was about to snap. Degraw rifled three *elbows into Driggs. Driggs was momentarily stunned and Degraw put the shotgun to Driggs's throat. But Driggs pushed back as the two men powered back up, getting back on their feet. They were locked arm to arm with the gun held by both as they stumbled back into the room. Driggs jerked Degraw hard and they slammed into the wall, busting through the lath and plaster. Degraw pulled back, then pushed hard on Driggs and drove him across the room, snapping the post from the footboard of the bed, as the muscled men smashed hard into the opposite wall. The two powerful men turned and turned again, going back out into the hall. Then Driggs picked Degraw up off his feet and charged back into the room with him and crashed out through the window. They landed, striking hard on the shingled porch overhang and instantly started to slide, and within a moment they rolled off the fifteen-foot-high roof. There was a short silence as they fell. When they landed on the hard-packed street Degraw gasped—his wind knocked out of him. Driggs was on top of him. Looking down at Degraw's eyes staring up at him. Driggs put his large hands on Degraw's head, and with a dominant twisting crack, he snapped Degraw's neck.*

Driggs stared at Degraw for a long moment, then glanced up and looked around. There was a crowd of people on the boardwalk that had come out of the Boston House Saloon who had just witnessed what happened, including Wallis.

"Mr. Bedford?" Wallis said.

Driggs pushed back his hair and tucked in his shirt.

"My God," Wallis said,

Off in the distance the whistle blasts of the evening train coming into Appaloosa echoed through the streets.

"Are you okay, Mr. Bedford?" Wallis said.

Driggs straightened his coat and tie as he looked to Wallis.

"Yes," Driggs said. "I'm fine."

Driggs looked to dead Degraw. He reached down, scooped up the double-barrel shotgun. Then he rifled through Degraw's pockets and found some shotgun shells.

"Are you sure?" Wallis said.

Driggs rose back up and broke open the double-barrel and slid in two new shells then looked to Wallis.

"I'm perfectly fine, Mr. Wallis, perfectly fine," Driggs said. "I have a party to attend."

Driggs snapped the break-over shotgun closed with a loud click and started walking off toward the Vandervoort Town Hall.

75

The train pulled into the Appaloosa depot at just past eight o'clock in the evening and Book was waiting there for us on the platform. When we approached, he removed his hat and looked down to his feet.

"Hey, Book," I said.

Book raised his head kind of slow-like and looked up to Virgil and me. He had tears in his eyes.

"I got some real bad news," he said with a quivering bottom lip.

"What is it, Book?" I said.

"Sheriff Chastain has been killed," he said. "Murdered."

"Goddamn," I said.

Virgil looked to me.

"By who?" Virgil said.

"Don't know."

"Well, how do you know?"

"He was found."

"Where?"

"In a building that was being built over on Main Street."

"How was he killed, Book?" Virgil said.

"I'm not real sure."

Book shook his head and looked away, fighting back tears.

"What do you know?" Virgil said.

"There is a building over there, the corner of Main and Third, that is under construction. Two workers found him there dead . . . along with another man."

"Another man?" Virgil said.

"Yes, sir."

"Who?"

Book shook his head a little.

"I got no idea who he is . . . was. I might have seen him around, but I'm not real sure."

"And you're not sure how Chastain was killed?" Virgil said.

"Not for certain . . . Looked like he was . . . was in a fight and he maybe was strangled. His neck was swollen and caked in blood."

"What about the other man?" Virgil said.

Book shook his head.

"Looked like the same thing, I guess."

"What'd the other man look like?"

"Oh, older . . . I say mid-fifty-something, sixty, maybe. Kind of a hefty fella. Dressed sort of normal, bowler. None of us deputies for sure knew who he was, but some of the others said they thought they'd seen him, too."

"Where are they?" I said. "The bodies?"

"Undertaker."

"Nobody saw nothing at this building?" Virgil said. "Any witnesses?"

"No."

"When the workers find them?"

"Today, this morning . . . they were down behind a door under the floor."

"What?" Virgil said.

"There is an opening to the building's floor. The sub-structure, there was a door in the floor. They, both Sheriff Chastain and the other man, had been dumped there."

Virgil looked at me and shook his head.

"Nobody knows but us deputies," Book said. "I told everybody to keep shut about this . . . I told them you two was coming back and that you needed to know first and we'd go from there."

"Get our horses," Virgil said. "Come to the Boston House."

"Boston House?" he said.

"Yes," Virgil said.

Book nodded and started off.

"And Book?"

Book stopped and looked back to Virgil.

"I'm sorry, son."

Book nodded a little, then moved on.

Virgil and I walked directly and with some pace to the Boston House. When we rounded the corner onto Main Street there was a crowd of people standing on the porch of the hotel and an ambulance was sitting out front.

When we arrived, Doc Burris was standing behind the ambulance, watching as a body was being loaded into the back. He turned, seeing Virgil and me.

"Hey, there," Doc said.

"What have you got here, Doc?" Virgil said.

He shook his head.

"Dead man," Doc said. "Nobody seems to know who he is."

Virgil and I looked inside the ambulance. I turned to the driver.

"Let me have one of your lamps there," I said.

The driver handed me the lamp and I raised it up some so Virgil and I could have a look at the man in the back.

When the light shined on his face, Virgil looked to me.

"That ain't Driggs," I said.

We studied the man's face for a long moment.

"I'll be goddamn, Virgil," I said. "Think that is . . . Ed Degraw?"

Virgil tilted his head a little, looking at the dead man with the wide nose and frizzy hair and nodded a little.

"I do," he said.

76

"Virgil, Everett," Wallis said. "Thank God you are here."

We turned to see fat Wallis. He walked as quickly as his big body would move down the steps and over to the ambulance.

"You know what happened here, Wallis?" I said.

Wallis nodded. He was out of breath and his eyes were wide.

"Damnedest thing . . ." he said, then inhaled followed by blowing the hair that was hanging in his eyes. "There was a loud boom, gunfire, upstairs. The whole saloon went quiet as hell. Then we heard awful banging around up above here and then two men, the dead man there, and another, Mr. Bedford, crashed out the upstairs window."

Wallis turned and pointed up the window.

"Any law here?" Virgil said. "Been up there?"

Wallis nodded.

"Just got here. Not seen Chastain or Book, but two of the young deputies is here, they went up there."

"You said the other man was Bedford?" I said.

"Yes, Mr. Bedford is a guest here. Him and that dead fella in the ambulance there busted out the window and landed here in the street. Then Mr. Bedford killed him. He snapped that man's neck, broke it with a crack. Right there in front of us. We watched the whole thing. Hell of a deal, I have to say . . . Mr. Bedford has been staying here for a good while. Hell, nice man, served him here near every day. Goddamnedest thing I ever seen."

"This Bedford?" I said. "Big strong fella?"

Wallis nodded.

"Was a woman with him?" I said.

Wallis nodded.

"Been a woman with him the whole time he's been here, a beauty, I might add, but she was not with him, not when he walked off."

Just then, Skeeter, the young Mexican deputy, poked his head out the busted-out window on the second floor and threw up.

Virgil and I stepped back and looked up to him.

Skeeter wiped his mouth and shook his head.

"Skeeter," I said.

He looked to me, shook his head, then threw up again. He wiped his mouth on his sleeve.

"Got a woman up here, dead . . . she's been ripped apart. I ain't never seen no dead person before, but I don't think in a lifetime I would see a dead person like this. It is God-awful."

"Young woman?" I said.

Skeeter nodded and threw up again.

"Oh my God," Wallis said.

"Any idea where this Mr. Bedford walked off to?" Virgil said.

Wallis pointed.

"Said he was going to the big party, at the Vandervoort Town Hall."

"The party?"

"The fancy party at the Vandervoort Town Hall."

Virgil glanced at me.

"He has a shotgun with him," Wallis said.

"What?" I said.

"A side by side," Wallis said. "He loaded it and walked
off."

"Said he was going to the party," Virgil said. "With a
loaded shotgun?"

Wallis nodded.

"He was kind of . . . intent, it seemed, like he had
something to do. Hell, I don't know . . . He had that
fucked-up look, you know."

"Goddamn, Wallis," I said.

"How long ago?" Virgil said.

"Twenty minutes, maybe."

Virgil looked to me and we started walking at a quick
pace toward the Vandervoort Town Hall. I looked back
to Skeeter as we walked.

"Leave her, Skeeter," I said. "Leave everything as it is
up there."

Skeeter nodded and threw up again.

We hurried the few blocks toward the Town Hall. We
heard the music before we turned the corner onto
Vandervoort Avenue, and as we approached the Town
Hall we saw a number of people standing on the porch
in front of the place.

All the tall double doors that fronted the street were
open, and toward the far end of the room the guests
were moving about through the doors, easing from inside to out and outside to in. Virgil and I edged up to
the first set of the tall doors and looked inside. The par-

tygoers were all looking to be having a fine time. We did not enter, we just stood watching, and after observing for a few moments Virgil shook his head.

"Don't see Driggs," he said.

"Nope," I said.

"Be hard to miss walking around with a fucking shot-gun," Virgil said.

"He'd be hard to miss without it," I said.

77

Most of the party crowd was toward the opposite end of the long room, but we had a good view of everyone. The majority of the people were spaced out, sitting in chairs around the edges. In the center couples were dancing to waltz music being played by a big band that was perched up on one side of the stage.

Virgil turned, looked around across the street, then looked back inside the room.

"What do you think?" I said.

Virgil shook his head a little.

"Don't make sense."

"Maybe he's off to catch that train when it leaves," I said. "Think it's at ten."

"Could be," Virgil said.

"Wonder what happened to the woman?"

"Been thinking that, too," he said.

"Think somehow Degraw might have got to her?"

Virgil nodded.

"From Skeeter's look and description, sounds like the

work of Degraw," he said. "But this is all pretty much a spiderweb if there ever was one."

"There's Allie and her friend," I said.

Virgil followed my look.

"Margie," Virgil said.

They were sipping champagne and talking to two young men near the front by the band.

"Allie looks to be having a good time," I said.

"She does," Virgil said.

"Want to go on in?" I said.

Before Virgil answered, someone from the crowd called out, "Here he is."

A lighted coach pulled by a big white horse stopped in front of the main entrance. The door was opened by one of the party attendants and out stepped Vandervoort, followed by his new bride, Constance. As always, he was dressed in a handsome long coat with gold buttons but now sported a frilly white shirt. Constance was wearing a gold dress that shimmered, and around her neck was a jeweled necklace that sparkled even more than the dress.

"The man himself," I said.

"Yep," Virgil said.

"Look like a couple from some damn painting."

When the waltz ended everyone clapped. It was as if it were orchestrated by some kind of divine order, the end of the waltz coupled with the arrival of the Vandervoorts.

Everyone turned and acknowledged Vandervoort and his wife with a round of applause when they entered. Then, after the long clapping died down, a chant started—*Speech, speech, speech!*

Vandervoort smiled and waved, then moved up the stage steps with Constance on his arm. Constance stood to the side and Vandervoort stepped behind the lectern as the crowd clapped. He held up his hands and resembled a Christ-like politician.

REVELATION   323

"Thank you," he said. "Thank you."

Everyone began to settle down, and once everyone stopped clapping Vandervoort put his hands together.

"Thank you, thank you, the fine citizens of Appaloosa . . . Thank you."

The crowd moved in around the stage to listen to Vandervoort and Virgil and I drifted in the door and stood just inside as he began to speak.

"Some of you know I just returned from New Orleans where I received a shipment of incredible goods that I procured from some auctions and estate sales overseas—from places like France and Italy and Spain. Fine merchandise, mind you, the kind of merchandise one might find in Philadelphia, Chicago, New York, or Boston. Nevertheless, the point is, this merchandise, in these two boxcar loads I brought back with me, will soon find its way into your homes and places of business. These goods, along with this wonderful Town Hall and this avenue with the fine stores and businesses, is what will separate Appaloosa from all the other hamlets that have sprung up during this country's western expansion. It has been my intention all along to build a city west of the Mississippi that will rival any of those aforementioned. It has been my intention since the first day of my arrival here to lift this community of Appaloosa out of the confines of backward culture. I see here among us some of my business and leasing partners. Please come up here with me, Bob Kirkwood is here, James Carlisle, Red Peterson, and Allison French. These are the owners and operators of new businesses along Vandervoort Avenue here. Allie, Bob, James, Red, come. Allie I am particularly proud of, our one and only woman business owner in all of Appaloosa. The tide is changing, folks, and we here in Appaloosa are on the forefront of that change."

Allie and the other men all walked up the steps. When

they were all there behind Vandervoort he turned and looked to them and clapped. This encouraged the rest of the folks in the room to start clapping, too.

Then, rising up the steps from behind the stage, came Driggs, with the double-barrel shotgun pointed at the back of Vandervoort's head.

78

The crowd instantly began to clamor and start for the doors until Driggs yelled with a booming voice, "Nobody move!"

Everyone did as he said.

Driggs was calm and commanding, and his physical presence was powerful and instantly convincing.

"Goddamn, Virgil . . . goddamn," I said.

Virgil and I were at the back of the crowd and any move we made, one way or the other, would not be wise.

Vandervoort turned slowly to see Driggs.

"Turn back around," Driggs said loudly.

The crowd gasped.

"Everybody quiet," Driggs said. "The first person that makes a move to leave here, this worm at the end of this gun will have his head scattered all over you."

Vandervoort turned slowly back and faced the crowd. His face was white and his jaw was slack.

"Put both your hands on that lectern," Driggs said.

Vandervoort did as he was told.

"This speech that he began was rousing," Driggs said. "But it's going nowhere. He's going to start over and tell you another story. Aren't you?"

Vandervoort said nothing.

"Looks like he's seen a ghost," I said under my breath.

Driggs moved up between Allie and one of the other men standing behind Vandervoort and put the barrel to the back of Vandervoort's head.

"Aren't you?"

Driggs popped him in the head with the gun.

"What do you want me to say?" Vandervoort said.

"Tell them who you really are."

Vandervoort said nothing.

"Tell them."

"No."

"Can't, can you?"

"Just do it," Vandervoort said.

"What? My God," Constance said. "No!"

"He might be right," Driggs said to Constance. "That might be the best. Certainly the easiest."

"Dear God . . ."

"God has nothing to do with this, lady."

Constance had tears streaming down her cheeks.

"Please," she said. "Please don't hurt him."

"Hurt?" Driggs said. "You don't know what hurt is."

"Please . . ." she said.

"Shut the hell up," Driggs said.

Driggs poked the gun again at the back of Vandervoort's head.

"Talk."

Vandervoort shook his head.

"No."

"I will tell them then, and you can fill in the blanks. Let's start not at the beginning but toward the end. Let's start with that necklace around your wife's neck."

Everyone looked to the stunning diamond and ruby necklace hanging around Constance's throat. Her hand instantly clutched the necklace as if someone were trying to take it from her.

"Don't worry, lady, it doesn't belong to you anyway. None of the jewelry belongs to you, or the gold, or the money. In fact, that necklace was what set all this in motion. Happened on the day you returned from your fucking honeymoon in France . . ."

Driggs poked Vandervoort with the gun again.

"I was not certain you were in trouble until I found out the Pinkertons were after your ass. Good thing I got to you before they got to you . . . They are here, you can bet your ass. You gave that necklace to her for a wedding gift and you end up with a photograph of the loving newlyweds in the fucking society news wearing the very necklace you stole off that ship from Spain eight years ago. Did you really think that they would stop looking for that? The fucking King of Spain hired the Pinkertons eight years ago and now they are here for you. They even paid for this party just so she would be an idiot and wear that or one of the other ones. That little cute woman there? She's one of them, too. Isn't that the truth? Tell him."

The crowd looked to Margie. They opened up as Margie moved a few steps toward the lectern.

"He's correct, Mr. Vandervoort . . . This does not need to end like this," Margie said.

"No?" Driggs said.

"And that fella over there that put this party together, he's one of them, too."

Driggs looked to Rutledge and his two men.

"Those two with him, brothers," Driggs said. "Them, too."

"I'll be goddamn," I said silently. "You damn sure called it, Virgil."

79

"But that is not the best part," Driggs said, then nudged Vandervoort with the gun. "Is it?"

Vandervoort said nothing.

"I was with him on the heist of that ship in Mexico," Driggs said. "Hell, it was my idea. I knew about the shipment and I organized the robbery. But what I did not count on was to be shot in the back and left for dead."

Driggs poked the gun again.

"But I'm not dead, am I? No . . . I am the first and the last. I am the one that lives. I was dead but behold I am alive for evermore . . ."

Driggs nudged Vandervoort again.

"You want to tell them who shot me?"

No one moved.

"No?" said Driggs. "It was him. He shot me."

The crowd gasped.

"I should have known that would have happened."

Allie was shaking so hard we could see the ruffles on her dress fluttering.

"Talk to him, Everett," Virgil said quietly. "Start a conversation."

I glanced to Virgil and he nodded some.

"Here's why I should have known it would happen," Driggs said. "Because he's been a ruthless killer his whole life. One of the first that I knew about was a man named Vandervoort, a Dutch salesman with a wagon-load of supplies. So what does he do? He kills the Dutchman and takes the wagon and then years later he takes his fucking name, too. He thought it sounded like Vanderbilt. He thought he could be just like him. The Commodore."

"Driggs?" I said.

He leaned out from behind Vandervoort.

"Hello, Everett," he said. "Welcome back. Who are you talking to? You see, we are both Driggs up here. This is Augustus Noble Driggs the first and I'm the second."

"Give it up," I said.

"That's right, this is my father," Driggs said. "He taught me everything I know . . . including killing . . . well, mainly killing. I think he killed at least five men that I know of before he killed my mother."

"Shut up," Vandervoort said.

"Or what?" Driggs said.

"Just shut the fuck up."

"Driggs," I said. "Just come with us."

The crowd parted some and Virgil and I eased forward.

"He taught me how to snap a neck," Driggs said. "Can you imagine your own father teaching you how to snap a neck? That is how he killed my mother."

"Shut up," Vandervoort said. "Just shut up!"

"Put the gun down and let us handle this," I said. "Listen to me."

"Do like Everett says," Virgil said. "Put the gun down.

There is nothing you can do to change what happened, but you can change what happens now."

Book came in the side door and pointed a rifle at Driggs.

"Drop it," Book said.

Driggs glanced at Book, and when he did Vandervoort spun on him with a powerful blow to the side of his head. The hard hit stunned Driggs. The people on the stage, the musicians and the others, scattered. Book had no shot and neither did we, as the people in front of us were all scrambling, trying to get out of the way.

Virgil and I fought through the crowd toward the stage.

Driggs was on his back. Vandervoort slammed a boot to his head, jerked the shotgun out of his arms, and stuck the barrel to his son's head.

"No!" I said.

But Vandervoort pulled the trigger and Driggs's head exploded, sending a spray of blood that shot up across Vandervoort's shirt and face.

Vandervoort grabbed Allie.

"Vandervoort!" Virgil said.

Vandervoort put the barrel of the shotgun under Allie's chin and spun around with her in front of him.

"Just let me walk out of here with her, or she will die."

"She dies," Virgil said. "You die."

Allie had tears rolling down her cheeks.

Constance, cowering on the floor, looked up to Vandervoort.

"My God . . . Vernon," she said. "Stop . . . Just stop . . . Let her go."

Virgil advanced on Vandervoort with his Colt pointed at his head.

"Drop the gun," Virgil said.

"Do as he says," Constance said as she got to her feet.

Vandervoort's eyes darted between Virgil and me as he backed up, all the while holding Allie in front of him.

"Drop the gun," Virgil said.

"Do it," Constance said. "Do as he says."

"No," he said.

"You got but one shot," Virgil said. "That's not for Allie, and you know it."

Allie's eyes were full of tears and her lip was quivering as she stared at Virgil.

"Vernon?" Constance said. "Please . . . *Don't do this!*"

"*Quiet, Constance!*" Vandervoort said as he continued backing up with Allie, edging toward the exit.

"You let me go, let me out of here," Vandervoort said. "I will let her go."

"No! Vernon!" Constance said. "Stop!"

Vandervoort looked to her.

"Stop this, right now!" she said.

He was perfectly calm as he stared at her.

"Just stop this!" she said. "Right now!"

Vandervoort snapped, "Did you or did you not say that I am nothing without you?"

"Dear God, Vernon."

"God? *God?*" Vandervoort then roared with a vituperative growl, "*LIKE MY DEAD SON SAID, GOD HAS NOTHING TO DO WITH THIS, BITCH.*"

Then he shoved Allie and turned the shotgun on Constance.

"*VERNON, NO!*"

Virgil shot him, three quick shots to the chest. Vandervoort fell back and as he did he pulled the trigger.

The double-ought buck hit Constance square in the chest, sending blood, diamonds, and rubies exploding across the stage as she stumbled backward, crashing through the fence of music stands and clutching the thirty-foot-tall curtain at the edge of the stage.

"Virgil," Allie cried as she hurried down the steps and fell into his arms.

"I got you, Allie."

"Oh, Virgil," she said as she buried her face in his chest.

"I got you."

"My God," Constance whispered.

She was still miraculously alive and on her feet. Margie moved toward her, as did I, and we stood side by side, looking up at her on the stage. Constance looked down to the hole in her chest where the necklace used to be. Then she looked at us wide-eyed and fell from the stage, bringing down the tall curtain with her. Margie and I rushed over and pulled the curtain back from covering her face, but Constance Vandervoort was gone, staring dead-eyed at the ceiling of the Vandervoort Town Hall located on the only avenue in Appaloosa, Vandervoort Avenue.

ACKNOWLEDGMENTS

As always, "much obliged" goes out to G. P. Putnam's Sons' president, Ivan Held, and my incredible editor extraordinaire, Chris Pepe, for making this escape possible. Much appreciation to Ed Harris, Viggo Mortensen, and Renée Zellweger for their continued supply of ammo. I could not have got out of the compound without the ladder and ropes from my partners in crime, Jayne Amelia Larson and mountain guide Rob Wood of Rancho Roberto. As always, I have to acknowledge the continued support of my mysterious sisters—the Clogging Castanets—Sandra and Karen who actually do nothing but laugh, which is beyond helpful. To Rex "Hook'em Horns" Linn for crying *Revelation* out loud. To James "Whatnot" Whitcomb for his constant toast to freedom. Thanks to manager Josh Kesselman, Allison Binder Esq., agent Steve Fisher, and the rest of the convicts from APA for helping to pepper the trail. As always, a smile up and around in the night sky to Robert B. and Joan Parker . . . and a shotgun salute to the late Helen Brann. Most important, a loud and grateful holler at the fullest moon goes out to my beautiful and loving—the good-looking brunette woman—Julie for being there on the other side of the wall with the horses—with love and deep appreciation—THANK YOU!